P9-EFG-253

DISCARDED

*July 2018*

# THE ICONOCLAST'S JOURNAL

Bruce County Public Library
1243 Mackenzie Rd.
Port Elgin ON N0H 2C6

# The Iconoclast's Journal

## TERRY GRIGGS

BIBLIOASIS
WINDSOR, ONTARIO

Copyright © Terry Griggs, 2018

All rights reserved. No part of this publication may be reproduced or transmitted in any form or by any means, electronic or mechanical, including photocopying, recording, or any information storage and retrieval system, without permission in writing from the publisher or a licence from The Canadian Copyright Licensing Agency (Access Copyright). For an Access Copyright licence, visit www.accesscopyright.ca or call toll free to 1-800-893-5777.

**Library and Archives Canada Cataloguing in Publication**

Griggs, Terry, author
    The iconoclast's journal / Terry Griggs.

(reSet books)
Originally published as Rogues' Wedding: Random House, 2002.
Issued in print and electronic formats.
ISBN 978-1-77196-229-2 (softcover).—ISBN 978-1-77196-230-8 (ebook)

    I. Title.

PS8563.R5365I36    2018        C813'.54        C2017-907309-5
C2017-907310-9

Readied for the press by Daniel Wells
Copy-edited by Emily Donaldson
Canadian cover and text design by Gordon Robertson
US cover design by Zoe Norvell

Canada Council for the Arts / Conseil des Arts du Canada

ONTARIO ARTS COUNCIL
CONSEIL DES ARTS DE L'ONTARIO
an Ontario government agency
un organisme du gouvernement de l'Ontario

Ontario
Ontario Media Development Corporation

Published with the generous assistance of the Canada Council for the Arts, which last year invested $153 million to bring the arts to Canadians throughout the country, and the financial support of the Government of Canada. Biblioasis also acknowledges the support of the Ontario Arts Council (OAC), an agency of the Government of Ontario, which last year funded 1,709 individual artists and 1,078 organizations in 204 communities across Ontario, for a total of $52.1 million, and the contribution of the Government of Ontario through the Ontario Book Publishing Tax Credit and the Ontario Media Development Corporation.

PRINTED AND BOUND IN CANADA

MIX
Paper from responsible sources
FSC
www.fsc.org
FSC® C016245

*For my grandmother*
Jane Crawford Scott

# CONTENTS

# PART 1

When I went to bed last night I fancied that something ran in at my bedroom door after me from the gallery. It seemed to be a skeleton. It ran with a dancing step and I thought it aimed a blow at me from behind. This was shortly before midnight.

*— from the diary of the Reverend Francis Kilvert*
JANUARY 23, 1875

# 1

# THEFT

N THE MONTH of May, 1898, on his wedding night, Thomas Griffith Smolders was chased around his hotel room, not by his bride, as you might expect, but by a ball of fire—luminous and strangely cool. Needless to say, this was a clandestine event, occurring as it did in a private room in a small hotel located in a provincial city in Canada. The world was looking elsewhere, already busily nurturing the Twentieth Century in its dark nursery. Mussolini was fifteen, Hitler a boy of nine, Franco, the "little sausage," only six. The ball lightning, that rare phenomenon, was scarcely moments old, having been conceived in the heat and humidity of the day, born out of the belly of omen and mystery. The thing sailed in through the open window of the Belvedere Hotel in London, Ontario, hissing like an angry cat.

Only moments before, Grif had taken off his shoes and arranged his morning coat on the back of a chair, fastidiously straightening it, dusting off a few specks of dandruff, attending to it as if he were dressing a younger brother. He was prepared to take much longer over the matter of his trousers, and had begun to pace the floor while he considered what their removal would ultimately entail. He suspected that his bride knew much more than he did about how the evening's scheduled pleasures were to be conducted, and he was right. She was waiting for him in the adjoining bedroom, dressed in absolutely nothing but her frightening knowledge.

Grif, pacing pacing, heard someone cry out in the street below, the voice plaintive and slightly crooked with wonder. He stopped and glanced toward the window, then stood frozen as he watched it float in, a yellow ball big as a head, haloed with white light. A live chicken would not have been unexpected, or a string of firecrackers; some of the wilder boys he knew might have ridden into the city to charivari the bride and groom with lusty drunken songs, and the odd boot or brick pitched through the window. But *this*. This was so far beyond being even the unexpected that it stripped him completely of comprehension. His eyes might have told him that, really, this was nothing more than a swarm of brilliant insects clustered tightly together in a mating dance. They did not tell him this. They didn't tell him a blessed thing, and he stood gaping, dumb as a doorknob, as the ball advanced toward him, sizzling and crackling, as if in the uncertainty of his newly married state he had become a magnet for impish and unruly phenomena.

The glowing sphere suddenly dropped and hit the floor with such a sharp whip-snapping *crack* that it woke him from his dreaming disbelief. It was then that he was struck through with a presentiment of danger—not merely from this fiery harbinger, but from the whole roaring marital furnace into which he had stepped that day so unguardedly. He took to his heels, and the ball lightning pursued him so closely that it ate holes in his socks and fried the leftover wedding rice that he was shedding profusely out of his trouser legs and shirt cuffs. A plucked Mercury, he made a dash for the open window and clambered out. The fire escape's rope burned into his palms as he slid down, but no matter, for as soon as he hit the ground, he was gone. He landed in a soft pool of street light, his stricken face illuminated briefly, and then he was off, running blindly into the night, certain that his life lay before him and not behind in that small, suffocating hotel room. The ball lightning, meanwhile, fizzled to nothing. It simply faded away, this amazing electrochemical manifestation, witnessed by no one but Grif Smolders and leaving behind only the trace of an odour, pungent and sulphuric, and a faint crescent-shaped mark on the floor.

Posed *puris naturalibus* on the bed like an odalisque, Avice Marion Smolders, née Drinkwater, heard the commotion in the adjoining room and smiled to herself. She pictured Grif in his virginal anxiety tripping over his own feet and crashing into the furniture. Then there was that noise, *goodness*, that sounded very like a shotgun going off. Someone playing pranks, no doubt, perhaps even Hilliard Forbes who was dead mad for her and would play them more seriously than some. Grif would be rattled by it all, and then more so if he ever got up the nerve to open that door and see her, *behold* her, stretched out naked on the bed. The gift of herself too beautiful for wrapping. Besides—she ran an admiring hand over her breast, down her thigh—she didn't need a man to undress her, to inch her nightgown up over her knees in the concealing dark, while they both pretended it wasn't happening.

Avice was a virgin too, of course, but she believed in research and had given Judith, the Drinkwaters' maid, the silver breakfast cruet from her trousseau in exchange for the details. A scene you might imagine conducted with much whispering, blushing and giggling, yet it was a fairly businesslike and frank transaction. Silver for sexual information—a bold if secretive female bartering, and all the more satisfactory for that.

"Avice!" her three sisters had chided, none the wiser about that chat with Judith, but disconcerted by her no-nonsense approach to the wedding, her wilful flaunting of custom. "*Not* in May," they had shrieked, that being the unluckiest month in which to marry, the month that fostered unpleasantly fierce relationships. "*Not* on a Saturday," the unluckiest day. "*Not* to him," misfortune's suitor, as they saw it. Delicate fingertips probed their vexed foreheads, finding nothing in those tiny furrows, not even the seed of an idea that would explain their younger sister's behaviour. Or lack of it. Tradition was a house she swept through, cool and brisk as a wind. No, she informed them, she would not be wearing mother's veil, nor any veil for that matter; she wanted no fogging sentimental mist in her eyes as she marched resolutely and defiantly down the aisle. Nor would she be taping a gold coin in her shoe, unknotting her laces or concealing anything blue upon her person. And yes, she would, and did, bake her own cake. The penalty for this? A lifetime of drudgery, at least according to Cecile, who stood by wringing her hands as she watched Avice slam the ingredients together like someone building a doghouse.

Avice was aware that she was living on the littoral, much closer to the edge of the new century than her sisters, who as it approached retreated further back, as if from a huge wave breaking on the shore. As far as she was concerned, if marriage was considered to be so perilously rickety that it needed the slant magic of superstition to hold it together, then it needed to change. And she would change it, a woman unafraid to lift her skirts and wade into unknown waters, however black and cold and high they might be.

The silence in the next room began to trouble her. She shivered. How long was she going to have to display herself like a glistening haunch in a butcher's window? What if it *was* a shotgun that she had heard, and Grif, even now as she waited for him to bring her warmth, to kindle her limbs, lay dead on the floor, much colder than she? That could not be, she decided. More likely he had stepped out into the hall beyond her hearing to settle his nerves. Or he was preparing a little surprise for her, as quietly as he could, betraying no secrets.

That's one of the things she liked about him—he was unpredictable, unreadable. Precisely what her sisters didn't like about him. Who *is* he? they wanted to know. Meaning who were his people, what were his connections. What kind of name *is* Smolders? He might be one of those anarchists they'd been hearing about, come to toss a bomb into the heart of their family, to tear apart their settled and prosperous Anglo-Canadian community. Wasn't there something Moorish in his aspect, something tinged and foreign, something of the moneylender, the gypsy? To them he was like the swarthy imp in a fairy tale, who by some enchantment was about to steal their youngest, their baby, and they couldn't bear to watch.

Truth to tell, Avice had enchanted and stolen him, or at least had chosen him like an intriguing and comely package as soon as she spotted him, a clerk behind the counter of Kingsmill's. She had been one of those children who always brought home strays, one-eyed dogs, three-legged cats—once even a monkey, fugitive from a travelling circus—and now *him*. Much better Hilliard Forbes, who was solid and reliable, a young man of conservative tastes and temperament, humourless perhaps, limited in romantic accoutrements, but a known quantity. Yes, Avice might have added, like lard, thinking of what filled the space between his ears.

Had they bothered to enquire of the groom himself, her sisters might have been surprised to discover that Griffith Smolders hailed from a village a scarce ten miles away from London, and from a family of good standing, albeit on a lower social rung than the Drinkwaters. The only very unfortunate thing about him—and this was serious—was that he'd been raised in the Roman Catholic faith. (It was well known that Catholics stole into people's homes late at night like darkness itself and slaughtered whole families in their beds.) Even so, when Grif's father proffered his quivering and purplish tongue at the altar rail, fully expecting the Host to alight on it, a certain amount of Protestantism also drifted in. This being puritan Ontario, it was in the air, a kind of ecumenical pollution. And when those sober, joyless sentiments drifted back out of his father's mouth, Grif caught the brunt of it. Utility, discipline, work, work, work. Grif did not mind the labour, only its wages. As a boy he had been sent several times a week to clean the church for Father Fallon, and on his return home would be soundly beaten, which was his father's way of keeping him morally rigorous and spiritually focused. Grif appealed to all the saints in heaven during these sessions, but no help ever arrived, not even from those who had themselves been most gruesomely martyred. If there was a point to this brutal exercise, he eventually decided to take its opposite. God's tenancy weakened in his young mind, and the Almighty became a squatter at best, in danger of being turfed out entirely at short notice to walk the streets like the unsightly and unworthy poor. When he arrived in London during the Depression of the mid-nineties searching for employment, he let his saint's name, Thomas, be struck away from him like a useless limb. He was simply Grif.

After about an hour had passed, Avice Smolders, her new name still light upon her back, still bridal fresh and alluring, rose from the bed and walked to the door that joined the two rooms. She opened it a crack, then wide enough to let abandonment flood in. She saw the raised window, the curtain stirring slightly. She saw Grif's shoes neatly placed by the wardrobe, his coat hanging on the back of the chair. She saw a sickle-shaped scorch mark on the floor, a black brand burnt into the hardwood, suggesting what? That Grif had been reaped right out of the world without a trace. Spontaneous combustion? (She had read her Dickens.) If she had known he was a Catholic, a religion rife with fantastic plots and absurd characters, she might have suspected Satanic foul play. Adamant belief, she knew, could turn the untenable into fact, the incredible into something hard-edged and real. Beware of what you open your mind to, was the gist of this thinking, for it might sweep in and destroy you. But Grif had been so evasive on the subject of religion when interviewed by her father, a member of the Protestant Protective Association, that he had been suspected of agnosticism rather than any credulous and childish popery. Despite the faint trace of sulphur that still lingered in the hotel room, Avice was certain that no devil had this evening passed through, for no one, not even old Harry himself, would dare take from her that which was hers.

Grif meanwhile had himself taken something—other than his freedom—that was definitely not his. Fleeing down Richmond Street, down Queens, ducking behind St. Paul's Cathedral to catch his breath, he spotted an open window in the church's manse, courtesy of the warm night, the beneficence of May in London, as well as the overheated bulk of the manse's occupant, the Reverend Elias Bee. As fortune would have it, Reverend Bee had with slovenly panache just tossed his jacket on the floor beneath that very window, and had followed up this gift with a pair of very fine shoes, which, after hitting the ledge, landed directly on top of the jacket. He had seated himself on a chubby horsehair sofa by the cold hearth and was presently admiring his hands and wiggling his toes like a baby. They were his best features, his hands and feet, delicate, fine-boned, small but expressive, his fingers plucking meaning right out of the air as he delivered his sermons, and his feet—well, they spoke too, in their way. Quick and agile, they were built for dancing, for mincing, for occupations requiring stealth. He clothed them in only the best imported shoes and boots, in leather that hugged, that took a high shine, natty enough for Sir Wilfrid himself. Unfortunately, his shoes were a poor fit for Grif. They pinched. The jacket was overlarge and overripe, as if Reverend Bee's pride in his person did not extend beyond his dainty appendages.

Grif had never stolen anything before. However, one church being as good, or bad, as another, he felt he had already paid more than enough for these items, the shoes especially, so

9

soft and supple they might have been made of his own flayed skin, his child's beaten-blue husk. He couldn't know that the Reverend Bee was the real thief here. Steeped in satisfaction, unaware of Grif's arm sliding through the window, the venerable man sat smiling to himself and regarding his own clever hands, thinking of the book he had snatched that evening from the archbishop's library. It was a very old book, an antiquity, and in splendid condition. A black market existed for such texts, one that he, a man most comfortable in black, found very useful. For one thing, this sort of trade paid for his exquisite shoes, beautifully crafted examples of which Grif now stole away in. To celebrate, Reverend Bee decided to treat himself to a finger, or two, of brandy—a light-fingered libation—before retrieving his latest find from his jacket pocket and assessing it more thoroughly than his lightning-quick side trip into the archbishop's library had allowed. How he loved old books, and the wealth they contained and, with entrepreneurial ingenuity, commanded.

Grif, a mere apprentice in this thieving business, had so far mainly taken himself away, up the road, beyond the city limits, beyond the limits of married life and of decent behaviour; beyond even the limits of the shoes' stitching, for the leather burst open like pods somewhere around Lucan, which only seemed to accommodate further his escape.

If Griffith Smolders had never felt so free before, his wife of several hours had never felt so arrested. The immense amount of time on her hands was acting very oddly, and moving more slowly than she thought possible for someone still supposedly alive to perceive. She was sitting up in bed, Grif's coat draped over her bare shoulders, the crumpled and undelivered speech she had discovered in his pocket (no one had asked him) long since torn into a storm of anti-confetti that had settled around her. She was finding the gulf between one minute and the next almost impossible to bridge, and she wasn't sure if she was going to make it, proceeding like this through time being such a tedious and endless labour. Hollowed was how she felt, struck open, like a shattered window through which a chill wind seethes. She sat so completely and utterly still that she might indeed have been dead.

At around four in the morning she began to stir, for by then she had begun to realize that not only was she still alive, but she was hungry. Voracious, in fact. It would seem that on her singular and astonishing wedding night she had developed a new and demanding appetite. She blinked a couple of times, as if waking from a strange dream, and looked about. Her eye fell upon a small dark shape crawling in the bedclothes, a spider that was struggling over the mountainous cloth waves. She reached down, plucked it out of the folds, and stared at the poor creature as it wriggled desperately between her thumb and forefinger. Her sister Cecile, who was terrified of spiders and yet maintained that killing one was bad luck, would certainly not have touched the thing, and would have leapt out of bed screaming. Avice smiled. Formerly, and sympathetically, she would have flicked it onto the floor so that it might continue its tiny pilgrim's progress. But tonight, without the slightest regret or remorse, she popped the spider into her mouth and ate it.

# 2

# PASSING THROUGH

A WOMAN can confide in a book, hold it up to her face, rub it against her cheek, whisper into its leaves. A daybook can absorb her secrets like a sponge. Her book might be the only one she tells about that man she saw walking through the river, through the black braided water, blossoms from the Nelders' cherry tree riding soft in his hair, on his shoulders. The secret here is not really the man she sees so much as the heat in her breath, her tongue slipping into the crack of the book, the virginal taste of paper uncontaminated by confession.

The particularity of this woman's life is rich; she could fill her diary like a bucket overflowing with detail. The larger sweep of it, however, can be summed up in a few words: spinster, elderly parents, walls of the house, fields, river. What she wants to write in her book is what she cannot see, what lies beyond in the dreaming distance, the places where the river flows. That man travelling it like a road, striding through the current, petals in his hair—was he even real? She half suspected that he had originated in her own reading, the hero of some romantic novel liberated by her yearning. ("'My Prince!' she cried.") How else could he walk with such certainty on what he could not see, the river bottom roiled and rocky? And surely such perfection loosed would come to grief in this hard country. Illusion or not, he was someone to capture, to press between the pages of her diary and keep forever. She might do that—snatch a bit of him, hair or skin, fuel to keep her desires banked. She knows he will haunt her anyway, his brief passing will harden into an enduring presence, the river-walking man, the stranger who always appears with a lover's persistence and loyalty, but who passes directly through her, through her life, as if she were the one who was the stranger, this woman whose days are as empty as her book.

Fuelled by impulse and premonition, Grif headed north, taking the coward's route between the lines (banks, back roads, fences), keeping out of people's way, avoiding even himself. He couldn't be caught, he reasoned (weakly), if he remained nameless, and while no one called him anything but drifter or tramp, his progress did not always go undocumented. This was an age of journal-keeping, and there were any number of diarists, not all romantically afflicted, who were scribbling away, revealing to their silent friends what they would never tell their mother or their sister. Journals know what they know, and don't gossip; they keep to themselves, unless of course one's mother or sister pries open the locked wardrobe door with a poker and reads:

21 May, 1898. After tea, slipped out back. Left Mother playing nap with Charles, Clara's intended. He is desperately smitten. Though not with Clara, rather with a certain someone who does not reciprocate. Saw Ann Danger, the new cook, sneak a flask into her apron pocket. Pretended not to notice. She wont last. Walked down to the lake, against orders. All the tramps, Mother says, five today at the back door looking for a meal. A lovely evening, warm, saw a red-winged blackbird. Wished I had brought my sketchbook. Then did see a man, bathing. Quite startled me. Should have run back to the house. Stood watching

instead. So absorbed was he in his ablutions, didnt even notice. Would Charles look so? Would he reach into the water as this man did, clutching at its very roots, pouring handfuls of it over his naked body like black silk? I think not.

There were other sightings of this not so rare creature, man on the run. A twelve-year-old boy in Blyth wrote:

Auntie went out at five this morning to fetch some barley to boil for the chickens. What did she get ahold of in the barn but a man's leg. Gave her a sore fright, and the man too he run away. Limping some. Auntie's got a fearsome strong grip.

A farmer in Grey County recorded his days with a strict verbal thrift, a taciturn economy:

June 1898. 2nd. Weather hot. 5th. Sun. Dehorned cattle. 10th. Sowed Johnson's field. 11th. High wind. 14th. Killed the heifer. 17th. Luella fine, but baby sickly. 18th. Started to dig new well. Rain. 22nd. Bad storm. Man come up the road. Stranger. 23rd. Baby died. Sold butter to Bert Winch 20c lb. 25th. Warm. 29th. Dog run off. Killed 2 chickens. 30th. Lost hand fixing thresher.

Grif himself had begun to feel like an epic written by the road, and not the hero of the story but its suffering and stretched body. Or perhaps he was only its grammatical flaw, his life solely constituted of one long winding sentence that goes on and on. Middlesex, Perth, Huron, Bruce, Grey. For days and days, turning into weeks, he worked these counties up through the soles of his feet—his stolen shoes worn ragged as cabbages—until the full knowledge of them, every stone and stem, burst in his brain like a huge puffball punched open. Intimacy is not marriage, he thinks, it is walking. *Walking, walking.*

Although he was unaware of it, Grif did have cause to be annoyed with the Reverend Bee, his unwitting benefactor. If the good man had been a more considerate and conventional thief, the pockets of his rank and sizable jacket might have contained something far more useful than what they did, something to spend, at least, to hock or to barter. If Grif, on first sliding his hand into the inside pocket, had discovered a wad of bills thick as a slice of ham, he would have been able to ride away on an animal more reliable than longing, or eaten a meal more substantial than dust (or sparrow filched from a cat), or slept on a bed kinder than rock or needling, bug-infested hay—and not been wakened by some shrieking harridan attempting to snap his leg off.

Out of one pocket he had drawn a voluminous and snot-bejewelled handkerchief, about the size of a baby's winding sheet. This he had hastily posted in a letter box before quitting London. In another, equally disgusting, he'd found a preserved plum still sticky and damp, which he had dropped instantly, for it felt like some kind of minute organ, a spare gland kept in reserve. Grif frisked himself like an arresting officer, raising an aura of lint and Bee scurf, but found nothing of value, only a book in the inside pocket that he took to be a breviary or missal. He didn't even bother to open it, and almost offered it to the pig he met on the outskirts of Stratford, his travelling companion for a stretch. It was a most personable pig, too, civil and well-mannered, deserving of an inspired—and inspirational—snack. The creature courteously gave him its full attention when Grif finally found the nerve to deliver his wedding speech, and it tactfully refrained from grunting where his father-in-law most certainly would not have refrained.

The pig had sharp, snappy eyes, like intelligent alleys stuck in its head, and an air of knowing what it was about. It had made good its escape from the Kingsleys' farm outside of Stratford, running straight as a blade through the wheat field, parting it down the centre like a green wig, then directly under a gap in the fence. No one had to issue the pig a telegram to inform it that it was in trouble, for it had correctly intuited that it was to be the intended at Miss Belle Kingsley's own wedding—intended for the banquet table. *Not this pig*, must have been its motivating sentiment. Grif found the animal to be a noble beast, clean and honest-smelling, warm to bank up against at night. He was sorry to part with it at Arthur, but the pig clearly had his own itinerary plotted, and headed east.

A biographical footnote, a few words about this "lively piece of pork," appears in Belle Kingsley's own journal. This prettily bound book was available in the sitting room of the Kingsleys' stately home for anyone to peruse, and in fact Belle had inscribed the words READ ME across the inside flyleaf. Such was the edge of Belle's wit that she felt it would be selfish not to share it. Thus she describes in her journal the adventures of their "fugitive bacon supply" and their "porcine rebel," who even as she writes is no doubt "advancing on Parliament to challenge the frog-faced knight of the realm."

Having gotten to know the animal, Grif would surely have been offended by such condescending whimsy, but then he had an evasive heart and tended to side with the shirkers and dodgers, while the young lady *had* been jilted by the centrepiece of her bridal dinner. Grif himself might have been a candidate for such a gustatory role, dredged as he was in dust and baking on the hot road. (An elderly woman in Listowel notes, "Last day I swear a ghost passed under our window. God help me, I felt my heart go cold in my chest.") He could picture the scene, his naked body bound and glazed, mouth corked with a Mac, a sumptuous spectacle appearing in the very centre of the Drinkwaters' groaning mahogany table. Like the other featured animals, he had been brought to his knees and bled white for this wedding. He thought of all those awkward flailing limbs, heads bludgeoned and lopped off, creatures stripped of their extremities and reconstituted as savoury dishes, a true domestication that rendered one plate- and tureen-shaped. The accommodating beasts: pressed chicken, pickled veal, jellied groom.

A bride was more like pastry. Little kisses made of meringue, ladyfingers, coconut cake smothered with a boiled and whipped white icing. (The bride's sisters, stiff yeasty buns.) Was it guilt or hunger that made him imagine so? Avice had worn a white muslin dress trimmed with oriental lace, orange blossoms in her dark hair, no veil, white kid gloves, white lisle thread stockings and white satin slippers. All this bridal whiteness, this purity, did not represent a consumable virginity, it seemed, so much as a death, an identity erased, the blankness of a new page. Avice must have worn her costume mockingly. So self-possessed was she that it was obvious— but only now, at this distance—that she had married herself years ago. He had been nothing more to her than a convenient device, a lever of some sort, used to free herself from the con- straining fit of her family. In the last sight he had of her in the hotel, she had whirled away from him like a waterspout into the other room, laughing, sharing a joke, but not with him. Amazing how that aisle he had walked down had turned into this long long road, and up ahead, the bride in her vaporous froth of white was nothing more disturbing than that cloud on the horizon dispersing.

If he had had the materials, and the ease, and a mind to, Grif might have kept his own record, a travel diary. A charac- ter would definitely form in it, a shape emerge, there would be a stepping forth. It wouldn't be him, though. He would write himself out of his own observations, as he had written him- self out of his life in London, the clerk behind the counter of Kingsmill's who had caught Avice Drinkwater's bold eye.

Crawling slowly up the face of the province like a fly, he could easily have captured the telling details, the features, that would compose a portrait of the place and its residents. An odd one, too, not what you might expect. Certainly not what he expected from the staid and dull Ontario that he knew, patriotic to its bootstraps—to England, that is. Although, as he passed like a shadow by farmhouses, through villages and towns, he instinctively avoided the homes that were virtuous-seeming and prayer-locked, and he gave a wide berth to those with oak boughs decorating their front doors in commemoration of King Charles's restoration to the throne, *only* two and a half centuries ago. He was drawn instead to the wavering lamplight that spilled at night out of houses filled with music and chatter and a sprawling, unkempt merriment. He stood at windows, munching handfuls of spinach or lettuce from the inhabitants' own gardens, observing those within playing cards, or getting boisterously drunk, or inventively amorous—on the kitchen table, no less. Once, entranced, he watched a whole line of men and women, crouched down and hopping along the floor like ducks, hands linked to waists, legs flying, faces hot and burnished as though buttered with pure joy. Laughing, dancing, shouting—it was heartbreaking, the lives that some people are given.

Flying limbs and soaring spirits—this was news to Grif. He thought of his own home: the altar-heavy and unplayed organ in the parlour, the confessional hush that rose out of the furniture, the prohibitive sheen of the oiled floor disallowing any frivolity that the feet might want to engage in, the plain black cross on the wall, the deity's illiterate signature sealing a grim contract on the souls contained within. One thing he had learned on his travels was that eccentric behaviour was not only widespread, but invisible to those engaged in it. In one farmhouse he had watched a woman perform her chores, pouring tallow into moulds, baking bread, her family going about their business; all the while she wore a fish around her neck, a trout it was, the red ribbon strung through its mouth and gills tied in a neat bow. In another he saw a man eating a newspaper, strip by strip, column by column, while blood ticked out of his nose into a basin balanced on his lap. If he were to stand outside the window of his childhood home gazing in, he wondered if he would see something that he had missed, something obvious to an objective onlooker. He might catch his parents smiling at one another, if only faintly, or exchanging a word or two, some banality at least symbolic of conversation. More likely his mother would be seated as usual in the most uncomfortable chair, sewing, lips compressed, the fine lines around her mouth like stitching sealing it shut. His father would be seated opposite, hands fisted but empty, quarrying the silence with his fierce stare. Grif had told Avice that his parents were both dead, and it had not been such a great lie as all that. Hearts have to beat, don't they? *Some* warmth has to be generated in the blood.

Was that what he was looking for: the fleeting, mysterious thing that licks like a flame through a room—or a journal—otherwise so stiff and still? He had caught sight of it here and there, but had no idea how to attract it. How was he to be inscribed by it, how endorsed? So seldom was he acknowledged by the man ploughing the field or the woman hanging out the wash, or only with disdain and aversion (even the dogs kept their distance, sensing disloyalty), that he began to take his own non-existence for granted. He must have walked clear of himself somewhere along the line without even noticing, a man who had slipped out of his skin as well as his marriage. But like a spirit still attracted to the living, he couldn't resist the heated spectacle of a gathering, the persistence of humankind, whether in church or at a boat race, in conjuring up that death-defying element that slipped like liquid, ungraspable, through his own fingers.

Near Tara, he was spying on a picnic in progress, a cyclists' club, some twenty or thirty people stopped by a lake to rest under the pines and refresh themselves with lemonade and potted meat sandwiches. He had encountered the abandoned machinery first, bicycles propped against tree trunks and scattered over the ground, a poignantly modern sight, like the scene of a benign accident, humans wholly tossed out of the picture. Since what he sought was not to be found there, glinting off handlebars and spokes, he crept down a path to the lake, pulled by murmuring voices so light they lifted easily and naturally into laughter. Gaiety was hard to resist, and why should he? He crept closer, concealing himself behind a screen of chokecherry bushes as the cyclists came into view. And there it was, quickening through the party like a nosy truffle-hunting breeze, the element he couldn't possibly define, bouncing off a china plate, off the tine of a fork, into a mouth silvered and full. It streaked among the visual clamour, the scattered dishes and bottles, then idled momentarily like something intentionally packed and toted along. It blessed a blade of grass, the crook of a cup's handle, a cuff, a swirl of hair, a peek of exposed bloomer, a moistened lip, a fingernail. It held all the discrete components of the day in an altered coherence. It was a game the partying cyclists played simply by being. He saw a packed and animate canvas (a *Dejeuner sur l'herbe*, buttoned to the neck), a work of art *and* life, both excluding him. So he decided to sneak back along the path and steal one of the bicycles.

That evening he sat by a campfire drying his socks, holding them out on sticks like flayed skins before the flames. Luckily, he had lifted the matches after, and not before, exploring the bottom of the lake on that infernal two-wheeled machine. How was he to know there was a trick to operating the damn thing? As it turned out, he had crashed that cyclists' party, literally, smashing plates and exploding a sponge cake on his wild lake-bound trajectory. He could still see the laughing faces of his rescuers, and hear the mock concern in their voices as they tried to catch him in a net of words. *Are you all right? Thought you'd try it out, eh, old boy? Who are you, anyway? What's your name? Yes, your name.*

He had made a dumb show of it, miming and gesticulating, shrugging, nodding, stretching his face in mute cheer. He pretended to be a foreigner, the sort given to intemperate acts, and indicated that he couldn't speak the language. Nor could he, not their language of palsy fun and heartiness. He escaped with his name (plus a box of lucifers and a lemon tart) intact, his soaked clerical jacket clamped around his body like an unbroken bud.

Grif planted the sticks in the ground by the fire, and the dangling socks smoked like censers, releasing their own complex olfactory story of his journey. He retrieved the missal from his jacket, also drying on a teetering homemade clothes horse, thinking it would give him some entertainment to see the book burn, to sizzle a few saints and preachments. To prolong the anticipation, he flipped the book open and riffled through it. He contemplated feeding the fire slowly, page by page. That's when the writing in it snagged his eye and he realized that it wasn't a missal at all, but a journal of some sort. What sort was beyond him, and in trying to figure that out he got enmeshed in the reading of it, as though an ancient gnarled hand had reached out of the pages and yanked him right in. The paper was buckled somewhat from his dip in the lake, and the crabbed script was on the verge of illegibility— but it was a verge to which he was nonetheless attracted.

He could figure out this much: that tubby, self-satisfied cleric from whom he had stolen it could not be its author; unless the man was even more depraved than he looked, for the journal was largely a record of mayhem and vandalism. Most entries described the desecration of churches, the destruction of statuary, holy vessels and relics:

> Clare. We brake down 1,000 Pictures superstitious; I brake down 200; three of God the Father and three of Christ and the Holy Lamb, and three of the Holy Ghost like a Dove with Wings; and the twelve Apostles were

carved in Wood on the top of the Roof which we gave order to take down; and twenty cherubims to be taken down; and the Sun and Moon in the East Windows, by the King's Arms, to be taken down.

Grif read on in the shuddering, uncertain light of his campfire, baffled but fascinated. The book also contained a few poems, notes on wills, passages in Latin, a recipe for how to make a Presbyterian ("Take the herbs hypocrisy & ambition. . ."), and detailed descriptions of whippings, brandings, beheadings, hangings.

His lips twitched as he read. He could feel heat rising in his throat, his tongue burning. The journal had nothing at all to do with him, and yet he saw himself reflected in it, as if he were staring at a mirror and not merely the faded pages of an old, lifeless book. The actions it described both deeply excited and troubled him. In the end he didn't toss it in the fire, but found himself clutching its black calf covers tightly, protectively, as if hanging on for dear life to his own hidebound soul.

"Griffith." His name dropped out of his mouth like a newborn. It was the first time he had spoken in weeks, outside of the speech he had delivered to the pig and the monosyllabic pleasantries they had exchanged. "Oh Grif," he said again, his soliloquy foreshortened by shame, for he had freely admitted to the crime of himself.

# 3

## NOMINUS UMBRA

So THE FUGITIVE, the scapegrace, admits to a name but has no plan, at least nothing he can attach a name to. Having yanked his name out of its place in the world, it seems an object adrift, like a head minus a body, a floating spectre trailing ripped tentacles and filaments. Possibly his name was his plan, one that carried him further and further north while he clung determinedly to it. It was the one thing in his life that he was faithful to, although not necessarily out of choice. If he could have dreamt up a convincing alias to hide out in, he surely would have. Erasmus Richardson? Raphael Dunsmuir? Utterly respectable fellows—*they* would never desert their wives—but as these names were so ludicrously weighty, Grif could scarcely launch them off his tongue, couldn't even get them past the barrier of his lips without laughing. Duncan Campbell . . . Lampman? *Ha, ha.* A good name, it appears, is harder to steal than a gold brick. Valentine Moote, Walter Thistle, Vespasian Nutting. Even the most ordinary and generic names he could think of sounded in his ear gimcrack and clumsily cobbled together, hardly credible and, like the jacket he wore, unconvincing concealment for an entirely dubious article.

He was not an actor—no name-haunter, or hustler—although nearly as contemptible as one. If anyone asked now, he would confess, *I am Grif. Grif Smolders*, and let them spit in his eye, or doctor him with a dose of cold lead. He would take what was coming. As plans go, this was a thin one, and did nothing much for his spirits, so perhaps it was useful that he did meet an actor, a villain as it turned out. Villains always have plans more robust and less mired in guilt than your garden-variety deserter.

This villain even looked the part, having only recently been chased out of Meaford for playing it to perfection in some cheesy little melodrama. To keep himself amused, he had adopted for the performance a broadly farcical French accent, and it may have been his provocatively stretched and slanted vowels that stoked the good Orangemen in the audience into an orange rage. Or it may have simply been the ambiguous spin he put on his part, complicating evil with a dash of goodness. Funny how a mere hint of moral confusion can incite in such a crowd an even deeper hatred than usual. They *loathed* him, a mass sentiment he always found bracing, even charming. How seriously people took him, *booing* and *hissing*, pitching the odd rotten egg, as he plotted and schemed his way through these mundane entertainments—*The Road to Ruin* or *Wages of Sin* ("Endorsed by the Clergy" and "Praised by the Press"). How little they required of their art, and what a triumph of simplicity. Jew-dark, moustache-twirling, forecloser of mortgages, despoiler of virtue, he became the locus of all dissatisfactions and resentments, a convenient scapegoat. Well, if he were a straitlaced, flush-faced citizen of Meaford, Ontario, wedded to one of those corpulent and jeering females, it would be understandable, wouldn't it? The blame for these dreary, constricted lives had to be allocated somewhere.

At least he was universally despised, even by his fellow actors. Ah, mischief. Had he really called Margaret, the lily-white heroine, a whore (she was), albeit under his breath, possibly a little louder than he had meant to? Thank God for the power of words, that, unscripted, they could still do the work of a hurled bomb. Men, enraged, rose up from the audience and actually stormed the stage to defend Margaret's honour, and by proxy the honour of their wives and daughters. It was so touching, which is why he'd cleared out, and hastily—the very thought of their meaty paws touching *him*... appalling. (And where was Frank meanwhile, the dashing hero of the play? Behind the curtain, dashing a quick pint down his throat. You had to be a hero yourself to receive the reeking lines he poured into your face.) There wasn't much point in being the villain if one didn't make off with the evening's proceeds, which he promptly did before disappearing in a puff of smoke, the latter usually a corny and unconvincing effect, except that the audience, in lieu of burning the words right out of his mouth, had to settle for torching the stage. A passionate lot in Meaford.

The villain was still wearing his top hat and cape when he came whistling out from behind Knox United on Murdock Street in Owen Sound. He'd nipped behind the church to take a leak and on emerging spotted Grif, who was gazing up at the bricks and mortar of the building as if there were some intelligible reading to be had in it, an early and invisible graffiti that might tell him what to do next. A likely-looking lad, the villain thought to himself, catching Grif's eye and flashing him a brilliant smile. A hearty meal, a wash, a decent pair of shoes (*heavens*, yes), and he'd be an even more likely lad. Good looks, a wonderful physique, a bit glum, but not beyond cheering up. The villain was feeling generous, public-spirited, in a mood to deepen his commitment to his fellow man. (He hoped he'd remembered to button himself up.) He smiled again at Grif, doffed his hat and gave his cape a natty little swirl. Self-parody ran so strong in him it was all he could do to keep his eyebrows from dancing off his face. He moved in on Grif, hand extended. "Fenwick Nashe," he said.

His name fit him like the skin on his arm.

Grif took him for a banker, and that a banker should want to make his acquaintance seemed likely enough at the time. In his long post-nuptial walk, his jailbreak constitutional, Grif's sense of what was possible in his life had unravelled and let in some light. Owen Sound itself had a kind of anything-goes atmosphere, fed by an unsavoury undercurrent that was not unusual to find in a port town. Corkscrew Town, he'd heard a man call it in passing, and Grif had noticed a prodigious number of taverns, as well as drunks, vagrants, reeling sailors and dock hands, loafers, gamblers, loose women. (He was a loose man, but that was different.) Easy to see how even an upright citizen might have trouble staying that way, how even a banker might have an eroded respectability. Fenwick Nashe didn't shun the public houses in any event, and by the end of the day Grif felt he'd been introduced to most of them: the American Hotel, the Queen's, the McWilliam House, the Clifton, the Comely. After a while the names no longer registered; they were washed down with quarts of Eaton Brothers' Golden Ale and Triple X Stout, then pissed out anonymously against the taverns' back walls, where a man *might* write something legible if he weren't too squiffed to handle the instrument in hand.

How strange it felt to Grif, being back in civilization, even this demotic version of it, after being wind-groomed and river-fed for days, tucked up under a star blanket at night, mosquitoes singing him lullabies. It didn't take long to become a wild man, which is why Fenwick's first move was to propel him into a barbershop, from which he emerged raw and blinking like a creature who'd just been dragged out of a bush. Groomed, fed, liquored and briefed, that's how the day progressed, but dreamily. The plan the villain slowly unfurled was a wavery one, submerged and ungraspable.

Around midday Grif milled down a meal—boiled beef, roast potatoes, pie—taking on this heaven-sent dinner as if it were employment. Serious work when it doesn't come every day. Then somewhere between one saloon and the next they stopped at a storefront to look at a chorus line of deer carcasses displayed in a window, and in another a bear: *This week exhibited live*, a sign read, *next week dead.*

"Empathy," Fenwick pointed out, keeping an eye on his charge, "is a ruinous sentiment."

At Grafton's, a dry goods store, they met two little people named the Winners, a major and his missus, who had come from Iowa to promote the store's camel-hair coats. Two little coats. The manager had billed them as *The smallest married couple and the world's greatest midgets*. Small and great, they attracted quite a crowd; and Grif, marvelling, could not help but reflect on the diminishing effects of the marital state.

For some undisclosed reason—a bank job in the offing?— Fenwick bought him a pair of shoes at Grafton's, and a suit of clothes to match, although Grif drunkenly insisted on wearing the Reverend Bee's noisome jacket overtop his new trim.

Grif supposed he would get the gist eventually. His patron was not reticent. He talked freely and ranged widely in subject matter as the watering holes they wandered into got progressively smaller and rougher, until they were practically nose to nose, facing one another over a table tottery as an outstretched hand. He could feel Fenwick's breath on his cheek, and he found it weirdly cool, smelling of nothing. But the barroom itself was too close, too warm, oppressive with the stench of men's lives guttering out in sweat and smoke. And vomit—there was a trench in the floor for sluicing it out the door. (Good chance Grif himself might soon be contributing.) The only other decoration in the place was a bucket in one corner that served as a spittoon and the pug-ugly faces of the men standing at the bar, who turned either to send a gob flying into the bucket or to stare with undisguised hostility at them.

Fenwick took not the slightest notice. He was absorbed in the current topic of conversation: himself. He was as open as a vault, but no banker after all, for he told Grif about life on the stage, about touring the Dominion, and where you could buy the services of a nine-year-old girl for fourteen cents, and a double-breasted suit sewn by her mother for less. He had met well-known actors, artists, politicians. Julia Arthur, May Irwin, the famous Canadian writer Gilbert Parker. He had escorted Pauline Johnson, the Mohawk Princess, to Shea's Theatre to hear the exceptional monologuist George Fuller Golden. He had dined at the Rideau Club, marched with the Knights of Labour, penned a column for *Busy Man's Magazine*.

"Do you believe that money is the handmaid of virtue, Grif?" His address slipped easily into American informality.

He didn't wait for an answer, not that one was forthcoming. Grif wasn't feeling backward, or out of his depth, so much as afloat. Fenwick provided a surfeit of facts, but there was a slippery ambiguity to everything he said. Grasping the precise point of it all was like trying to hold a freshly plucked eyeball between your fingertips. Nor was he any the wiser about the man's views. Was he for or against privilege, the safety razor, child labour, the coin-operated phonograph, zippers...? Grif honestly couldn't say, and didn't.

"Have you tried one of these telephone devices yet?"

Hah! Grif knew all about the perfidies of that invention. It was said that the telephone transmitted false information and lies.

"Electricity is the coming thing, though, eh? I know a fellow in Quebec..."

Even worse! The devil's own veins and arteries creeping through your house. Grif's parents had been terrified of electricity, yet had embraced it readily enough, infernal light to extend the working day.

"Superior to gas, mind you. Do you realize how many people that kind of lighting has killed off? A chap prepares to retire at night, blows out the flame, forgets to turn off the gas, goes to bed and never gets up. Asphyxiated." Something about that word pleased Fenwick, and he took a moment to linger over it while stroking his gums with an ivory toothpick. Then he said, "You're on the run. Tell me why."

And, *Bless me Father*, he did, confession being an old habit and a hard one to shake. The villain may have worked some colourful embroidery into his autobiography—that bit about larking with Oscar Wilde in Toronto—but Grif had no need, his story was fanciful enough.

Fenwick was sympathetic, exonerating him for his marital defection with a dismissive wave of his hand. "You're well shot of that one, my boy, she would have eaten you alive. Sounds like one of these New Women." He shuddered. "Once the ladies have the vote, we *will* be done for."

As for the ball lightning, the fiery, heel-igniting orb, he also eased Grif's mind. Where Grif had been worried that the- ology and retribution might be involved—a divine messenger lobbing a sizzling knuckleball at his confused and sinning head—Fenwick offered a scientific explanation. "A high-density plasma," he suggested, "or gas trapped in the atmosphere. You are fortunate to have witnessed such an unusual thing. And to have survived it. One does hear of it happening; there are documented reports. I recall reading about one such that occurred in the seventeenth century, in England it was. A yellow flaming ball, just as you describe, rolled into a house right through the door and killed eight people. And a cow—don't ask me what it was doing in the house. Fresh milk, I suppose."

Seeing as his actor friend was not shy of knowledge, it occurred to Grif that he might also be able to enlighten him about that peculiar book he had found in the cleric's jacket, what its provenance might be, what exactly it was, why, even, it seemed to engage him the way it did. He began to say something about it, but Fenwick's attention had been diverted elsewhere.

"Knuckle-walkers." He nodded toward a group of men who had tumbled out onto the street to play a game of hot cockles. One man, blindfolded with a black neckerchief, stood braced while the others proceeded to ball up their fists, then took turns punching him. The object of the game being that the blindfolded man had to correctly identify the one who had hit him, and when he did so, it would then be the identified man's turn to be blindfolded and punched, until he too came up with the name of his assailant. There were some subtleties in this game, perhaps difficult to locate—that even the wielding of a fist was done with a certain style and could leave an impression clear as an incriminating fingerprint. Also, there was punishment in full for not knowing who your friends were.

"Knuckle-walkers?" As Grif watched through the grimy window this brutal give-and-take, blood already streaming out of the blindfolded man's nose, he figured it wouldn't be too long before the game broke free of its rules and they got down to brawling in earnest.

"Primates. I wonder, does such an activity prove or disprove Mr. Darwin's theories?" Fenwick smiled, trying to retract the iniquitous edge of it. "We are progressive men, are we not, Griffith? You agree to what I have proposed today."

Statement or question, Grif nodded, although it was more like shaking up a jar to get a view of the contents. What had Fenwick proposed? Something about making money, piles of it. But he hadn't meant actually *making* it, had he? Grif could already see his own grimacing mug printed up on one of those handbills he'd seen posted around town, men wanted for robbery, arson, trespass, murderous assault and "furious driving." Surely he was in enough trouble already.

"Excellent." Fenwick rose from the table and grasped his hand briefly, giving it an efficient contract-sealing shake. "Tomorrow it is, then. At the pier. I'll be waiting."

Grif watched him stride out, and suddenly he seemed so unlikely in his actor's gear, he might indeed have been nothing more than a figure loosed from a melodrama, a fugitive from the script. It's a wonder he didn't walk right through the wall. A man propped up against the bar, a hairy lunk with few teeth and even less charm, sneered as Fenwick swished past, and sent a sloppy wad of black spittle after him, which disappeared into the folds of his cape. Someone less accustomed to critical review might have taken exception to this and sent the man's few remaining teeth down his gullet to nibble on his equally unattractive insides, but Fenwick merely walked briskly out the door and up the street.

The game of hot cockles was in full swing.

"Percival!" the blindfolded man bellowed. "*Unhhh.* Archibald? *Anhhh.* Jesus fucking Christ! *Ufff.*"

I won't meet him tomorrow, Grif told himself. The man was up to no good. Even beneath the caricatured impression of danger Fenwick had given him, he sensed something else, truer, darker. On the other hand, he knew he would show up. Not so much because he was a man of his word—hadn't he proven otherwise?—but because he was deeply curious to know what that word might be.

# 4

# A SCREAM

GRIF sat up abruptly, pulled out of sleep, and listened. He wasn't sure whether it had come from somewhere within the boarding house or from within his own head—a scream, high and sharp, a briefly sustained note of pure terror. He did dream sounds sometimes: the peal of a bell, a door banging shut, phantom voices whispering, laughing. The place seemed quiet enough, hosting only the usual creaks and groans a house is allowed to make for bearing its human cargo without complaint through the long day. No indications that a woman was suffering some indignity within. All was silent, even in the room next door where earlier its occupant, a lumber man, had been planing the already thin walls with a snore as rough as a ripsaw.

Outside, he could hear the shush of the water in the bay, the inevitable dog barking in the distance, a cart being driven up the street, one of its axles squealing—but not screaming. It was not out of the question that he had made the noise, that he was its author. The very moment of waking he had been dreaming that a bird, black and glistening, was emerging from his mouth, being born.

All those nights outdoors he had slept warily, provisionally, light as mist on the ground. He was tuned to danger—wild animals, roving thugs. *Lord knows*, something might have dropped out of the heavens and pressed him flat as a tattoo onto the earth. Feeling safe enough between these walls, he had let sleep plunge him under. But how foolish he'd been and, more to the point, how stupidly piss-eyed. The only thing he remembered doing before crawling into bed was lying on the floor for what seemed like hours, puzzling over a pamphlet he had discovered flush up against the chamber pot. It was an advertisement for a club that was about to open in Owen Sound called the Young Men's Christian Association: "Our object is the conversion to Christ of all young men and the strengthening and development of those who love His cause, in all Christian powers and graces. Also, the social and mental elevation and improvement of young men by such secular means and appliances, which though wholly secondary, are still important objects in the scheme of our organization." *Powers and graces*, he had mused, *powers and graces*, before retching into the pot and wiping his mouth with the pamphlet.

It occurred to him that he was still wearing his new clothes and shoes. He jerked his hand up quickly to touch the pocket where the journal lay, a tic he had developed, like an old gaffer repeatedly seeking the reassurance of his purse. Not lost. Grif traced its outline with relief. Earlier in the day, while fingering his lapel and murmuring something about the shiny coats of clerics, Fenwick had slipped a crisp bill into his pocket. What *did* the man want—his own bridal night with Grif? Coming from him, the money hadn't seemed like a gift, more a reverse form of theft, something more interesting than generosity anyway.

Grif did not like being beholden, but after Fenwick left, he took the bill out and gazed at it with such raw admiration you'd think he'd never seen money before. He let it pull him right out of the tavern and through the streets like a planchette in hot pursuit of a spirit, and where it brought him—and what it bought him—was a tenancy in this room that almost broke his heart with its spare and simple welcome: a spindle bed covered with a patched woollen blanket, a jug and basin on a small washstand, a drugget on the floor, a hook on the wall. (No mirror to harass him with his own sorry image.) Why had he ever wanted more? He could live here forever like a monk in a cell, penitent to the point of erasure. He had no need of gaudy word-encrusted prayers. No need of marriage and the noisy clattering cascade of goods attached to it—silver mustard pots, necktie cases, clocks, buggies, cigar jars—or of the jumble of duties and responsibilities that fell upon a man and buried him in a suffocating avalanche. Such a fate would make anyone scream.

Fenwick had assured him that his marriage would most certainly have been dissolved by this time—*Unconsummated, did you say?*—and that Grif's fear of the law on his heels was nothing more than vanity. His bride's momentary shame would have been promptly extinguished by the family's enormous relief at having gotten rid of him, and so fortuitously, with no blame falling upon them. Grif's claim on Avice's memory even now had to be tenuous; she would very likely be enjoying a restorative tour of England or the Continent, his debonair replacements waiting in the wings to whirl away with her heart. The rate of a husband's decay in such circumstances was phenomenal: from his stature as a titillating piece of gossip, Grif would shortly dissolve into a dark secret, then into a forgotten one. Soon, to his former and fleeting mate, he would be nothing at all, not even enough dust to get up her nose.

Naturally, Grif had been consoled to hear that this might be the case. Yet it had also bothered him a bit and made him shift uncomfortably in his seat. It was like hearing tell of your own death, then looking carefully at yourself and not finding much evidence that it wasn't so.

As he settled back in the bed, a pre-dream image drifted into his mind of a woman's face, mild and gentle, wearing the slight dash of a smile. He then saw a wooden staff raised and the face smashed open, leaving behind a gaping and jagged black hole through which a cold wind hissed.

A dreadful thought possessed him. What if a man were to wake up one morning with a woman's voice instead of his own. The utter humiliation of it—would he dare speak again? What if he woke up with Avice's voice alive in his throat, and when he spoke, it berated him endlessly. Her accusations would flow out of his mouth like venom, would splatter onto his chest like spilled acid.

He shuddered, and very softly, and hoarsely, said aloud, "Eeeeeeee." Sounded familiar; the tone was right. He tried again, this time louder and deeper, with an exaggerated manliness: "EEEEEEE." Then, as if a disgruntled mate were addressing him, he said to himself, "Shut up, will you, and go to sleep." Advice he wisely and swiftly followed.

Why Fenwick had chosen the dock for their assignation was a mystery that would come clear, Grif supposed, when he found him. If he found him. Grif was late, and the place was packed. He didn't think there could be a busier spot in all of Owen Sound, with one steamer arriving and another preparing to depart. The harbour was dotted with tugs, sailboats, fishing boats. The dockside was even busier, and traffic on the land just as thick. Wagons jammed the road as passengers spilled out of them to join the milling throng on the dock. Children streaked through the crowd, dogs, a chicken on the loose; a young man barged through carrying a skeletal white-haired woman in his arms who was dressed in purple satin from toe to bonnet as though rigged out in her own coffin lining.

It was a carnival of apprehension and excitement. Hoots, shouts, shrieks, braying both animal and human. Deckhands were loading cargo onto one of the boats: mailbags, crates of flour and sugar for the northern settlements and the lumber camps, horses and cattle, all sensible beasts, and sensibly terrified. He was aware of the fear in people's voices, too, although it was less straightforwardly expressed, diverted into chatter or a strained, shrill laughter almost painful to hear. True, these steamers did have a bad habit of catching on fire, and you wouldn't want to be dwelling on that if you were a passenger or had a loved one on board. In his search for Fenwick, the man's inscrutable features hidden somewhere in this crowd, he glanced into many faces more readable, several taut with worry, even premature sorrow. There were families gathered here who were about to be broken open by a great distance, a wound of space inflicted that would never be healed. So much talk about the sanctity of home and family, yet the truth was, people couldn't stay put, couldn't wait to leave. Free land out west, gold in the Yukon, factory jobs in the city. Material betterment might be the excuse, but restlessness was the drover.

For a time Grif was wedged between two stout fellows, one sniggering to himself, the other quietly weeping—both solid as bookends. Being stuck, he took the opportunity to gaze up at one of the steamers, the *Northern Belle*. She was a beauty, too, with her burnished brass and fancy mouldings, decorative as a birthday cake. And he thought, why not line up for his share, his serving of the journey? Fenwick had insisted that he was a free man ... *insofar as that is possible*, he had added. Philosophy aside, this boat could further that freedom, stretch the bounds of what was possible. It was what he wanted, wasn't it: to stoke the fire in his breast that his impulsive departure had ignited? He *had* to go forward, on and on, and dare not look back where he knew she was standing, staring after him, granite-eyed and unforgiving. He did not believe that she was to be found in Europe enjoying a tour of forgetfulness. She was at his back, always at his back, waiting, like death itself.

Someone tugged firmly at his sleeve and it made him jump; a shiver ran up his arm. His stout props, Comedy and

Tragedy, seemed to have melted away, and he turned expecting to see Fenwick (not that he really wanted to see him anymore). His brief travel reverie had him almost convinced, and he could see himself stowing away in the belly of this boat, living on crumbs that fell through the cracks and the odd rat. No wait—he would work his way across the lakes, disembarking at the Sault with a pocketful of honestly earned wages, then head out west where there was plenty of land and space under the stars to lose yourself in. A prairie sky renders a man practically invisible.

It was not Fenwick but a young woman standing before him, very pretty, if somewhat pale and agitated, and wearing the most alarming hat. A madwoman's hat. It was widebrimmed like a picture hat but made of bones wired together, wrapped in a gauzy material and decorated with flowers, tassels, a stuffed finch and a sprig of cedar. He couldn't help but stare. The thing was like a bad dream she might be having, exhibited on the exterior of her brain. No wonder she looked troubled. Avice's hats had all been trim and stylish, functional as punctuation, a brisk nod to convention without being subsumed by it. Everyone in possession of a head, whether lively or dull, required a hat, but *this* was cause for concern.

"Do excuse me," she said, sanely enough, unclasping her fingers from his sleeve and sizing up Grif's own incongruous appearance: *two* jackets, the outer hardly a match for the flashy boater he was wearing (purchased only that morning, for he had been shopping, not sleeping in). The hat was pushed back on his head, rimming it like a halo, and giving him an open, innocent look, an approachability. Certainly he was the most handsome man in sight, and Amelia Kennedy did have a reputation among her friends for being a desperate flirt. "I am so sorry to bother you, but I need some assistance. You see, my boat is about to leave and I have all these to get aboard somehow." She gestured helplessly at a leaning tower of hat boxes. "I can't find a steward anywhere. Fred was supposed to be here to help me. Fred, my brother. And—oh dear, it's no use, I *am* going to miss it."

She is very pretty, Grif thought. I wonder whose bones she's wearing on her head, he also thought, while smiling gamely at her.

A boat whistle sounded, a throaty, resonant blast that made Captain Peter Campbell—"Black Pete" —of the *Northern Belle* stop to listen, fingers lightly grazing the dark beard that foamed around his face. How he loved that sound. It excited him like a woman's hot hand sailing up his back, and the *Echo's* whistle did have a lovely tone, so pure she might sing in a church. Which is about all you could say for her—a ship of slight construction, its wheelhouse built too high, fitted with the wrong kind of propellers for lake navigation. Besides which, the boat was mismanaged, understaffed and overloaded with freight, driven more by the company's greed than by skill or any concern for its passengers.

Standing on the hurricane deck of his own ship, he watched a young couple race past on the dock below, weaving through the crowd, then up the *Echo's* gangplank. Honeymooners, most likely. He shook his head and snorted, "Hats." The young man was running blind, struggling with a slithering, cascading armful of boxes, while the girl, her skirt hitched to keep up (fat ankles), chattered non-stop and directed the fellow as if he were a dumb beast. Captain Campbell leaned over the railing slightly and narrowed his eyes. He couldn't quite tell what she was wearing on her head, but it looked suspiciously like a chicken carcass. With dressing. His own hat he sometimes cinched to his head with a length of rope when he raced Basset's *City of Midland* up to Collingwood. But his hat was never screwed on so tight that he couldn't see what was happening on his own ship. In fact he was downright omniscient, with the capacity for wrath that can accompany the all-knowing. More than once he had found it necessary to throw a passenger overboard, his luggage following, for smoking in a stateroom. A steamer can keep afloat only so much human stupidity. He knew that he would never be the dictator of these waters, but on them he managed well enough. It was said that he had the luck of the devil—twenty years a skipper and still breathing air—but he thought what he had rather was the devil's good sense.

He wondered if the captain of the *Echo* was sober enough today to read his barometer. And he wondered too, not without sympathy, where that young couple might find themselves this night. In heaven or hell? Both were distinct possibilities.

Captivated or captured? Ruefully, Grif had begun to ponder the distinction as he placed the last of the boxes in Amelia Kennedy's room. He tried to edge out the door, but she held him fast, pinned to the spot with a non-stop monologue. He couldn't tell whether it was simply nervousness that made her rattle on—fear of travel, or water, or a woman's well-founded anxiety about travelling alone. She might simply be a compulsive talker, a bleeder of words, her mouth a gash in her face through which her whole being poured. He was not so charmed as he had been at first.

He marvelled at the amount of information she imparted in so short a time: her father's gout, her mother's needlework, her brother Fred's accident involving the tuba, her sister's confinement, a distant cousin's engagement to a military man, which was, even to her it seemed, of distant interest. He was almost beginning to feel like an intimate of this family, a suffering member yearning to escape its claustrophobic banality. She filled him in on her various likes (glove sets, hat brushes, magic pencils) and her dislikes (mourning pins, conversation tubes, vest chains made of hair), confided her spiritual ambitions (trite) and her secular ones, which included the present venture. The hat boxes represented neither an obsession with her appearance nor with the joys of haberdashery itself, but were a professional investment. She was a milliner en route to Fort William to work for a Mrs. Dorcas Small, although only temporarily, as it would not be long, she assured him, before she had her own shop and several girls working for her. Admittedly, her confidence was as remarkable as her hat, and probably as skewed, for he couldn't quite see the ladies of Fort William gliding into their church socials or at homes adorned in femurs, twigs and paws—however fitting were the head-dresses of savages for those rigid and chilly rituals.

There was something to be said for reticence in a woman, for a seemly reserve. Indeed, there was a great deal to be said, and he didn't doubt that she would get around to it. He longed to place his fingers on her plump lips to staunch this flow of pointless, useless chatter. He wanted to halt this promiscuous clacking of her tongue; surely that organ was pure muscle, strong enough to lift and hurl the whole of the language in one try. Instead, inching backwards, one hand behind him, he groped for the handle of the cabin door. Ever since he stepped on board this boat, he had felt uneasy, troubled. He noted how shabby it was, and dirty, with garbage banked in corners, its brass smudged and filmy as if mauled by an army of grubby-fingered two-year-olds. Not only that, but it rode too low in the water for his liking, and he figured there was no point in adding further ballast.

"Excuse me, Miss Kennedy," he interrupted, "but I really must—"

And then she screamed. "Ohhh, did you see it? Behind the bed, a *rat*, oh, not in my room, a *rat*, do something, please, get it out!"

But it wasn't a rat. Or rather, it wasn't the rat that contained the truth of the matter; it was her scream. The *same* scream that had woken him during the night, the high, sharp cry that had slit open sleep and dream. A premonition it must have been, a warning that he had left undeciphered and unheeded. If that rat carried the bad news about this boat in its verminous heart, then Amelia Kennedy's scream carried a bleak certainty. Finally she had told him something worth knowing.

He scrabbled clumsily at the door, flung it open and ran, hoping he could rely once again on his cowardice to save him. He tore along the deck but it was no use, he was too late, the *Echo* was already steaming twenty, thirty yards from the dock. He stared into the churning water, wondering whether it would buoy him up if he leapt in, or would he hit bottom like an anchor? What chance did he have? He couldn't swim. Surely someone on the shore would see him go overboard and rescue him. But no one was watching. Already backs were turning away, eyes redirected inland. There were no lingering goodbyes or wistful looks following in the wake of the *Echo*.

Except one. There *was* one, a man on the dock standing alongside a medium-sized wooden crate. He was waving at Grif, shouting out, trying to tell him something. Fenwick. *Lord*, it was Fenwick Nashe. He had found Grif after all. He was waving his arms strenuously, and shouting loudly, with urgency, his face knotted with effort. Grif strained to hear, but the boat's whistle kept blowing and blowing as though a madman were in control of it, annulling all other sound, dispersing Fenwick's words like smoke.

Hearing it, Black Pete of the *Northern Belle* paused but did not turn to watch the *Echo* leave the bay. He shook his head sadly, as he considered the equivocal nature of such instruments, why they call to us so irresistibly and yet are so deceitful.

# 5

## MAL DE MER

A MAN attuned to what the weather was bringing him might feel it in the texture of the wind—a freshening, a stiffening; no longer a cool soft silk pouring over his skin, but a material more ruched and abrasive, like that handful of lace he sank his face into one time. Grif stood on the deck of the *Echo*, letting it rush over him, the wind like an endlessly unfurling bolt of funereal crepe, rasping cloth that told him a thing or two. Not that he needed to be told, since the ship's name said it all (twice). The *Echo*—it practically invited misfortune on board. It seemed more the title of some dreary elegaic poem, thick with tragedy, one he would turn away from instinctively, because who needs to be entertained with a mind-crushing wallop of sorrow? The problem was that Grif was in this tragedy, riding on its very deck, his hands clutching the railing so hard he might have been wearing white gloves, formally attired for the occasion with fear's accessories.

He was only a boy when the *Asia* went down in this lake, on this very run, up past the Bruce Peninsula and into the Devil's Gap. One hundred and twenty people had drowned, corpses spread from Flowerpot Island to Manitoulin. Like many women at the time, his mother wouldn't serve fish for months afterwards, fearing that by some ungodly jigging of the food chain they would indirectly consume some of the victims. There had been two young survivors, Duncan Tinkus and Christy Morrison, saved most likely by their impervious adolescence: death may not have occurred to them. Their ordeal made them celebrities. Reams of poetry about them had appeared in the papers, and a song had become inescapably popular. Grif did not expect that he would survive as a lyric let alone as a minor character if the *Echo*'s foundering got written up as a story. He wouldn't cause the faintest smirk of grief before the page was turned and he was forgotten. Literature could scarcely claim him if life had already dropped him through the cracks—he wasn't on the passenger list. He wasn't even on the devil's list of the carnally experienced.

He whipped off his hat and fired it into the lake, that unsettling brew of black, churning water. It rode for a while, jaunty on the crest of calamity, then was carried away out of sight. *Horse Turd*, he thought. That had been the name of a tug he had seen at Owen Sound, and it struck him as a far more honest name, uncontaminated by the pretensions of mythology. He wished to God he were riding on that piece of excrement rather than this one.

Amelia Kennedy was completely surprised to encounter him again. Given the ungentlemanly haste of his departure— he hadn't even said goodbye—she had assumed that he liked vermin even less than she did, and that once out of the cabin door he had put a good distance between himself and this ship, disembarking easily enough at the dock. Yet here he was, still on board. She had come out of her room to take in some scenery and air—mostly air. That rat had upset her and she had begun to feel queasy. She discovered Grif leaning against a railing on the quarterdeck, gazing moodily into the water as if mesmerized by his own broken reflection. It was her fault, of course. In assisting her, he had missed his own boat, or his day's work, or whatever had brought him down to the dock in the first place; she hadn't enquired. He must be furious, taken so far out of his way, and penniless perhaps, his absence a cause of panic and worry at home.

She moved toward him, staggering to keep her balance. How rough the lake was getting. The waves were lashing the sides of the boat like black tongues.

He was studying the water so intently, she didn't think him at all aware of her approach. But he turned to her, and said, grimly, "I need to . . . fornicate. You. You'll do."

Well, there were prettier ways of putting this, less direct and certainly less crude. The whole social machinery of courtship and marriage hummed along so that these words did not have to be uttered at all. Grif didn't have time for that, though, and he was married already, and he was going to die, and he had never done it, and he was a man after all, and he was astonished at what he had just said.

He fully expected her to be so outraged she'd give him a ringing clout on the side of the head, knock him flat; and that too was a form of intercourse not unwelcome.

Amelia gasped, and her fantastic hat trembled slightly, absorbing the aftershock of the request. There was a charged pause as she stared at him, hard, and then she threw back her head and laughed—too loudly, her lips too relaxed. He caught a glimpse of decay in her back molars, and with her bellow of laughter came a sweetish, offensive mortal smell. Her breath betrayed her, and he hoped to hell she would not say yes. Unfortunately, assent at this moment seemed all too likely; he caught a flickering lascivious gleam in her eye like a cat's. It might be wiser, he thought, to travel virginal into the dark, letting innocence light the way.

He had succeeded in diverting her, in any event. After her laughter subsided, she still wore a pert, knowing smile on her face. The vulgarity had pleased her, warmed her, but she side-stepped it nonetheless in asking, "What is that you have in your hand, Mr. Smolders?"

He glanced down. "A book."

"A present? It is very oddly wrapped, wouldn't you say?" She was having some difficulty in suppressing her merriment. Apparently he stroked a woman's funny bone, if nothing else.

"Yes," he said, "it is."

Grif had enfolded his journal in a square of canvas and then secured it with a length of cord, materials provided by the boat itself. Earlier, after watching the shore recede and Fenwick dwindle to a fly-sized speck, he decided that he had better take a tour of the *Echo*. One thing he definitely wanted to do was count the number of lifeboats. *Three*. Given the number of people on board, the sums were not promising; things did not add up. Using a knife he'd picked up in the dining room, he cut the canvas and cord from the tarpaulin covering one of the lifeboats. No one stopped him from hacking away at the ship's property, not a steward or a deckhand, for the boat was eerily short of crew. No one seemed to be in charge, and yet there was no shortage of passengers: on his way through the dining room he had stepped over men, women and children stretched out on the floor, and then discovered even more down in steerage, readying crates to bed down in.

Amelia persisted. "What kind of book? A novel of some sort, something full of adventure and romance?" she teased. "Is it Mr. Zangwill's latest? 'Her white teeth flashed' twixt laughing lips. His voice was hoarse, faltering. . . She came nearer and her eyes wrapped him in flame.' No, wait—you're not a preacher, are you? It's not a bible, surely?"

Grif didn't have the energy to lie, or the interest in doing so, but before he could respond they were distracted by something that hit the railing, a substance soft and wet. And red, red as blood, some of which spattered onto Amelia's dress.

"Oh!" She leapt back. "What is it?"

"Beets," said Grif. He surveyed a group of passengers further up, several bent in misery over the rail. They were speaking their dinners into the wind.

Amelia clapped her hand to her lips, and the colour drained from her face, as did her amusement.

He slipped the packet, the journal, back into his pocket and grabbed her arm. "Listen, Miss Kennedy," he said. "The lifeboat on this side, can you remember that? This side. You must get to this one, and not the other two. I've checked, they're not built properly. Without watertight compartments built into them, they won't right themselves in a high sea."

"High sea? What in heaven's name are you talking about?" She was annoyed now, and cross, wrenching her arm away. The gauze on her hat, undone by the wind, had begun to rise out of her head like smoke. "You *have* been reading too many adventure stories. The lake is a bit rough, I agree, but really . . . ohhh." She stumbled to the railing and gripped it like a wrestler. She was going to be sick, but not in front of him.

Grif stared at his shoes, trying hard not to hear her, thankful that he had forgone breakfast himself. After buying the boater, he had spent his last few cents on a shoeshine; at least he would be a dapper corpse. He honestly couldn't see any use in having this advance knowledge when it wasn't going to save his life or anyone else's. Soon enough an awareness of their common fate was going to spread from mind to mind like fire and there would be a democracy of terror on board. Even now he could hear the horses and cattle in the hold, stamping and bellowing, could almost see their eyes rolling, their nostrils flaring, awled with the scent of death. They *knew*, and as she turned back toward him, wiping her mouth on her sleeve, so did she. Her eyes had gone cold as stones in her head. The wind whipped off her ridiculous hat and smacked it against the deck, bones snapping. Unpinned, her hair was flying wild. To him, her head looked so pitiable and vulnerable he wanted to cup it in his hands and crush it.

"Come," he said, reaching out. "Let's wait in your room. We'll pray if you like."

She accompanied him back, both weaving along the deck like drunks, but she did not want to engage in anything as submissive as prayer. He might have expected her to be docile and malleable, yearning for sanctuary in his arms, but fear had an unusual effect upon her, and she became suddenly furious. She smacked him on the side of the face, then glared at him, as if in a delayed response to his earlier request for intimacy. She made a fist, which she was clearly about to drive into his chest when he grabbed her by the wrist and they began to struggle. What she needed to do most of all, it seemed, was fight—with *him*, as if he were responsible, as if he contained not only the secret but the means of her death, and she was determined to wrest it out of him and obliterate it, like a mother tenaciously and brutally digging into a child's heart for a suspected lie.

While the wind rose higher, and the waves, and the ship began to pitch and roll, and voices outside the cabin rose in alarm—men shouting, women screaming—they tumbled on the floor, locked in an embrace that looked like love but wasn't. She attacked him, viciously. Grif did all he could to protect himself from her kicks and thrusting knees and clawing hands. She was a brute. She swore shockingly. All he thought he knew about women, which admittedly wasn't much, she ripped to shreds. He had been ready to offer her comfort, kindness, even the illusion of hope; the ship might make it through the storm, who was he to say? But all she wanted was this dressing down of the starkest truth that by some bad fortune he had come to represent.

The *Echo* had become like a huge cradle rocked by a lunatic's hand. Furniture skidded past them, and luggage, and hats leapt out of boxes like wild surprises. Locked together, steamrolling from one side of the cabin to the other, they crushed silk roses, flattened crowns, got entangled in ribbons and were stabbed with the quills of ostrich feathers. Anyone would have taken them for soused revellers, rather than desperate strangers pointlessly exhausting themselves.

Abruptly, she stopped struggling. Not that she was done with him, but he could sense her listening, attending to something outside, a noise more providential, she must have hoped, than bellowing humans or the howling wind.

"What is that sound?"

He didn't want to set her off again, but answered, "Below deck, they're dumping cargo overboard. The animals too, they're being driven into the lake. God, listen to them."

"Will it save us?" she shouted at him, her face only inches from his own, her mouth wrenched and ugly.

"No, Miss Kennedy. It's not likely."

"Call me Amy," she said.

That is when he thought he might strike her. He certainly wanted to, wanted to ball up his fist and smash it into her face, and watch with satisfaction how it shattered—now that their relationship was a little less formal.

"I have blood on my hands," she said.

Grif glanced down at himself in case it was true she might have injured him. But the only blood on her hands was invisible, its weight borne with a slight trembling, as she sat up and brushed a strand of hair from her face. "I've murdered a man."

He didn't doubt it. By this admission it was clear that she was on the run too, and for a crime far worse than his own; at least Avice was still breathing (down his neck, like an arctic wind). Yet this was hardly the time or place for the felonious details, and besides, he was thoroughly sick of her. Did she think he was really a preacher? If so, he had no absolving words. Salvation, if there was even a glimmer of it available to either of them, lay not in this room, in this death-trap confessional, but outside, where all hell had broken loose.

"Look, *Amy*," he said, slapping down the curse of her name. "Somewhere here, under the bed, there should be life preservers. Have you checked? If there is only one, you take it. Remember that lifeboat I told you about. Get to it. Don't let anyone stop you."

Not, he thought, that anyone would dare.

When Grif and Amy stepped out of the stateroom, uncertain and afraid, awkward as children strapped in their bulky life preservers, they stepped into sheer chaos. The world had been upended. The day was as dark as night, the waves had mounted into enormous towers of water, the wind sawed through their heads, the boat itself had become one huge cacophonous instrument of the devil. As for the human element, it was dissolving. People raced pointlessly every which way, frantic, pushing, crying out. Many were on their knees shouting prayers, imploring God for deliverance, for mercy. Some were howling, clutching at themselves, at their mates or children, tearing at their clothes, their hair. Some had already thrown themselves into the lake, and others had been swept in by the waves that were crashing over the railings.

If only Grif could have stopped up his ears. The scene had already been scored into his eyes so deep he would never forget it. But the *sound*, he thought, was going to kill him. The collective voice of despair was overwhelming, the black and leaden weight of it enough to engulf and sink him before even one drop of water entered his lungs.

He knew he had to act, even if there was absolutely nothing he could do and nowhere in this churning world around him that was safe. He flattened himself against the wall of the deck and inched along, recoiling from the crates that hurtled past, and the bodies. In the confusion he had lost track of Amy, she had vanished from his side. He thought she must have ducked back into the cabin rather than confront this—as many other passengers had probably done. There was no hope. They were all staring into the featureless and terrifying face of eternity.

The *Echo*, quaking and shuddering against him, felt so tenuous it seemed as if the winds might pluck it out of the water altogether and launch it like a paper ship into the sky. Or smash it to pieces. The boat had been labouring for some time in a deep trough between tremendous waves, which had now begun to sweep overtop of it. Grif's mind went numb, stupefied with fear, anaesthetized for what was to come—a mercy so small you could hardly credit it as such.

Only his devious heart was haring along, beating so fast in his chest that, against all odds, it seemed determined to outrun death itself.

# 6

## MODERN HERO

I T WAS the work of a moment, but a moment split open,
cracked like an atom, its forces unleashed. The *Echo* was hit
with a sixty-foot wall of water and rolled over on its side,
slowly, like an animal defeated, lying down. A deep rending
noise resounded within: the boat had begun to break up. And
then it suffered another wave, this one composed of pure
sound as the passengers joined in a cry of horror. When the
ship began to sink beneath them, they swarmed upward in a
solid body, a group as cohesive as the pounding water itself,
screaming like gulls. Then, as the last of the *Echo* disappeared
beneath the waves, this community of the terrified flew apart,
and the real life-and-death contest began.

Someone, possibly some member of the phantom crew,
had released the lifeboats, and they were floating free. The thing
was to get to them, and the protocol was savage. In the water,
people were thrashing and flailing, grasping onto whatever
they could, taking a flying foot in the mouth or a fatal helping
of the lake. Three people attached themselves to Grif and clung
to him like leeches. For the first time in his life he had become
a valuable man, a potential saviour, but only because he was
one of the few in the water wearing a life preserver—wreckage

with a human aspect. What none of these hangers-on seemed to realize was that they were all going to drown if they didn't let go, or he didn't get rid of the thing. Desperately—and desperately trying to forget that he couldn't swim—he grabbed at a hunk of board torn loose from the ship and, hanging on to it, managed to struggle out of the life preserver and thrust himself away from the clutching hands of his admirers. Let them fight over it.

Head empty as a buoy, he struck out toward one of the lifeboats. Later, when it no longer mattered, he would tell himself the bad news: that survival was not possible, and that he was unworthy of it anyway—the prize of life fine as a mote and too elusive to seize. Such thoughts, he knew, weighed very little but could take you straight to the bottom. Doubt, not good; compassion and chivalry, both deadly. Having gotten rid of his shoes (his *new* shoes) before the ship foundered, he kicked his feet freely and vigorously, holding on to his board as if born to it, while trying to keep the lifeboat in view. He passed a woman and saw her go under, dragged down by the weight of her sodden skirts. He wasn't sure, but it was possible that he had struck her with the board. He could have grabbed her swirling hair and pulled her back up, but he didn't. He wondered if he would stop to rescue a child, but then refused to consider it. Thinking was an indulgence—and indulgences killed you.

Undeterred by obstacles moral or physical, he managed to reach the lifeboat, and called out to those on board for help, adding that he was a man of the cloth. (He was wearing clothes, wasn't he?) This was a ploy that could easily have backfired, as it might have been a boatload of atheists, or *should* have been by now; but a hand was extended to him, and then another, and he was pulled on board, gasping his blessings. These benisons didn't cost him anything but breath, and the shaken passengers were grateful to receive them. The boat was already overloaded, and others clamouring in the water, begging to get on, were not going to be so lucky. Those scrabbling at the sides, pitiful and imploring, would be by necessity ignored, their clawing hands smacked away with an oar. Grif caught sight of one of the other lifeboats and saw that it had flipped over and was floating upside down, a struggling mass of limbs and bobbing heads boiling around it. The other boat was gone, probably swamped and drifting to the bottom of the lake. Again, the sounds that filled the air were wrenching, unbearable. The roar of the storm, the agony of the dying. Grif feared that something essential in him was about to be ripped out through his head. He clamped his hands over his ears and tried to bury his head between his knees, but someone yanked roughly at his arm and shouted in his face, "*Hold on to the life-line, man, for Christ's sake, we're going over.*"

He grabbed blindly at what was offered, fingers closing tightly over the coarse bristle of a rope, and almost immediately the boat was broadsided. He felt himself being thrown into the wind like a scrap. A sharp object struck him on the head, and then a wave smashed him back into the side of the boat. The water pounded him, dragged him away, sucked him under—but he didn't let go. In this wild, shifting element the simple material reliability of the rope seemed miraculous. *Blessed be the rope-makers.* He gritted his teeth and kept his lips clamped shut. He knew better than to pray; open your mouth to plead for divine intervention and half of the lake would waltz in. He suspected that God had an unsophisticated sense of humour, roaring at these vaudevillian entertainments, the pratfalls and comic disasters to which humans were given. At least fortune, or dumb luck, had delivered Grif to the one lifeboat worth its name. All he had to do was stick with it, clinging to the rope with one hand and his life with the other.

The lifeboat did right itself as he had thought it would, unlike the other two. The passengers who had survived the dunking began to pull themselves back in, those younger and with fewer injuries lending a helping hand to the others. Grif saw that there weren't as many on board as before, but he also saw, incredibly, that one of them was Amelia Kennedy. *Amy*. She sat soaked and shivering in the stern, her hair plastered to her head, her face blank with shock. She was the only woman among them. A sprig of affection stirred in him. Or relief. Or perhaps it was only gratitude to see a familiar face.

"You made it," he shouted at her.

"Yes." Her voice was flat, toneless. "You're hurt."

Grif touched his temple, dipping his fingertips into a wetness that was not water. Feeling the tug of custom, he almost crossed himself with it, with his own blood, as if his head were a holy font. Instead, he stared at his fingers, stained black in the storm light, wondering if the disease of mortality was going to spread and engulf him.

A man seated beside him said, "Take care when she goes over, she'll knock you senseless."

He was referring to the lifeboat, but Grif thought for a moment he meant Amy, her capacity for violence possibly visible on her pallid face. *I've murdered a man*, she had confessed, and it occurred to him only now that she might have meant him. Maybe it had been a prediction, an admission of culpability.

Another fellow, about fifty years of age, white muttonchops thick as brushes sprouting on the sides of his head, was cursing richly, and kept it up, repeating the same profane sequence over and over, each word a hard bead of blasphemy in a rosary of oaths.

"Stow it," someone finally ordered. "Save your strength, granddad, yer gonna need it."

"Mary," someone else was moaning. "Mary, Mary."

The man beside Grif nudged him sharply in the ribs and pointed at something that was riding the waves, a boxy vessel—not one of the other lifeboats, which had both disappeared, but the ship's wheelhouse, which must have broken off from the *Echo* when the boat went down. A man stood balanced on its roof, laughing raucously, his arms outstretched, hands poised and waving gracefully as if conducting a symphony. He *was* conducting a symphony, commanding the raging elements, orchestrating the whole storm.

"The captain," Grif's companion snarled. "Drunken jackass. If that thing gets blown this way, I swear I'll kill the bastard. I'll rip off his arms and shove them down his bloody throat."

Grif felt he would gladly assist in applying this bit of marine justice, but he didn't get the chance. Nor did the *Echo*'s captain get the chance to sink them once again, which would have been the more likely outcome had the two vessels met. The man was abruptly spirited away, driven completely out of sight as another wave separated them and swept them in opposite directions.

Also gone from view, mercifully, were those passengers still struggling in the lake, still clinging to the wreckage and crying out for help. Their last words, stark and unanswered, whipped bare by the wind, were finally blown entirely away.

If those remaining in the lifeboat were spared this final scene and silencing, they weren't spared much else. At first a surge of guilty relief passed through them. What could they possibly do to help the others now? It was beyond them, beyond human strength and ability. The Lord Himself had chosen them, for what reason they couldn't guess, to be the survivors. Or possibly not. Perhaps they had been chosen for something more prolonged and cruel, a thought that must have occurred to more than one spiritual vagrant on board the lifeboat when it was struck hard and capsized again. And again, repeatedly. They were in the water and out, hands raw and bleeding from being sawed by the rope or from scrabbling up the sides of the boat. Their bodies were bruised and cut, and bones broken. Exhaustion, exposure, concussion, despair were the black cards slapped down in this game, in which there seemed to be only one wild card, one joker: Grif.

He caught on quickly to what was necessary, dodging whatever harm was being dealt to mind or body. When the boat flipped, he learned how to go with it, and then how to get himself back on board with the minimum of fuss—sometimes with a ruthless efficiency that meant others weren't so lucky. So be it. Once back in the lifeboat he sat quietly, canny and contained, watching as the handful of passengers who remained prayed or wept or talked compulsively, draining themselves of life, making caskets of their own bodies. In the extremity they had voyaged into, in this borderland near death, he had sniffed out a survivor's secret. Oddly, no one else had discovered it, although he couldn't see why, as it was obvious to him. He felt he must be shining with the certainty of it, even though no one took particular notice. Except Amy, who occasionally turned on him a wondering and pitying eye.

It was fairly straightforward, and involved a hardening, a turning away, a willed invulnerability. He would summon up his worst attributes and make use of them. He saw it so clearly. A window was open, like that window at the Belvedere Hotel on the night of his wedding, and he was going to escape through it even if no one else did. He did not intend to let anyone else's chances of survival diminish his own. If there was a hole in his heart through which emotion flowed, he would stop it up. He himself would become an unsinkable vessel, tightly caulked and containing a mechanism that no one would dare tamper with.

In other words, he was destined to become the hero of this disaster, but only to himself, his individuality so firmly outlined it was impermeable.

From his point of view Amy had launched herself on a fool's course, for apparently she had decided to head in the opposite direction and become a saint, a Florence Nightingale of the lake. When the storm finally blew itself out, and the lifeboat no longer bucked and turned turtle, she regained some spunk, which she poured into a new role, sisterly and ministering. Five men, not counting Grif, remained, and to these she applied her attentions. She spoke softly to them, and listened sympathetically to their mother and wife stories, their anguish and regrets. She sang hymns to them, her voice pure as a child's, and they joined in. What she helped them face was the long drift into the night, the knowledge that they might never see land again, or if they did wash up on some uninhabited island, they might never be found. No supplies, no oars (long since lost), no hope—this is what she had to work with, these non-existent materials, and yet she cobbled together something to give them.

Grif knew what that something was, too: enough ease and comfort to die with. Her kindly ministrations weakened them, her warming blankets of sentiment made them unwary, and he watched as they fell one by one into the deepest of sleeps. Never mind about him—the trouble she had caused, the harm done—she was murdering them all. Hers were the last words they heard in this world, her hypnotic whispering in the dark, her voice like a drug, a lethal lullaby.

Before he died, the man seated next to Grif, the one who had earlier offered him the lifeline, broke a lengthy silence, saying to him, "My name is William. William Ferris."

Grif wasn't having anything to do with this. He knew what the man wanted: his own name echoed. *Ah, William, yes. Bill, is it? Bill Ferris?* His little self gently placed and cradled in his ear, or clutched to his breast like a doll, the pathetic comfort of one's own self acknowledged before giving it up for good.

He said nothing in reply and the man's quiet expectancy soon died on his face.

Grif did not want to know these men, even minimally; and what would it signify if he did, since they were all sailing straight into anonymity? They—not he. That man with the muttonchops, he was long gone, his oaths, no matter how strong, having failed to save him. The handsome fellow with the British accent, lost overboard. The government man with the horseshoe cravat pin lay stone cold on the floor of the boat, an anvil-shaped gash on his forehead. And now his neighbour …

"Please," Amy spoke from the stern, "that man beside you, say something to him."

He didn't, though.

Much later she said, "Will you hold me?"

Grif did not think this was a good idea. The boat could easily tip if he were to stumble down to that end. So unsteady did he feel, he might even pitch into the lake himself.

Even later, when everyone else had fallen completely silent, and the waves had stretched out satiny and black—the night so beautifully clear and peaceful that it was almost impossible to believe it had been the scene of such fury and destruction— she spoke again. She said, very quietly, "Forgive me."

He thought about answering. He seriously considered it— but never did. He was distracted from offering her anything, even the smallest and emptiest of consolations, when his eye was caught by a glimmer in the water, by a light. He turned and saw a lighthouse signalling in the distance, its bright stroke scything through the dark.

"Amy!" he said, jumping up, rocking the boat and hastily sitting back down. He touched his fingers to his eyes as if seeking some assurance that he could trust them. He looked again and said, "You see it too, don't you?"

He turned back to her, feeling that his own face must be lit like a lamp, but this time he had to leave her name hanging, because she was gone. Dead. She had slipped away into the night, was drifting out over the water, stealthy as an owl, no creak of wings to betray her. She left when he wasn't looking, or speaking. *Call me Amy*, like a bird's cry.

"Amy," he said again, softly, but only to himself.

# 7

## FLOTSAM

WHAT WOKE Grif was a faint *tap tapping* against the soles of his feet. His *bare* feet. Lord, but it was hard to keep shod a wayfaring man. It seems his shoes got into the habit of movement and couldn't stop. He had forgotten that he himself had taken them off and thought they must have deserted him, danced away across the water. Not only that, but they took his socks along for company.

*Tap tap tap.* If he were really awake, if he were alive even, he would get up and see what that was knocking against the bottom of his feet so insistently. But his head was too full of the night and its horrors. He couldn't lift it. It was heavy as a rock, packed tight, recollection and hallucination jammed together, one embedded inseparably in the other. The storm had gotten into his head, the wind and the lake, and thinking tore through it like screaming. He had assumed death would be quieter, less troublesome, more final. He should not be able to feel that thing at his feet, whatever it was, tapping with a gentle persistence, calling him back. During the ordeal, he had been so determined to live. Why that might have been, he couldn't remember.

What he did remember, he wished he couldn't. How the lifeboat and its cargo of corpses had drifted away from the lighthouse and salvation. They had drifted into an endless stretch of night and time, during which the dead refused their peace. They twitched and rustled and groaned. He would have thrown them overboard but was too terrified to touch them. They stared accusingly at him, especially Amy, her cold eyes following his every move. They wanted something from him, wanted to pluck some bright fibre out of his being, mix their ashes with his living flesh, like Father Fallon's thumbprint on his forehead, his father's hand wiping it out, and out, and out.

Grif opened his eyes and saw the whole magnificent vault of the sky ranged above him, a clear and beneficent blue, cloudless, devil-routed, a sky out of which you'd think only good news could come.

He lay numb as a plank on a bed of rocks, feet in the water, shod now in the whole lake. By rights he too was a corpse, but sensation was insistent, slowly returning, called up by that messenger at his feet, some piece of loyal flotsam trailing in his wake. He began to feel the sharp, uneven lay of rocks at his back, and the heat they radiated into his legs and hands. He could smell it too, baked rock, and a faint perfume of evergreen, and another fragrance—chamomile. Somewhere not far above him he heard a *scritching* noise, a bird picking through dried reeds. He heard the water lapping, felt the silky warmth of it caressing his feet. Far above, a single gull wheeled in that perfectly blue sky. He raised his hand in front of his face, and his own shadow marked it. Sea wrack plays sundial. He saw that his nails were beautifully clean—held at a certain angle, sunlight glanced off them—but he knew his hands were dirty.

Alive then, though not much better than sentient rubble. (No miracle of sumption overtaking him, no flickering presence of the Divine.) He was nothing and had landed nowhere. As an unregistered passenger, he was more missing than the missing. He was the ultimate stowaway, in his marriage (just try to find him), in his life—but no longer in his shoes.

*Tap tap.* The pesky, nagging thing might be his hardened conscience, which had slipped out through the bottom of his feet and wanted re-entry.

Why wasn't he dead? Obviously, he had no talent for it. Only a creator as perverse as the Almighty would have dreamt that one up and offered it as a gift, something a man would be grateful to receive in a situation like this. But Grif didn't want any gifts from God. He'd take his punishment, if this was it. He had tried his best to drown, finally hurling himself out of that wretched lifeboat, no land in sight, his lazy crew exacting their grim mutiny, staring him overboard. But life clung to him like the dressing on a wound, a curse he couldn't shake. He had thrashed and clawed his way through the lake, ungainly as a monster. His had been no victor's swim, and no contest, but somehow he had won himself a stretch of shoreline.

*By Christ, piss off.* He gave the thing at his feet a kick, and it sailed a few feet away but soon was back, barking up against his soles. It wouldn't let him be. Or rather, it wouldn't let him not be. He raised himself stiffly, head woozy, stomach uncertain, to have a look. When he saw what it was, he jerked his head aside and retched into the rocks.

A baby, stiff as statuary, swaddled in its own blue skin. Its face was twisted in anger, set in the shape of its final complaint. Not only were its eyes squeezed shut and its tiny hands fisted tight, but its whole body was clenched, as if determined to hang on to something from this world, if only the injustice suffered. When Grif was able to look at it again, he tried to see it merely as an object floating among other objects, a purely inanimate thing knocking against that barrel close by or the overturned kettle—shipwreck souvenirs. He needed to rob the child of its humanity, but it continued to bump up against him as if he were its miscreant and unresponsive parent. The dead do make their wishes known, and he was appalled to think that he was being asked to gather it up and hold it close, to be its cradle of pain, groaning like old wood as he rocked it. Just because his heart had turned to stone didn't mean it couldn't break.

"Is it yours?"

The voice drifted down quietly, but the surprise of it was great enough to startle a shout out of him, or the beginnings of one that turned into a choking cough.

"Forgive me." The voice was all around him. "I thought you were dead."

A figure crouched down before him. Grif saw a man dressed for the occasion of death, in a black suit, high-buttoned waistcoat, white pocket square, tie, hat. This attire was surely more formal than one would expect for the middle of nowhere, some deserted island, some distant shore. His luck that he should wash up in a place where the only citizen was an undertaker, or the Lord's own bounty hunter.

Grif found he couldn't speak. A snare had tightened around his throat, and so he shook his head instead, more to deny the man's presence than anything.

"Not yours, then." The man regarded the child, sorrow fitting his face well enough. "Poor little wretch. I have a couple laid out up above and will put him with them. They'll make a family of sorts." He moved to the water's edge, scooped the baby out and carried it away, dripping, its northern baptism complete.

He returned shortly, this time with a silver flask in hand. "Whisky," he said, "compliments of the late Theodore Rudd of Chatham, Ontario. My guests don't always arrive so well provisioned. Nor are they so easily identified." He held up a calling card in his other hand. "I'm afraid we can no longer drink to Mr. Rudd's health, although we can make an attempt at yours." He offered the flask to Grif.

Grif accepted it, fingers fumbling as he unscrewed the top. It took both hands to bring the flask to his lips and fill his mouth. The drink didn't unlatch his tongue, but gave him a searing, resuscitating kiss that struck deep.

"Come," the man said, extending a hand to him. It was an offer of assistance, of welcome, possibly even solace, and as such was a foreign language to Grif, a human hieroglyphic that he could scarcely understand. It was an honest and uncomplicated gesture, but male hands had rarely dealt him a kindness, and women's were either grasping or withheld. He thought briefly of his mother, arms frozen at her sides, and of his wife, whose touch he had eluded. Oh God, *her*. He closed his eyes and saw her standing before him, so readily and whorishly summoned. She had her arms clamped across her chest, as if concealing something, a wound perhaps. A cold hissing filled his ears and he fell back against the rocky shore, certain that if he opened his eyes again the man would be gone and she would be there, eyes livid and gloating. Grif didn't want to see it, the spectacle of this stranger—his wife's guise—dissolving. He chose darkness instead.

Grif's body was moored safely enough, but his untethered mind had wandered off. Avice was to blame. Her figure stood in the light, unentreatable, blocking the way, and he had no recourse but to escape, tumbling backwards into himself, into fever dreams and a willed madness. He let the tide take him and off he went, broken and bumping up against the objects jettisoned out of his own head: a bicycle wheel, a tuba, a boater (his own), a cassock, a cabbage with a human face. He heard Amy cursing, but could not see her. And then there was that dreadful baby, his very own stillborn, except that it wouldn't *stay* still. Awake in the middle of the night, Grif felt an oppressive weight massing on his chest, a tumour growing slab-heavy and crushing the breath out of him. That horrible unholy infant had found him, had crawled up from the shore, its skin grey and shredded as a rag. Needy, as babies are, it gnawed on him. With sharp pointed teeth, it ate a hole in his chest through which it disappeared with the slithering ease of a snake. Opened, at least he was able to breathe again.

His caretaker was patient and did what he could, understanding that his guest was afflicted with brain fever. Shipwreck can take a mind far into unnavigable territory, the return not so easy. Or certain. He had seen it before, as he had seen much else. Each day he brought Grif a gift from the island—a stone, a small stick, a seed pod—and placed it on a low table beside the bed. It was a calendar of objects that had in its arrangement an appearance of primitive magic, a shaman's device, but was gathered more for the man's own amusement than anything else, and his love of simplicity, what cures life's many griefs. *Hell*, he thought, maybe it was magic he was proferring, a low and unacknowledged source. *Hold on to this, son, this abbreviated bit of the world, and I'll pull you back in.*

Grif saw this unknown figure standing over his bed and he couldn't interpret its meaning. He sensed that it wanted to help, that it meant no harm, and yet he had watched his wife overtake it, inhabit it, her nacreous skin crawling over its surface like a rapidly spreading disease. *Sleep*, she whispered, and he dared not in her presence. *Eat this*, and he knocked the poisonous dish out of her twisted crone's hands. *Don't try to speak.*

She was threatening him, but how could he speak anyway? He was mute with selflessness, with absence. There was no point, there was nothing to say, there was no one there to say it. His mind had shattered like a mirror in which he was once clearly reflected, and day after day he sorted through the fragments. He shuffled and reshuffled them, laid them out in different patterns like a fortune teller, although he never came up with much of a future, or even a present. He did occasionally see that stock figure of fortune, the dark stranger, looming over his bed. For a mystery man he had the most remarkably unthrilling conversation. *Sleep. Eat this. Don't try to speak.*

Speak? All the words he knew in the world had been rammed savagely down his throat. He'd have more luck shitting them out than speaking them.

"You're smiling, you know. I only mention it because people do not always recognize the fact that they are perfectly sane. Or imperfectly sane would be the more usual condition, I suppose."

Grif thought about this. He raised his fingers to his lips, traced their veering curve, and it was so. His mouth had broken into something you could call a smile, which surely meant that he was crazy. His fingers trailed to his chin, his cheeks, and struck a thicket. While he'd been shirking, refusing to collect his wits, his body had been getting on with its job; but then, even the dead can grow hair.

"Not quite a hundred years' growth."

Grif looked around, looked out from himself. He saw a ladderback chair, a pair of boots, overalls hanging on a hook, a pot-bellied stove, a cot at the other end of the room covered in a Bear Claw quilt, a bucket and a dipper, a pile of driftwood, a grease lamp, a teapot, an anchor, a spoon, its bowl filled with light. The whole room in fact was filled with light, for nothing was keeping it out. A door stood open wide, thin curtains were pulled aside and knotted. The bright day—and whatever else was out there—could gain admittance as he had done, easy as air drifting in.

He tried to imagine the fashionably congested parlour in Avice's home stripped and opened in this manner, swept clear of its knick-knacks, photographs, paintings, hunting trophies, ostrich eggs, the immense bible, the antimacassar, the heavy furniture, the Oriental carpets, the layers of lace and red velvet curtains hanging on thick wooden poles, completely shrouding the windows. It was a shrine to the Drinkwaters' belief in industrious activity and acquisition, and no one dared trespass in it, not even the pagan sun. Poverty had its own style, which was nothing but trespass, and his boarding-house room in Owen Sound had been frugally appointed for the improvident—but here he sensed deliberation. Beside him on a small table lay a suspiciously precise arrangement of objects:

a crow feather, a cigarette-sized reed, a perfectly round white pebble... For all its light and breathable air, he wondered if this room didn't also have a design, as did his wife's parlour, a webbing too subtle to perceive fully, in which he was caught.

Grif turned his attention to the man who had been tending him. He was seated about four yards off at a pine table, hulling wild strawberries. A glass bowl resting on the table before him was filled with the glistening red fruit, tiny as birds' hearts. The man's fingers were stained pink. He worked with ease and precision, deftly plucking the calyx from each strawberry, and at a pace that suggested he was enjoying this sensuous task—the feel of the fruit, the fragrance, the vivid colour.

"Jam," he said, pausing a moment to look over at Grif and smile.

He was no longer wearing his Sunday best, his undertaker's uniform, but had on dungarees and a white, collarless shirt rolled up at the sleeves. Grif judged him to be about fifty, old enough at least to be amused by most things. His hair was closely cropped, his beard and moustache neatly trimmed, more salt than pepper on balance. He seemed plain as the table at which he was working. No mystery man after all.

Clearly, that was Grif's role. He was the one who had washed up on shore, nameless, half dead, his whole story still contained within him like a message in a bottle. Speak? Of course he could speak. But he was biding his time, waiting to break his silence significantly. He searched for the right thing to say, as one might scour a beach for the perfect stone— round, flat, fitting flush in the crook of the finger, a stone that would scale the surface of the lake lightly, a gravity-bound piece of the earth basting together sky and water.

He couldn't find it, though, that revelatory word, and so with a shrug he said only, "Griffith. My name is Griffith Smolders."

"Ah," the man replied, plucking another calyx, like a tiny green star, and placing it neatly in a small pile beside the glass bowl. But then he frowned slightly, and asked, "Which one?"

# 8

## LIGHT-KEEPING

EXACTLY one hundred wooden steps down the bluff to the beach, and Grif was taking each one so slowly you might think he was christening them as he went, naming them with his own sins—*faithless, faceless, feckless*—words of descent. The bluff was steep, the woods thick on either side, the stairway overgrown in places with vines. He couldn't remember having climbed up these stairs in the first place, but he must have done, as he didn't think that Jean Haitse, so slight of frame, could have hauled him up on his own. Then again, he could fool you, the light-keeper. *Jean*. It was the first French word Grif had ever spoken, and he couldn't get used to pouring it through his nose like a damn teapot, spilling it abruptly into the air. The name was spelled like a woman's, yet spoken like a duck. As far as he could see, which admittedly wasn't too far, it was the only French thing about the man. Grif had asked him if he was Catholic, and Jean had said no, he was a blue-domer, he worshipped under the heavens, believed only in the sky.

Grif stalled about midway. The anonymous steps fell in a cascade before him. He wasn't actually naming the stairs but staring at his feet, getting better acquainted with his newest pair of shoes, two odd ones he had chosen out of the light-keeper's store of salvaged goods. Jean had built a shed by the dock where he kept whatever items washed up on the beach, if he had no immediate use for them. And what use would he have for a woman's corset, or the picture of a solemn and unknown married couple in a gilt frame, or a pillowcase embroidered with the insignia of a ship silt-mired and rotting on the bottom of the lake? Entering that dim shed was like stepping into someone's plundered dream, and Grif had not wanted to touch any of it. There was something obscene about this continuance of people's possessions beyond them—and yet he needed shoes. Jean had warned him about walking barefoot. Rattlesnakes the main reason, which made Grif wonder if he had somehow drifted clear of his own safe country, and then he stopped himself, his wondering ceased. He didn't care where he was—better not to know.

The shoes were a stiff, water-cured leather, and not a bad fit, considering that one was a size bigger than the other. He had been fortunate to find a left and a right, although each was so different he thought his confused feet might just walk off in separate directions, to the east and west of him. The only identity this pair shared lay in being drowned men's shoes, and it seemed to Grif that neither had entirely shucked its former owner. The left and larger one was moulded into an impression, all toe bumps and corn knobs, that defined a man's foot clear as a death mask. It was a mud-brown brogue, worn at the heel, broken at the cuff, laceless (he'd secured it with string), its ripped tongue lolling like a tired old dog's. Surely a foot phrenologist, if such existed, would have a heyday with it—criminal tendencies, lewd predilections—and wasn't the state of a man's shoes supposed to be revealing of character? (What did it mean that he couldn't seem to keep them on his feet? That he had no character of his own?) The other shoe, the right one, was sleek and black, smooth as an otter, sunlight winking off its toecap after he'd given it a polish with his sleeve. Its owner might have been a clerk or a lawyer, someone proper and dutiful and decent (its lace had been double-knotted), while the other fellow with the unkempt and shoddy footwear was clearly lazy and suspect, an untrustworthy oaf, a blinkard. Or maybe it was the other way around: one was simple and honest, while the other was sly and scheming. The greater question, though, the only one he needed to consider, was: which shoe fit *him* best?

*Which one?* Jean had startled him in asking. *Which Griffith Smoulders was he?* Jean had seen the name very recently on a supply run to Collingwood, noticed it inscribed in the register of the hotel he had stayed at. He said that the signature had caught his eye because it was written in a hand that was ornate and flashy, drawing attention so insistently to itself he had to pause and look at it. Given the arrogance and advertisement of the signature, he had assumed it to be that of a salesman or politician. He remembered thinking how ironic that was, since the name "Griffith" means "man of great faith." *As you must know,* he added.

He didn't know. Besides, his name was clipped to Grif— man of little faith.

"But that could not have been you," Jean had continued, "for you came up from Owen Sound."

"I did," said Grif, attempting to look perturbed. "It's ... odd, such a coincidence. And to think there is someone else in this province, and nearby, with my name."

He knew who it was, too. Fenwick Nashe. All the details of the terrible mishap, invented or otherwise, would have been in the papers by now—the foundering of the *Echo* and no survivors. Fenwick was the only person alive, outside of Jean, who knew he'd been on board. Since Grif no longer had any use for his name, and couldn't defend it, the villain had obviously stolen it, had taken it like a wife, or a grave robber, a resurrection man. What a convenient banner (if already soiled) under which to conduct his unknown and illicit business.

Any troubling introspective questions Grif might ask himself were no longer quite so personal, now that he was sharing his name. The central question—Who *was* he?—had taken on a more universal application. With Fenwick's theft, Grif's self was split, twinned—an other set loose in the world, a Griffith Smolders over which he had no control.

He took the steps at a brisker pace. *Duplicitous, equivocal, double-crosser.* The empty water buckets, one in each hand, clanked against his legs. The rifle slung over his shoulder tapped him on the back like a loose wing. Grif raised his chin as if preparing for a blow, but received only a puff of wind coming off the lake, off its shimmering, slightly ruffled surface. Lake Urine, his father called it, fouling it, but unintentionally—which made Grif smile. His father's only joke and he didn't even get it.

The lake was the source of other jokes as well, but darker ones, and Grif himself didn't get those. Jean had told him about a former light-keeper's wife who had insisted on being lashed to a tree near the water's edge during a storm. Huge waves washed right over her and she claimed to have seen the very bottom of the lake, miles of it revealed as the vast watery skirts lifted. The man stood back clutching himself, terrified that his wife was going to drown, while she roared with laughter and shouted out, amazed at what she was seeing. Did all women have a streak of wildness in them? Perhaps it was only because she was stuck on this island, married to it, which would drive anyone mad. The isolation, the ghosts. Grif had no doubt that the place was haunted. It had to be with all the bodies that were buried on it, all the unquiet deaths, some very recently, his fellow travellers. Jean had not uttered another word about that dead baby and his makeshift family, thinking possibly that Grif, in his delirium, would not remember. But his memory was a very crypt.

When he was first up and around, he noticed that the Indians who stopped at the dock to sell blueberries or fish transacted their business with uncharacteristic haste, refusing even to step out of their boats, their faces wary and evasive.

"Up on the bluff beyond the light tower," Jean explained, "there's an ancient burial ground. A sacred place."

Old bones, restless spirits. Yet Grif suspected it was the newcomers who were the troublemakers. His race, dead or alive, was hungry and dissatisfied and forever on the move. He could feel it here, could sense them moving through the undergrowth. At night sometimes a candle flame would flicker out suddenly, extinguished for no reason. Or a door would open with a crash, letting a chill rush into the room.

Jean had pointed out to him two mounds behind the storage shed down below where a lighthouse keeper of a few years past and his dog lay buried. They had starved to death over the long winter.

"Why didn't he eat the dog?" Grif asked.

Jean shrugged. "Would you eat your only friend?"

Nearing the bottom of the stairs, Grif stopped again, paused with one foot momentarily suspended, which he then very slowly retracted. On the third step from the last a snake lay basking in the sun. A well-fed fellow with a blotchy appearance, dark brown markings on tan, like splashes of cocoa. Unwind him and he'd be about two and a half feet in length. Or she, maybe it was a she; and maybe she was a water snake and not a rattler at all. Jean had told him that the two were often confused, and people killed both anyway, usually clubbing them to death with a Christian fervour.

Grif would have been happy to give this one the benefit of the doubt, but it was taut with awareness, and raised the tip of its tail in warning, giving its rattles a menacing little shake. Gently, carefully, he set the buckets down, then reached a hand back for the rifle. According to Jean, this island was thick with them—the massasauga rattler—especially near the tower, where they drew close in the evening, biding their time, waiting for the dazzled birds that knocked themselves out hitting the light. A man could stand in the kitchen and pick the snakes off the rocks for gun practice, his aim truer if he feared and hated them. Killing rattlesnakes might somehow help fill up that empty and dangerous space within that deepened and got more dangerous in a remote place like this. It was not a hobby that Jean himself subscribed to. He had no need, being spiritually amused.

Grif cocked the rifle and took aim. The snake had amber eyes, like doll's eyes but very much alive, and they seemed to look directly at him and through him to whatever lay beyond. He was reminded of a cat, ears and limbs and fur smoothed away, all extremities eased flush into its compact and sculpted body. Studying it, he decided that the creature was better-looking than most humans he had ever encountered; certainly it was more perfect, almost an ideal form. He had no desire to blast it to bits, to tear open that cunningly wrought skin in which its being was so seamlessly sealed. Besides, he didn't even know how to handle a rifle and would be more likely to shoot himself in the foot, thereby ruining another worthy pair of shoes, no matter how eccentrically matched.

He lowered the gun and felt immediately the tension in their relationship slacken, after which the snake simply slid off the step and disappeared into the bushes. It probably went away sniggering, he thought, having sensed the tremors that his knocking knees sent through the wooden stairs.

Again he gazed out over the water, its shimmering surface. *Fiat lux.* "Let there be light," he said aloud, which is what he had taken to saying every evening when Jean climbed the stairs to his priestly tower to light the lamps for the reflectors.

Once the words were out of his mouth, Grif was sorry he had said them, for he'd forgotten that speaking came at a cost. Since his bad spell after Jean found him on the beach, he had acquired a follower. It was nothing corporeal, nothing he could actually see. But he could hear it, barely, a small voice that rode in his own, that was plaited into it like a thin twist of hair. It seemed to come from a distance, as if a child were calling him, and he heard it only when he spoke. His own voice obscured the message it was trying to deliver, if indeed it had one.

For a long time he stood stalled again, quietly, listening.

Jean had been observing Grif's halting descent. This was easy enough from the light tower, where he'd gone to polish the mirrors. The catoptric reflectors were beautiful and a pleasure to work with, and the system—the concentration of light required from the lamps, the principle of reflection it was based upon—was interesting. It all had to be carefully maintained. He had tried to involve his guest in this process, in the science of it at least, to keep his mind from becoming as diffuse and useless as scattered light. Not that such light wasn't lovely, the poetic effects, but it was very hard to live by.

He pitied the young man and regarded him as someone frozen and gradually thawing. He certainly looked it at the moment, standing motionless on the stairs that led to the beach. A man could die up here of thirst before Grif got to the bottom and back with a couple of pails of water. Jean had to wonder, as he often did, about the genius who built this lighthouse. He could have split the idea in two and constructed the house near the shore and the tower above; but that would not have been economical, and the government was famous for its economy. Say what you will about the Yanks, they gave their light-keepers training, uniforms, assistants, supplies, holidays and a regular wage, whereas the Canadian government stuck theirs on a rock with a sack of beans and forgot about them. They encouraged their light men to marry and have a brood of young ones so there would be more free labour. And married keepers were not carted off quite so soon to the laughing academy from having walked around and around their chunk of rock until their wits were entirely unravelled.

Jean hoped he had not made a mistake giving Grif that rifle, such an efficient instrument of self-delivery. He was only trying to do . . . what? Sober the boy, give him some simple work to do, put the feel of metal and wood in his hands so that he might weigh in closer to the earth. To Jean it seemed as if Grif had exceeded some limit, as a murderer does when he transgresses a moral boundary. It was unnatural how Grif folded himself into the dark at night, letting it take him. He never reached for a lamp, never lit a candle. How could a man not desire the light? Jean could not resist; it was his profession, after all, possibly his vocation. He felt moved to ignite his guest as well, to spark some small flame, to keep a living fire in him, however slight.

This was why, even though he didn't have any need to hear the sound of his own voice, he had begun to tell Grif stories—hard-luck ones mostly, parables of misery and misfortune, just to let him know that he was not exceptional. Grief is a country that everyone gets to visit at one time or another, and some are genuine natives of the place, born and bred. Grif hardly spoke anyway, so Jean did, his honest, unadorned words lighting the dark.

He talked about homesteading out west, which he had tried for a while until he got tired of eating dirt and dodging the hailstones as big as fists that pummelled his livestock into the ground. He described running a hand over their prone bodies afterwards and feeling how their muscles had been pulped to mush. He told Grif about farmers who went berserk in their sod houses and axed their families to bits, or of those who got lost walking from the barn to the house during a blizzard, a journey measured in feet. They might be discovered in the spring, lumps thawing in the field, or never seen again. No need to tell tall tales about the West because the weather there, summer or winter, could be so extreme it pulled a man apart like taffy. Once, Jean said, he woke in the morning with his beard frozen to his shirt, his hair completely white with frost, even his piss in the pot frozen solid. There had been a snowstorm during the night, which had practically buried the house, snow drifting over the eaves and onto the chimney. The quiet was unearthly, and the sense of being interred was *all too* earthly; and the memory of it made light-keeping on this open, far-seeing bluff like glorious resurrection itself.

Jean had also worked as a cowboy for a time, until he noticed that at about thirty years of age most cowboys were maimed somehow: legs broken, shoulders busted, fingers ripped off in the bight of a rope, not to mention the fun of getting kicked, bitten and rolled on by your horse. Next he'd tried the rail lines, where the work was tough but the evening entertainment even tougher. The men loved to fight, bare-knuckle, John L. Sullivan style, and didn't think anything of it if their noses got flattened, their eyes blackened, their jaws cracked. Sometimes bets were placed, sometimes not; they beat each other stupid for the sheer joy of it.

Grif listened to all of this with interest, and for a time it stopped him from attending to whatever it was that otherwise diverted and absorbed him, his ear slightly cocked as if he were trying to catch some telltale scratching in the walls or a signal issued from the other side of the world.

Jean couldn't decide what was more troubling about his young friend: the fact that he was so incurious and failed to ask even the most obvious of questions—*Where am I? What is this island called? How far is it to the mainland?*—or his habit of sleeping at night with that ragged and bloated parcel of his clutched to his chest, as if it contained his numb and displaced heart. Jean had given some thought to what it did contain. Not a bible, he decided, or a thick wad of cash. Letters most likely—yes, a cache of love letters once rich and sweet as butter, but with death's touch gone rancid and stale. Letters from some dear one lost on the *Echo*, a young wife possibly, someone he could not bear to speak of, someone who had in fact taken his powers of speech with her.

"You know," he'd said to Grif at dinner that day (Jean had made a Fidget Pie—onions, apples, bacon), "the trouble with ghosts is not that they haunt you, but that they do not. Let's say a person has lost a loved one, and to see them again in any faint form, even a wisp of them, would satisfy a great longing. But they do not appear, ever again. Not even in those spirit photographs you've probably seen. Those are fake, a real swindle. Grif, what you have to worry about in this world are the quick, not the dead. People are capable of great harm. One man alone can cause unbelievable damage."

Grif only shook his head slightly. Whether in disagreement or because he was bound too tightly by memory, Jean couldn't tell.

Looking down toward the stairs again, he saw that Grif had finally made it to the beach, and was walking unsteadily over the stones, making this ordinary task look perilous. It was almost as if he were made of some watery substance himself, and was moving forward with necessary caution lest he spill and drain away through the cracks.

No, Jean thought, he should not have given him that gun.

His benefactor needn't have worried. Grif had no intention of decorating the beach with the contents of his head, even if it was a sure way of silencing what dogged him. He had been mulling over Jean's admonitions about the spirit world. Such rationality was a discipline the light-keeper had to adhere to if he wanted to maintain his life here. He was a man who had withdrawn from the cruelties of human society (the real theme, surely, of those Wild West stories), and who had become self-sufficient with his garden, his goats and chickens, his slab of mossy bacon hanging on a hook in the larder, his rack of books from the Upper Canada Tract Society, his daily consuming chores, and his mind as certain and concentrated as that beam he cast upon the water every night. No doubts, no missteps. Even the entries in his logbook were calm and matter-of-fact. He recorded details of the weather, supplies used, all incidentals pertaining to his job. The most unsettling aspect of that log, to Grif anyway, was that he appeared nowhere in it. He flipped through it sometimes when Jean was up in the lightroom fussing, cleaning, refilling the lamps with oil. The corpses were in the book, sure enough, their discovery and burial duly recorded; but he was not. Grif supposed that Jean was protecting him, granting him an immunity, a respite from the record. Yet it would have been a relief to see his name listed there among the rust scrapers and monkey wrenches, the hard-edged and undeniably real that had earned a place in the log. Or possibly the keeper regarded him as more of an absence than a presence, a no one drifting beyond the pale, just one more of those pestering ghosts he absolutely refused to acknowledge.

Other light-keepers had not been so careful and exclusive. Dipping back far enough in the log, past hands bold or shaky, Grif had encountered those unafraid to record strange or supernatural sights. One man had seen a sea monster with fins and a sinuous neck and red knobs the size of cauliflowers on its sides. Another, mermaids. . . *In a strong wind you hear them, plain as gulls crying.* In Lake Huron! How charming other people's fantasies, and terrors, were. Grif did not think that those old-world fishergirls would have lasted long in the cold waters of this rough and prim country.

Nearing the water's edge, Grif hopped onto a rock that sat a few feet out, in order to more easily scoop up two clear, grit-free pailfuls. He saw then a boat in the distance moving toward the island. Lonely Island. He had read that in the log too, but the weight of sadness in the name made it too heavy to repeat. That boat, it could be anyone, although he knew that Jean had been expecting an official search party. Bodies had to be identified.

Quickly now, Grif filled the buckets and hurried along the beach to the stairs. Water brimmed, flashed with caught light, brilliant as a woman's dress, spilling over, flouncing down, as he ran up, and up, to the tower.

# 9

# SKELF

GRIF lay listening to the water slapping the belly of the boat, applause for his daring. Or for his trusting nature. His gullibility? That he could ride in a boat at all amazed him, but what other way was there to escape the imprisoning shore of this island, since he couldn't sprout wings and fly, and Jean wouldn't be making a supply run for months. He was not like the light-keeper, who had achieved a solitary and saintly contentment. Grif was abraded by the calm, unnerved by the quiet, which was not pure quiet at all but infested with small, indefinable and accusatory sounds. Nor could he shake the feeling that he was being stalked, hunted. Which is how he came to be stretched out in the bottom of a homemade skiff, one that was held together with a lick of paint and crossed fingers for all he knew, and skimming through the night like a bug on a leaf.

It was his hope that the lake was going to be as selective as lightning, in that it wasn't going to strike twice and send him to the bottom. Never again did he want to be caught on the wrong side of the waterline, like an image trapped in a mirror. The lake had rejected him once, had not wanted his body defiling it. No place was reserved for him in its army of the drowned. And if he believed that, he really was gullible.

Grif had in fact invested his trust elsewhere: in Ned Hawke, who was at the helm and had let it be known that he was unsinkable.

"I'm a floating man," claimed Ned, explaining how he had discovered this talent when he went overboard on a side-wheeler up near Spanish, carried either by the wind or by sheer exuberance. At the time, ashes and burning motes from a shore fire were being blown onto the deck and the passengers had been placed on "spark duty." Issued with wet mops, their job was to extinguish those bright spores before they burst into full flaming blossom. Ned pitched in, and with such enthusiasm that he also pitched over into the North Channel and floated away like a pine chip, a wee skelf riding buoyant on the waves as if he were adrift in the salty Dead Sea.

"Ah," Jean had said, watching Ned's caddis-fly contraption slide ashore and the man himself leap nimbly out onto the beach. "A visitor." He had expected a search party, but this was better, much better. "Come," he said to Grif, who was about to melt into whatever background would have him, "he's a good man, you'll want to meet him. You might want to bring those buckets again, too. Now that the stairs are washed so beautifully, we could use a little of that wet stuff to cook with."

"Ned." The man doffed his name like a hat, informally, drawing it right off the top of a longer nominative—Edwin Tobias Hawke. The hand he offered to Grif in greeting was small, warm, dry as a stick. He was slight and weathered, and gave an impression of living lightly in himself. To Grif's young eye, Ned had reached an age where age no longer mattered—his hair white as a dandelion clock's, his skin tanned as a boot; his body had arrived where time intended to take it. He himself had arrived on a whim, in his whim-built boat, having travelled a great many miles across the water for nothing more complicated than a cup of tea with the light-keeper.

Ned ranged widely over the north, walking or sailing, and more or less lived out of doors, having at one point in his life gone outside and discovered that he had no inclination to go back in. He might squat on an uninhabited island for a while, dragging his skiff ashore, flipping it over, propping up the bow with an oar and setting up house underneath. It didn't seem to trouble him to sleep on the rocks like a handful of earth scattered overtop. Ned would leap from his stony bed, limber as a child, fossils imprinted on his cheeks. *Ammonites*, he would say, fingering the shapes before they faded like stars in the morning light.

That cup of tea Ned came for *was* more complicated, as it happened, and outsmoked the usual Smoky Oolong and Darjeeling. Declaring that leaves were for the cloven-footed, Jean rooted around in the shed until he'd collected up the tailings and tag ends of several orphaned flasks and bottles. He then poured these into a bailing tin, indiscriminately marrying the grain, the grape, the juniper berry and the lowly potato. An evil brew it was, a bilge cocktail, and they sat on the dock in the beneficent afternoon light passing it from hand to hand, bailing it in with a gentlemanly relish.

Ned also passed on what news he'd picked up of late, telling Jean about a mutual acquaintance of theirs who had contracted blackleg at a logging camp in Blind River.

"Landlubber's scurvy," he said to Grif. "They eat nothing at those camps morning and night but salt pork sandwiches smothered in corn syrup."

He told them about a couple of young fellows who broke into the light at Mississagi Strait and downed a crock of wood alcohol, and by the time the bodies were discovered they had turned *completely* black.

His news had a restlessness, a propulsion of its own, and Grif noticed how it moved outward, further and further afield. He related a story about a ship in port at Windsor that had exploded and sent a two-hundred-pound radiator sailing into the town's funeral parlour, where it flattened the director and made blood squirt out his ears, like a man who'd had a date with Skevington's daughter. ("Who?" said Grif. "Torture device," Jean explained.) Ned then ranged across the river to Detroit, where a prominent senator was himself boiling mad. The local papers were having a field day with a story about a boat named after the senator's daughter that was in dry dock having her bottom scraped.

Talk then turned to the disaster of the *Maine*, blown up in the Havana harbour in February, and to the trouble in the Transvaal following the Jameson raid on the Boers. And honestly, it surprised Grif to hear them go on. These old hermits, how removed they were from the world's troubles, free of it all, and yet they were keeping such a close watch, canny as small animals in a large predatory field.

"You know," said Jean, "some say we will soon be seeing the end of war, that humankind is getting to be too advanced for such barbarism."

"Some say, yes," Ned laughed, slapping his hand down on the dock. "Arbitration is the new way, and reason. We'll all sit down together and talk things over. Somebody might have told the Yanks that, though. Never seen a country more feverish for war."

"Canadians were happy enough to join 'em. Signed up by the thousands, I hear."

"A noble cause, the Spaniards being an inferior race. Like the French, eh, Jean?"

"Hah! Here's to the French. Least they had the sense to scupper that temperance plebiscite."

"What I don't follow, boys, is how this idea of everybody working in factories and making a few industrialists rich contributes to mankind's moral progress."

"Everybody's too worn out working sixteen-hour days to fight. Makes them less aggressive, you see."

"Is that it? Well, here's to reason, then."

"To world peace."

"Did you say peach?"

"Peace. Clean out your ears, man."

"Ah, I guess that's why those factories overseas have been so busy."

"Read about that new Maxim machine gun. Sixteen rounds a minute it can fire."

"They've improved the field gun, too. Has an automatic recoil."

"And now there's smokeless powder."

"Torpedoes, mines."

"Hell, we must be in for a whole shitload of peace."

"Hmph, a new century, hard to imagine. Never thought I'd live to see it."

"Don't count your chickens, Ned."

Ned spat into the water and they all sat in silence watching the foamy topped-up gob gently undulate, until out from under the dock a quick, shadowy form emerged, darted to the surface and snapped it up.

"Did you see that? A bloody great sturgeon."

The sight reminded Grif of someone taking communion, a greedy beast gorging on the insubstantial—for all the good it would do him.

Ned patted his vest pocket lightly, reached in with two fingers and pulled out a harmonica, a small, thirteen-cent, nickel-plated Hohner, which he put to his lips. Those chickens he had been advised not to count—they appeared. He pulled them out of their tiny roosts, the harmonica's ten slots, birds beaked and feathered and rounded with pure sound to peck and scratch on the dock before them. Then, as instantly as they had appeared, the shape of the musical creatures changed, metamorphosed into a form less comic, more graceful, and, compact as sparrows, they lifted into flight and vanished.

Appreciation was as hearty as two happy sots could produce, and Ned inclined his chin in a modest bow. He told Grif that he was the occasional organist in a settlement on the north shore, by which he meant mouth organ, the only instrument the congregation could afford. There was no church, either, and the services were held in the schoolhouse—Methodist in the morning and Anglican in the evening, but everyone in the community attended both.

"Let your Sabbatarians fight it out in the city," he said, "some people just want to get along and have a good time."

Ned then played a few of his sacred tunes, lively and raucous, more suited to a saloon or a sporting house Grif was clearly thinking.

"Son, the Lord can hardly find the place on the map."

An appealing approach to sacrilege, but what struck Grif even more was the appeal of this music. He couldn't see how it was accomplished, how Ned, simply by blowing on a sliver of wood and metal buried in his hand, by sucking the weightless substance out of it, could produce such antic or sad or languorous melodies. He looked to be drawing music out of his very flesh and bones.

Listening, letting it pour into him, Grif felt roused, lightened. Jean, too, leapt up, hurried back into the shed, and returned with a bashed-up two-string fiddle and a homemade bow, which he began to saw away on, extemporizing with a few yips and howls.

Grif gazed at his empty hands, wanting to add something of his own devising. If he could just widen it, hold it open, make room for *more* pleasure to flow in. He was untalented, untutored, but he could clap along at least, could build a bracing, echoing cairn of sound with his bare hands.

Ned, eyeing Grif, paused for a beat and said to him, "Why don't you show us which one of those shoes of yours is a better dancer? I'd put my money on that hobnail one on the left."

"Dance? I can't."

"I've never played this thing before," said Jean. "Come on, lad. The fish won't laugh. Not so loud as you'll hear them, anyway."

So Grif rose to his feet and, *what the hell*, partner to himself, started to stomp around on the dock, trying to chase down what the other two were recklessly tossing out. He clumped and shuffled, awkwardly at first, a foolish grin on his face. Then he began to lose himself in concentration, the grin dissolving into intentness. The feel of the air swirling around him, pouring through his widespread fingers, the groaning sounds the wood made under the punishment of his heels, the dock's vibrations, Jean's boat bumping up against it, the disturbance he was creating in the water—how the proximate world was being pulled into his orbit.

He had attended a dance in Ingersoll once. Coaxed into dancing with a friend's kindly and patient sister, he had clumsily rattled through a two-step like a squirrel caught in a cage. The rules of that damn measure were understood and adhered to by all except him, and here was his chance to smash those rules to pieces. He let his shoes, with their differing dispositions, argue it out. His heels hit the planks of the dock like mattocks as he danced, truly danced, an anarchic northern flamenco. His shoes filled with fire; beads of sweat flew off his forehead. Peculiar noises were struck out of the wood like cries. His performance (he thought) was sheer artistry. Certainly it was ephemeral, never to be replicated, evaporating the very moment of its expression, an escapee's choreography that vanished straight into his soles like a high-noon shadow the second it was laid down.

The music ceased when he began to spin, and the two older men watched, impressed, as Grif followed himself around and around, faster and faster. They half expected him to bore a hole through the dock, or fly off twirling like a spout across the lake. Instead, he fell flat on his face, and a sharply pointed splinter of wood, about three inches long, shot up his left nostril and pierced clean through the skin, decorating him like some exotic South Seas native carried in the high winds and dropped suddenly out of the sky.

Grif reached up to touch his nose, which still throbbed, although it had finally stopped bleeding. Once the splinter had been plucked out, he had spent the rest of the day with various objects stuffed up his "nose-thirl," as Ned called it—handkerchiefs, cobwebs rolled into soft gauzy balls, even a cork. Jean offered to sew up the gash with one of the violin strings, a medical procedure he'd seen performed on a horse, but Grif declined the doctoring, saying the fiddle needed the string far more than he. It was no more than he deserved anyway for his prideful hoofing. The way he saw it, his blood was so embarrassed to be found in his body, as in some collapsing structure, that it wanted out, and had crowded through that small portal of a wound in a panic to escape him.

As evening had drifted toward them out of the forest on the bluff above, so had clouds of mosquitoes—and what a sound they made, like someone honing an axe to drive a wedge into their party. Hands that earlier had made such sprightly music and had birthed stories right out of the air now turned on their owners, swatting and slapping. Grif started hitting himself so aggressively his partners wondered if there wasn't something else he was after, some other thing cleaving to his skin that required punishment. They were afraid he might do himself more damage than he had already done.

"I'd say it was time to go," Ned announced, jumping up.

"It is getting late. I have to attend to the light," said Jean, holding out a hand to Grif, then hesitating. "Wait, there's one more thing before you leave."

Leave? Apparently some understanding had arrived more surreptitiously than the droning insects. But of course he had to leave—flight was what kept him alive. Gently, with the lightfingered touch he had once used to make the sign of the cross, he felt his jacket pocket for the journal, still bound in its protective canvas wrapping. It was a square of ice cut out of the frozen past, a small black window that admitted a limited but thrilling view of a lost and haunted country. His view, his book. He was packed and ready.

Again Jean had ducked into the shed, and this time he returned with a woman's change purse, which he held out to Grif.

"It's not much," he said. "Corpses are poor employers. Might help along the way, just the same."

The purse was made of a gunmetal mesh that poured into his hand, and the design of its clasp was that of a mermaid stretched out and feeding a lobster with a spoon. It had a pleasing weight, like a sack of plums, and surely was of some value in itself, for it was a striking object.

He smiled and slipped his hand into Jean's, and now wondered, as he lay stretched out in the bottom of Ned's boat, why his hand didn't glow. He was suffused with warmth, radiant, a human lantern ignited by the light-keeper. Perhaps it was only a shirker's surge of relief he was enjoying. Or the unexpected decanting of an ideal into his physical being, and the sense that he had achieved something impossible—a true freedom, however brief it might be.

Ned advised him to settle in, to sleep if he wanted, and not to worry about travelling at night, for he knew every rock and shoal in these waters.

"I'll be, and that's one of them right there," he said, as the boat made a sudden grating noise. He slid an oar into the lake, gave a push, and they continued, gliding over the smooth black water.

Grif wasn't worried. He didn't care. Wasn't that the secret of being a floating man—jettisoning all care? He thought of a story Jean had told him, about sailors in treacherous seas throwing statues, their resident saints, overboard when all supplication and prayer had failed to calm the waters. This spiritually brazen act must have been intended as a warning to the powers above of a more acute danger: that the divine will lose their hold on the earthly if they do not better serve.

Grif slid down and stretched out, making himself comfortable. He didn't even glance back to watch Lonely Island, its lighthouse and keeper, recede from view. Open and receptive as a flower, he stared up at the immense sky, the stars beginning to appear. The chill of the lake penetrated his back. He lay shallowrooted, a dreaming keel, at one with Ned's claptrap skiff as it headed further and further north.

# 10

# THE IRISH CONSTELLATION

I T WAS an education travelling with Ned Hawke, but Grif wasn't sure what degree he'd graduate with if he survived the trip: Master of the Minimal? Doctor of Wonders? Ned was as full of information as the lake was water, most of it about as trustworthy. For the first time in his life Grif wished that he weren't so ignorant of what existed beyond the edges of practicality, so that he could contest some of what Ned told him. His teacher seemed at times to be like those ancient sailors who returned from their explorations with stories of fantastic peoples and distant lands rich with marvels. Yet Ned claimed that science was his subject, not fancy—except when he was teasing Grif, who was entertainingly credulous.

Grif's instruction began late one afternoon, early into their journey, when they were setting up camp on a small island in a mazy stretch of Lake Huron's North Channel. Dotted with reefs, shoals and islands that boats had to weave and waggle through, this part of the channel had come to be known as the Turkey Trail. Ned was constructing a steeple of kindling for their campfire and asked Grif if he wouldn't mind fetching a branch of cedar. *Arbor vitae*, the tree of life. A handful of cedar was better for a man than a bag of oranges. It could cure snow blindness, scurvy, nasal congestion and possibly what ailed his young companion. Grif was happy to comply, and wandered up the beach and into a small stand of trees, where he snapped a branch off a sapling, easy as breaking a child's arm. He was glad of it, too, for a couple of horseflies, thugs of the fly tribe, attacked him on the way back and he was able to do battle, using the branch as a switch to drive them off.

Ned regarded the branch—and him—with curiosity. A pileated woodpecker concealed in a bush nearby began cackling loudly, derisive as any schoolyard bully.

"White pine," Ned observed. "You will get to know it by its carcass, heading south. The Americans make mail-order catalogues out of it."

The old man's look was almost vocal: how was Grif ever going to find his way if he couldn't tell the difference between one thing and the next, between where he had been and where he was going?

"This won't do?" Grif waved the branch.

"Not at all. Why don't you sit down on that rock there and I'll tell you about what's under your very arse."

"Huh?"

"Lichen, two plants. Living symbiotically. Like man and wife."

"What, *this*?" Grif pointed to a greenish leprous scale on the rock. "It's not alive."

"It's alive all right, and has been for years, likely for centuries. The manna that fed the Israelites in the desert was a species of lichen. The stuff blows off the rocks in the lowlands there and people do eat it. Miraculous matter indeed."

Grif protested, as well he might, because Ned had begun to pull him through a grain-high, hair-wide passage into the world of particularity.

Tree, plant, bird, rock. What more did a man need in the way of definition? Vast and plain, categories as large as continents, these words sufficed. You could navigate through a whole life, incurious and detail-blind, without requiring microscopically subtle distinctions and directions. Ignorance had its uses; it kept things whole, and easily comprehensible. But not for Ned, who believed that all animals, especially the arrogant two-legged ones, needed to stay alert. To attend. What if Grif ended up marrying the same woman twice without even realizing it? Ned knew what he knew (Grif talked in his sleep) and had decided that this was not the time to be beggarly with the world's infinitesimal wealth.

It took Grif a while to catch on. As they travelled through a labyrinth of islands—some nothing more than a hump of smooth rock with a scattering of vegetation on top, like a giant's bald pate emerging—and dipped into dark-water bays, and as they camped and fished and swam (Grif with the help of an inflated moose's stomach), he found his attention constantly diverted by Ned to the oddest and most insignificant of things. To the veined wing of a mayfly, or the wriggling bluish legs and orange claw tips of a crayfish, or the papery bark of the birch, encoded as a roll of music for a player piano. He listened, and occasionally grunted to prove he was listening, but then would purposely forget what he had been told, would shake it off as though ridding himself of a smattering of dirt and grit. Not that Ned's "facts" weren't interesting, even captivating, for he touched magically on this and that with the slight wand of himself. Grif just didn't care that every bloodsucking bug he might encounter—and did—had been distinguished with a Latin name. Higher classification didn't improve their manners in the least. Take *Chrysops callidas*, the deer fly. Black-banded wings, iridescent green eyes, half an inch in length, quick in attack, tenacious, transporting you away in small burning chunks— Grif might learn everything there was to know about the deer fly, yet it still ate him alive. It knew him more intimately than he would ever know it, unless he happened to swallow one. So much for knowledge and the deflecting power of words.

Grif liked Ned. How could he not? The man was personable, easy to get along with, undemanding. He had a cricket for a pet. During the day it lived in his pocket, and at night he placed it on his knee so that he could speak to it. And the darn cricket answered. Truth was, Grif had gotten to the point where he would much rather hear the cricket's monologue than Ned's. Irrational, no doubt, and ungrateful, but he had developed an aversion to the sound of his companion's voice, of what it carried, like pins and bits of broken glass that scraped against his inner ear. It was like listening to a wind at first melodious, then monotonous, then causing a deep ache in the head. He made excuses to get away from him. When not sailing on the lake, or drinking as much of it as his gut would hold (giving him a reason to go off and piss privately in the woods—he'd made a nuisance of himself zinging streams scattershot off the rocky beaches, wetting Ned's pant legs), he began to spend more and more time in it, submerged, ears stuffed with muffling water. As a consequence of being driven into it, he was—incredibly—mending his relationship with the element, and mending himself into it, stepping from water to land and back again as if crafting for himself an amphibious existence.

One day he wandered off to dry himself on a baking haunch of rock. He tilted his head back, opened his mouth and stretched out his tongue, letting the breeze move in and the sun lay down a warm host of light. Despite the lessons, this transient life was not so bad. Ned was only trying to help, after all, and although he had told him a great many things, the subject of a destination had not come up. Grif wasn't about to suggest one, either. Nowhere in particular was a safe enough place to be. If attention—or some semblance of it—was the tuition he had to pay for this errant life, then he supposed the fee wasn't beyond his means. He glanced down and watched his wet footprints fading on the rock, as if he himself were evaporating, lifting into the air, stepping up and away, being translated directly into spirit. No man, nowhere. Touching his cheek, though, and his brow, skating his palm down the length of his arm, he felt himself to be solidly, ineradicably present.

He then noticed the blue flower of a harebell that was growing in a narrow crevice beside him, and reached out to touch it instead. *Campanula rotundifolia*. Grif knew that now, and knowing it didn't make it less delicate, or less hardy for thriving in this barren spot. He placed a finger under the bell and raised its tiny blue chin to peer inside. Curse the man, he thought, it's becoming a habit. He was expecting to see lavender stamens tipped with yellow dust, but saw instead a thing dark and twisted, a writhing black seed. He drew closer, eye to flower, body stretched out flat, and distinguished two insects (unnamed even by Ned) stuck together to form one crude and misshapen unit. Disgusted, he ripped the plant up by the roots and smeared its blue bower into the rock with his bare heel. *Everything* mocked him, even creatures so small you could scarcely see them.

That evening as they sat together by their campfire finishing supper, Ned pulled a pike's bone out of his mouth as if out of a sheath, ran it over his upper lip, combed it through his beard and said, "You know the Wise Man who brought the gift of myrrh to the Christ child?"

"Yes-s."

"Think what better shape we'd be in if he had brought mirth instead."

"Christ would have been telling funny stories instead of parables?"

"Jokes, yes. And the Apostles might have put on skits instead of long faces. There's no comedy in religion, is there?"

"None that I've ever encountered. Except once, when Father Fallon knocked a chalice over during the consecration. Turns out he was having his morning coffee in it."

"Ha. A sense of humour produces a critical mind, is why. Liberates you to think your own thoughts. Can't have that where faith is concerned."

"Does the Pope believe in God, do you think?"

"That old monkey? I'd be very much surprised if he did. Too clever by half."

"He's infallible."

"So's my cricket." Ned twirled the fish bone in his fingers, then, pointing it at Grif, said, "Why did you leave her?"

Grif sucked in air, rammed by the very conversation he was cruising along so comfortably in.

"Didn't you love her?" Ned persisted.

Grif snatched up a chunk of driftwood, flat as a paddle, that lay beside him. It seemed for a second as if he were going to swipe it across Ned's face—erase the question and the inquisitor both—but instead he drove it into the fire. A spray of sparks leapt up, a tendril of smoke.

"I didn't even know her," he said.

Mercifully, when Ned was asleep, he neither snored, nor philosophized, nor interrogated. At night Grif kept himself awake as long as he could to appreciate all the uninterpreted sounds on offer—waves lapping the shore, wind in the trees, bats squeaking. Gazing up at a sky thick with stars, he thought about something Ned had told him: that mariners once possessed the power of seeing the stars during the day, an ability gradually lost with the discovery and use of navigational instruments. Grif didn't know whether to believe this or not, but he wanted to. Ned had also told him that human beings are made of the same material as the stars, and this he didn't believe at all.

Lessons in astronomy had come his way too, and he could pick out the constellations—Pegasus, Perseus, Cygnus—most of which had tragic stories attached. The night sky was god-infested with Olympian memorials. How oppressive this was.

The stars were more beautiful, he had decided, as abstract splatter, their designs loose and unresolved. Once you saw the patterns the constellations formed, you always saw them, ancient and changeless (although Ned claimed they did change over time); they rode ceaselessly overhead, dragging their sad stories with them, no matter how rent their forms.

Clouds. He preferred clouds, which were too rapidly changeable for the mythmakers to do anything with. Try to stop one with an imprisoning story and the sky would clear instantly.

But there was one constellation that he had grown fond of, and he sought it out this night: a giant who strode across the heavens in a drunken, rangy swagger, his being like glinting shards of broken bar glass tossed up into the sky, his open self a wild lament burning into the darkness. O'Brien he was called, or at least that's what he thought Ned had called him. He had a red star embedded in his right shoulder and a blue star in his left leg. Around his waist he wore a belt of pearls, and from this a mirror-bright dagger depended. O'Brien had two dogs following him, and was himself standing on Lepus, the hare—which did not seem like inconsistent behaviour for a rogue Irish star man who must, with blather and charm, have elbowed his way among the Greeks. When sleep finally claimed him, Grif drifted off secure in the knowledge that although the giant continuously pursued those girls, the Pleiades (Colleen, Sheila, Emer . . .), the chase was endless. He'd never catch them—nor would he know what to do if he did.

The morning after Ned so irritatingly questioned him, invoking his wife, Grif woke pulling and scratching at his chest. In sleep he had been clawing at himself, trying to remove a holy medal, hot as a brand, that was sinking into him as if his flesh was as soft as butter. With dream cognition he recognized this medal as one that had been given to him at birth, his first possession, long since lost. The medal was about the size of a child's thumbprint and on it was embossed the figure of the Virgin Mary, tiny and ghostly.

He sat up suddenly, jerked out of sleep, and looked toward the fire, suspecting that a flaming spark had landed on him; but the pit was cold, filled with nothing but grey ash and charred chunks of wood. He rubbed at the spot, stinging and itchy, and unbuttoned the top of his union suit. A red, angry lesion had risen in the centre of his chest like a bull's eye. I'm a marked man, he thought. And aloud, "Hey Ned, does that infallible cricket of yours bite?"

Ned was out of earshot, up to his knees in the lake and standing perfectly still, concentrating, poised as a heron, ready to catch their breakfast with his bare hands.

A spider, then. *Lycosidae gulosa*, which is Latin for "sneaky bastard." *A smother of spiders*. Grif shuddered to think what could have passed over him in the night. He reached for his jacket and the journal, thinking he might just go arachnid hunting, stub out a few sons of that furtive night-walking family for the offence of trespass. Then again, maybe it was hard not to trespass when you have eight legs.

Weighing the book in his hand, it occurred to him that he hadn't held it for some time, although he was ever aware of its weight, like an extra hand riding in his pocket. He supposed he could actually use it for something more dignified than squashing bugs. The journal was only half full, and what a waste, how incomplete. There wasn't any reason not to write in it himself. *Throw enough mud and some of it will stick*, as his father was overly fond of saying; and although he meant aspersion rather than knowledge, Grif felt that in this case knowledge applied—and had been applied, liberally. Ned had thrown it at him by the bucketful, and it *had* stuck, some of it. Observing, learning, *knowing*, might even be another bolt-hole, another way out. It wouldn't hurt to record some of what Ned had told him, what had truly begun to interest him, and perhaps to add to that an account of his days. He could pick up where the original writer—so methodical in his account of ecclesiastical destruction—had left off. In doing so, he would bridge a hiatus of centuries, grafting his own experience, his green growth, onto that old, twisted stock. The liberating dissent and mayhem would nourish him like black, tilled earth. That he might deface an object of considerable historic value did not trouble him overmuch. Like the roving creature that had nipped him during the night, trespass was a sin of freedom he had become comfortable with, if not entirely reconciled to.

Ned plunged his hands into the lake and an arc of silvery water flashed up.

Grif felt a thrill of rising excitement possess him, as if he were a hunter about to skin an animal still faintly warm with life. He slipped the cord off the package and began to divest the journal of its canvas wrapping.

# 11

## UNNATURAL HISTORY

G RIF ENTERED the journal on the sly, like so many dust motes drifting invisibly into a room, materializing quietly, unobserved, particle by particle, on a shelf, under a bed. He entered like a roach scuttling into a dark corner. Like a moth disguised as a leaf sailing in on a breath of air. Why he had to creep and flit and sift into his own book, a procryptic man, he couldn't say, except that it seemed a sensible and shrewd thing to do. The *saturniid moth*, he wrote, *has antennae that resemble feathers, and large eye-spots on its wings to alarm predators.* What pleased him most about scientific observation, now that he had succumbed to its allure, was how exact it was, and how evasive. Only a very keen reader might discern in his description of a wood nymph or a painted lady the camouflage of the naturalist himself, the one peering warily back through an insect's eye.

For weeks he and Ned followed a meandering path struck through the water. The quiet was at times unnerving, the channel's surface black as a bible's binding. They passed limestone islands smooth as bone, towering virgin stands of pine, white quartzite cliffs, luminous in the sunlight. They passed a lumber mill that broke the silence thunderously, and filled the air with smoke and the lake with log booms that made navigation dodgy. They skirted fishing camps where huge piles of trout were stacked like cordwood, and in one, herons and grebes strung up, hanging from a tree. They waved to a man who was sitting on the end of a dock eating doughnuts, about twenty looped on the end of a broom handle. Another man rode right by them mounted on a swimming moose. He tipped his hat in passing, and said, "Howdeedo." Pleasure craft, yachts sleek and polished, also slid anonymously by; and in one a young man, stocky and resolute as a bull, stood on the bow and stared down at them with interest. (A guest on board, and not of the moneyed class himself, he was trying to negotiate his own way through the labyrinthine channels of influence and privilege. This was the young Mackenzie King.)

Grif kept his eye turned from the human element when it presented itself, for he had become absorbed in his task of observing and recording, collecting small but potentially essential pieces of information. He'd decided that these were all clues to some mystery of which he might be a part, all forming some pattern that was sunk deeper and was less predictable than anyone before him had possibly discerned. The more closely he observed the natural world, the more fantastic and unreal it appeared. A damselfly wriggled out of its own skin like a girl out of a ball gown. Springtails flew through the air like animated specks of dirt. Fireflies addressed one another in a code of flashing lights. Sphinx moths carried their own deaths on their backs, portable packages laid by the Braconid wasp that, when opened, devoured the recipient.

Ned was satisfied to see him anchored, moored with a written line to that daybook he had unexpectedly produced and begun beavering away in. His grimoire, as Ned thought of it, his book of spells and black magic. The thing looked old enough to play the part, although Ned didn't say so. Now that Grif did not run away every time Ned opened his mouth to speak, he no longer opened it quite so often. The writing exercise had a grounding effect at any rate, and the young man's nervous habits that were at times pronounced—of smoothing an unruly eyebrow, scratching an elusive itch, running a finger tentatively along his nose, tracing its outline as if surprised to find it still lodged on his face—these had been diverted into the book. There he was free to search and probe, and to reassure himself of his own existence.

Ned, however, foresaw a technical problem. This was not difficult and required no occult talents. The pencil he had offered Grif when he'd first noticed him frowning into the blank pages of his opened diary had been whittled to within an inch of its own life. He had watched the instrument disappear in Grif's hands, and presently his fingers were bunched on the point of it, as if his whole being were balanced there. Curious how something so insignificant, a nub of wood encasing a fraction of graphite, had the power, like other small, danger-packed objects—a poison capsule, a bullet—to alter one's destiny completely. There was going to be a death sooner or later, either in their journey or in Grif's account of it, and as his partner did not want to stop scribbling—or could not, for he clung to the book as if it were an extension of his own skin— Ned made an agreeable suggestion. Agreeable to himself anyway, for he was beginning to feel crowded by Grif's company, nostalgic for his own fleet and unobserved peregrinations.

The suggestion was straightforward—and not unwelcome, he thought—and involved dropping Grif off in a bay on the east side of Manitoulin Island, the most accessible spot to land the boat. Ned knew of a family named Cormany who lived on the outskirts of a small village there. He had met them on only a couple of occasions, but found them to be genial and hospitable people—a bit eccentric perhaps, but harmless; and he was certain that they would put Grif up for a day or two while he got his bearings, and might even have a writing instrument to lend him. Or he could buy what he needed in the village store. From the Cormanys' it was a short walk, fifteen miles or so, to Little Current on the north shore, where the steamers stopped on their way to the Sault and on the return trip to the south—in other words, to whatever destination Grif's weathervane of a conscience might lead him.

Grif glanced up from his book to nod in agreement—he'd been thinking, whimsically, about what secrets he might reveal if he could dip a pen into the ink of these waters, into their black or indigo or gold—and the next thing he knew he was nodding again, more than a bit surprised to be watching Ned sail away at a buoyant clip, hand raised in a parting salute, fingertips reaching into the air as if the open sky were a font of freedom. He had been dumped, but not without directions, which he supposed he might as well follow. He didn't want to squander the money Jean had given him—the currency of the drowned after all, and not to be frivolously spent—and so decided that he would try to cadge a meal, maybe even something to write with, from these people and be on his way.

He slid the journal into his pocket and began to walk along the beach, which seemed to consist entirely of slate, pieces the size of dinner plates and platters that broke like crockery as he picked his way over them. It made him feel oafish: here he'd just arrived and already he was wrecking the place. He made a beeline for a bank and clambered up. A path on the other side brought him before too long to the village Ned had mentioned.

In keeping with his newly acquired interests, Grif paid more attention as he walked to the skimming dragonflies and the tumbling sulphurs than to the wharf and fishing boats on his left, or the grist mill and hotel up ahead. He was recalling what Ned had told him about the fritillary larva and its preferred menu—the tender leaves of violets—and didn't notice the villagers, who had ceased all activity and stood motionless, as if caught in a photograph, to watch him, a stranger who had apparently stepped right out of the lake. Even a woman hammering shingles onto her roof, a rope tied to her skirts to hold her dress down, paused in mid-swing to stare. He was unshaven, had long hair, was oddly dressed—and shod—and was as preoccupied as any phantom on a midday patrol. He brought with him an unsettling chill, a breath from the grave that rushed through them as he wandered by.

The only citizen unaware of the passing stranger was a young man, a pianist who had retired to this obscure corner of the world and to the loving care of his sister due to ill health (consumption). Enfolded in the gloom of his parlour, he was sunk up to his elbows in a Chopin nocturne (no. 6 in G Minor, op. 15, no. 3), and was as intently focused on the technicalities of this passage as Grif also happened to be on the entomological minutiae of his. As he walked by the young man's house, Grif was startled by a brace of beautifully articulated notes that drifted out of an open window and into a net of dancing midges. Looking around, taking in a wider view for the first time, he began to wonder what sort of enchanted shore he had been abandoned on. And indeed, the people of this village were standing around stock-still, arrested and staring, as if bewitched. He could easily guess who was responsible, too: that woman tied like a witch to her roof.

His impression of strangeness wasn't alleviated any as he approached the Cormanys' residence, which was located several miles beyond the village. It was a four-square frame house, two and a half storeys high, bracketed by tall chimneys and graced with several large windows in front, each decorated with arching eyebrow cornices. This architectural detail made it seem as if the house were watching him, as the villagers had watched, although this was not what struck him as unusual. What did were the three grown men in the front yard playing leapfrog, bounding through the long grass, hurtling over one another and roaring with laughter.

He paused, and studied the scene. He shook his head, dismissing it as if it were an illusion, and was about to move on towards the town, thinking it might be wiser to forgo an acquaintance with this family, when he paused again in a stutter of indecision and the gambollers caught sight of him. All the energy the men had been pouring into their game was instantly directed at him. They laid a welcoming siege, shouting greetings and motioning him in with large arm-swooping gestures. To Grif, an uncertain, flickering figure on the road, the force of their inexplicable friendliness was irresistible, and against all caution he was drawn down the lane toward them.

One of the men was older, but each bore a striking resemblance to the others. The elder gentleman was a vintage version of the younger two, who were handsome, pale-eyed and fair, and all displayed a great many white teeth—a fleck of pink dentifrice powder evident in the older man's gums—as they took turns clasping Grif's hand and introducing themselves. William Cormany and his sons, Edgar and Albert. The sons brimmed with health and high spirits, and Grif was intrigued to see such delicate, beautiful skin on these young male faces. He doubted if they even shaved. Like angels, they seemed, or overlarge cherubs. Beside them he felt like a plate of leftovers, a man woven together out of hair and creases and stains.

When he mentioned Ned's name, the welcome was amplified and extended, and he was swept into the house to meet the rest of the family. The men led him down a hallway, past an unoccupied drawing room, and into a dining room where four women were seated around a thick-legged cherrywood table, the surface of which was cluttered with a welter of objects: unwashed dishes, a pile of mending, an apple skewered with a knitting needle, magazines, a pipe, orange peels, a scatter of chess pieces and a half-eaten butter tart in which a dental impression was clearly visible. The women's hands might have been idle, but their chins weren't, for they had been busy wagging them in an excited whispered conversation that stopped dead the moment the men appeared. They turned very slowly and all at once, as if the act were choreographed; and Grif saw it was a planned jest, for each woman had a maple key, split at the seed base, stuck to the bridge of her nose. They looked as fetchingly peculiar as any of the insects he had lately become smitten with. They began to titter and laugh, and the Cormany men joined in, and Grif too caught on to the tail end of it, but with a faltering grasp, like that of a flying child who is last to latch on in a game of crack-the-whip.

"You must forgive us, Mr. Smolders," said Ina Cormany, the mother of this merry crew, when he was introduced, "but we do like to have a bit of fun."

The daughters—Victoria, Maud, Polly—shared in the limited but excellent range of features that were allowed this family, and all were lovely, especially Polly, the youngest. Grif judged her to be about sixteen, and perhaps to distinguish herself from her neatly coiffed and carefully dressed sisters, she wore her hair down, an unruly reddish-blonde blaze, and she had on a dress she'd grown out of.

He had to turn his eyes away from her (no corset)—the burning rims of his ears shame enough—which is when he spotted another member of the family, tucked up in a bucket and presently putting in service as a doorstop. It was a baby with a sooty tuft of down on its head, a poet's sideburns and a very serious expression on its small, ugly face. This child didn't seem to belong here among them—dark, glowering, an imp in a pail—nor was anyone paying it the slightest bit of attention. But the baby drew Grif's eye as if it had some magnetic power to which he alone was susceptible.

"Who is this little fellow?" he finally asked.

"That?" said Edgar, the elder brother. "What's it called, Polly?"

"Why, Master Rumwold, I believe."

"Fitting. He is a rum one."

This sally provoked more laughter from the family, as if the ridiculous lay all about them, discoverable in the most unyielding places, even in Master Rumwold's grave demeanour. Not that they worried the baby for any further entertainment; the full glare of their attention, especially the women's, was turned upon Grif. He was offered tea, brandy, a cigar, a chair, a bed for the night, for as many nights as he wished. They pressed him for news of Ned and of his own travels, and listened with rapt expressions to everything he said.

They were such a lighthearted family, and so gracious, and yet he didn't feel much at ease. More the opposite—a niggling sense of alarm was growing in him, a tiny screw of apprehension tightening in his gut. That baby, so sober and silent and unregarded, troubled him. Wasn't Rumwold the saint who had preached a sermon when only three days old? This child looked as though he could easily be the guardian of some terrible secret that he would reluctantly but dutifully divulge to the world as soon as the shattering power of speech was conferred upon him.

At dinner that evening Grif was surprised to find the dining-room table cleared, set and displaying a range of savoury dishes that might well have appeared there by magic. After spending the early part of the afternoon with the Cormanys, he had not had the sense that work took up much of their day, nor had he encountered any hired help. Yet the room he had been given on the top floor was clean and pleasant. Someone had set out a change of clothing for him on the bed, and a bowl and pitcher filled with hot water sat on a pear-wood washstand, along with a bar of caraway-scented soap, an ivory comb, a pair of scissors, a silver-handled shaving brush and mug, and a straight razor. He took the hint.

As he laboured away, shaving, snipping, combing, divesting himself of his vagabond guise, watching with a sinking heart as the same old Grif Smolders showed his face in the mirror, he puzzled over the nature of this household. It was possible that the Cormanys did all the work themselves, but secretly, keeping the indignity of it hidden, as people kept hidden the procreative act. Given their manner, dress and possessions, they did appear to have a social position, or pretensions to one, but this was a remote place in which to enact it. He had expected to find stalwart homesteaders, or poor scraping farmers, or trappers living in windowless wattle-and-daub shacks, with a rifle slung on a peg in the wall, and a squaw for a wife. And mouths full of carious teeth, not at all like the ones that flashed at him throughout dinner and, frankly, had begun to give him a headache.

"Mr. Smolders, are you pained?" asked Victoria.

"Not at all, Miss Cormany. Only a bit fatigued, I think."

"You should rub your head with an onion, then," offered Albert.

"Oh?"

"Father's cure for complaints of the head."

"I thought that was your cure for baldness, Father?" said Maud.

"Bad dreams, my dear. A superlative cure for bad dreams."

"Pop the old incubus on the noggin, eh, Pater?" This was Edgar, smirking.

"You know that ancient couple who live down the road…?"

"The Buckles."

(Laughter.)

"Yes, the Buckles. They wash their feet every morning in the contents of their chamber pots."

(More laughter.)

"Good heavens."

"Polly, I don't believe Mr. Smolders—"

"Are you sure?"

"You're inventing."

"It's supposed to cure chilblains."

"Can't do much for their smelly feet. Or their souls."

"Haw, haw. Albert made a joke, Mother."

"Fancy that."

The dinner conversation skimmed along in this nonsensical way, glib and quick, plumbing no depths. No talk of politics or worldly news. For all their teasing they did obviously take pleasure in their own company. How different this was from the dinners in his own forsaken home, which were achieved in complete silence as he and his parents shoved food heavy as earth down their throats—except that there was something equally airless and crushing here, perhaps just the relentless cheer itself. He had certainly heard more varieties of laughter, more range, than he'd thought possible in one sitting: booming, gulping, chuckling, samples great and small, a selection broadly peculiar enough for a lunatics' museum. The baby might have been cleared out with the rest of the clutter, but a nursery atmosphere prevailed. At one point William Cormany had been chastised by his wife for not finishing his dinner—"No dessert for you, Father!"—and not long after Grif spotted him slipping a piece of ham into his pocket, and harrying a slice of turnip under his plate. When Victoria, the eldest daughter, began buttering a slice of bread, the activity so beguiled her that she didn't stop until she had buttered her arm clear up to her elbow. This made Albert laugh so hard he snorted ginger beer up his nose.

"I've seen Albert squirt milk out of his eyes," said Polly to Grif, as she wiped her face with a bun. "Do it, Albert."

"Not with this stuff, it stings. Stop kicking, Maudie."

"That's not me."

"'Tis so."

"Mother, Edgar flicked a pea at Mr. Smolders with his knife."

"Did not."

"Children, children."

"Mr. Smolders,"—Polly addressed him again—"aren't you ever going to enquire about the two vacant place settings?"

Naturally, Grif had noticed them—the unoccupied chairs, the empty plates, the unused crystal and silverware sparkling in the candlelight—but he had no intention of setting himself up by asking who was missing. He had come to suspect that he had been welcomed so warmly into this household because what this family needed most was a dupe, a gull, some living fool to feed into the voracious maw of its humour.

"The one is for Hattie," Polly told him.

"And who might that be?" he said.

"Our sister."

"Another?"

"Hattie's the shy one. She's been hiding behind the wood stove since you arrived."

"Oh."

"The other setting is for Grandmother Cormany."

"And she is…?"

"Dead."

"I'm sorry, I didn't know," he said softly.

"Two whole days now."

"I beg your pardon?" He knew she couldn't be serious, that she was pulling his leg; otherwise the house would be swathed in crepe, and the women too. A wreath on the door, black ribbons tied around handles, all the usual paraphernalia that signifies a death in the house.

"Yes, we were all so fond of her. She's in the larder. We didn't know what to do with her. I mean, we always play games in the drawing room after dinner, so that wouldn't work."

"Darling," said her mother, "you know very well that Grandmother Cormany is in Toronto."

"As good as dead, then," said Albert.

"Mother," said Polly, her cheeks colouring, "*you* know she's not."

Grif glanced around the table into faces indifferent, unreadable, strange in the candlelight, while keeping the muscles around his mouth tensed for laughter, waiting for the joke to strike.

Readying himself for bed that night, Grif tried to concentrate solely on a pleasure that awaited him: oblivion. After sleeping rough for so long, he knew that stretching out on this feather tick mattress was going to be like sinking into a bed of cream. The servant who operated silently and invisibly in this house had even turned down the covers for him, and had placed a warmed stone at the foot of the bed. His clothing, washed and folded, had been set on top of a pine blanket box, along with the Reverend's jacket, which looked as if it had been given a good thrashing with a rug beater. He might wonder if this shy sister, Hattie, was the resident Cinderella, but he avoided the thought, not wanting to be roused by perplexity. Wetting his fingers and pinching out the flame of the candle by the bed, he found sleep almost immediately, a pure self-dissolving dark, absolute as the night around him.

Not long after, however, he was awakened. Something small and soft, a paw it felt like, smacked him on the temple. He lay there, disoriented, blinking himself awake, listening closely. Whatever it was, he could hear it thudding into the walls, bumping up against the ceiling. It was not large enough to be a bat, he thought, but was likely a fair-sized moth, a noctuid of some sort. He knew he should light the candle and properly identify the creature, but only lay listening to its intermittent searching patter. His journal. He hadn't turned to it once during the course of this unusual day. His reason for coming here in the first place—to borrow a pencil—now struck him as being utterly ludicrous, like travelling halfway around the world to borrow a cup of sugar.

He pulled the covers up over his head, not liking the idea of that moth parking in his snoring mouth, and prepared again for sleep. He might have been close to it, too, his mind drifting off the path of logic, for he suddenly saw Avice. More particularly, he saw that pattern of moles she had on her left cheek, fast by her ear, and the few freckles that trailed onto her throat, the lesser stars in this constellation. More might even be concealed beneath the black velvet ribbon she wore cinched around her neck. The remarkable thing was how similar this pattern was, this insignia of imperfections, to the figure of O'Brien he had often watched striding across the night sky. How horrible. What if he were to gaze up into that sky henceforward and see not the glorious open space between the stars, an eternity of the undefined, but *her*, gigantic and lowering, the scattered diamonds of her wedding band embedded in her cheek, and her furious black eyes forever staring down?

After this, Grif tossed and turned in the bed until the sheets were wrapped around him like a tourniquet. When he did finally drop off, he was visited by dreams, brutal in their intensity and cunning, that pressed him to the very edge of wakefulness without granting him release.

# 12

# THE GORGON'S MOUTH

HER VOICE was level, and had heft, as if weighted like a sling with a chunk of rock or glass—something that might hurt if she lobbed it at you. It belonged to a woman he had not encountered the day before, and unless she was the unobtrusive servant finally showing herself, it could only be Hattie, the missing sister, the "shy" one. If she *had* been hiding behind the wood stove, it must have been on account of its iron-hearted companionship, or to enjoin its heated force with her own, for she did not fear company by the looks—or sound—of her.

Grif had come down early to the dining room, dream-driven, and doctored—scored, cupped and bled dry—his face pale and his hands shaking. The table had not been properly cleared from the night before, and on it were the congealed remains of a roast, a tower of greasy plates, a scatter of smeared cutlery, skirts of solidified wax encircling the bases of the candlesticks. The door that led to the kitchen was closed, but he could hear someone banging around in there and wondered if there was any hope at all for a cup of tea. Master Rumwold was back in his bucket, inert as a block, and it occurred to Grif that the child might be addled, despite its black and avid eyes.

He took a seat at the table and cleared a space for his journal. This he set before him and opened to a page empty as a fallow field. He still had nothing to write with, and the inclination to do so was beginning to drain out of him. His hand hung over his book like that fern—what was it called? ... *dead man's fingers.* He glanced at the cherrywood sideboard and caught sight of a mouse skittering beneath it, then watched as it hustled along the base of the wainscotting. A nervy and surreptitious hunter of crumbs. Like himself. He thought how, with the right instrument, he could lift the little creature right off the floor, right out of its scant grey existence, and set it free in his book. A writer's harmless fantasy.

"There's a fine waste of time." A curt nod toward the journal. "You would do better to get yourself some breakfast; no one else will."

Hattie. She had come into the dining room quietly enough, but the lead sinkers in her voice struck hard and cold in his ear. Grif stood. Had she come from the kitchen? He hadn't noticed. He did see that her features were unmistakably Cormany ones, even though the eyes were smaller, the mouth larger (she was what his mother would call muckle-mouthed), the colouring darker. Physically, she seemed to be putting up resistance to the family design, straining her body away from the rest in opposition. The Cormany charm had soured in her, the sunniness dimmed. It wasn't difficult to figure out why this might be. Master Rumwold was her child; that was obvious. He surmised that whatever humour she once possessed had drained straight through him and disappeared, as through a sinkhole. But who was the father, and where was he?

"I can't write ..." he began to explain.

"How unfortunate," she cut him off. "Then you might as well breakfast. You'll find something in the larder."

With that, she walked out of the room, and shortly afterwards he heard the stairs complaining as she ascended in her sharp buttoned boots. He glanced at the baby, as if for an explanation of his mother's surly behaviour, and found no joy there. Master Rumwold was like a tightly sealed wallet in which a cache of worry and pain had been securely stored. Of the two of them Grif knew that he, Grif, was the more likely to break down and cry.

He had not forgotten Polly's claim from last evening, and so didn't doubt that he would find *something* in the larder. Not that he believed her—it was preposterous, you didn't lay your granny out in the larder like a wheel of cheese—but an image had been evoked nonetheless. He had encountered it in his harassing dreams, and found on waking that it was not made of the usual ephemeral material. Like a stubborn ghost, it had refused to fade with the morning light. Closing his eyes, he could see the corpse still: an old woman, naked, stretched out on a narrow slatted shelf, her hands tied together with black ribbon, as were her knees and ankles. A silk handkerchief, slash red, was looped around her head and jaw. Grif had never in his life seen a naked woman, and had to wonder that he could make one up in such detail. He knew he was making one up, though; not because he doubted the details, which had a convincing plausibility, but because the woman, despite her body's slack and loosely worn skin, had a face that was unmarked by age and still animate with Cormany beauty.

Was this how it began, the mind losing hold, with these sorts of visions moving into your head and taking on an undismissible authority? With the screen between what was real and what not becoming worn and permeable and letting anything imaginable drift in? He didn't know, and was not so hungry for the truth, or even for breakfast, that he was going to enter that larder and find out. The very word *larder* chilled him, as did such other—*root cellar, ice house*—damp underworld spaces with trap doors that locked from the outside.

Grif took one more look at the baby, who was boring a hole through his head with its hard little eyes, and fled from the room.

His destination was the front door. Some air, a morning walk, would do him good, especially if it was a long walk to the next town, and onward. He knew that what he really hungered for this morning was the vast blue relief of the sky, the lane that rolled out straight as a runner to the main road. But in passing by the open door of the front drawing room, he noticed Polly seated by a window, sewing, or about to. In her lap lay a square of blue cotton set in an embroidery hoop, and in her raised hand she held a bright needle from which dangled a piece of thread long and black as a hair.

She looked up quickly, and smiled warmly at him, shadows from the lace curtains brindling her face. "Mr. Smolders, good morning."

He apologized for interrupting.

"Please do," she said. "Come in, come in. This needlework, believe me, is not my idea. I haven't the faintest notion where to begin. I'd rather be out climbing trees or playing tennis. Or canoeing on the lake. Do you know, I took an absolute header the other day, got thoroughly soaked. Buckets of fun, though. Do you canoe, Mr. Smolders?"

"No," he said, driving the word like a nail into the floor between them. She disconcerted him. She might speak with the candour of a child, and wear a dress that belonged to a twelve-year-old girl, but she was mature enough in figure to make his collar stick to his neck. He tried to keep his attention to her physical presence light and delicate, observing only as much of her as decency permitted.

"Did you notice these?" she said, pointing at her chest as she leapt up to face him, letting her embroidery slide to the floor.

He immediately took an interest in the maidenhair fern in the corner, then in the collection of bird skulls that were arranged on a library shelf according to size, from raven to wren, like the descending notes on an avian scale. He began to read titles of books shelved below the skulls: *Chatterbox* for '96, *Little Women and Good Wives*, *Wild Animals I Have Known*, *The Untempered Wind*, *The Turkish Messiah*.

"Mr. Smolders?"

"Oh, sorry, Miss Polly. I was just...reading."

"Do you fear them?"

"I beg your pardon?"

"These. Spiders. I understand that some people have a dreadful terror of them."

"Spiders? God, so they are."

Polly laughed, and gave the embroidery hoop a good kick. It shot under a sofa that was upholstered in a material pink as a tongue.

He saw now where her real sewing skills lay. Her necklace was more a kind of charm. Threaded through the abdomens, bodies clenched, a few legs trailing raggedly, were about twelve or thirteen spiders. Common house spiders, orb-weavers and a few harvestmen were all snagged in a web like none that nature itself would be perverse enough to devise.

She laughed again, delighted by his dumbfounded expression. "Quite mad, I agree. But honestly, it does work."

"Work?"

"For ague, chest colds. You see, I caught a chill last night. I'm afraid Father does not put much stock in modern medicines. You won't find any Cosmoline or electric liniment in this house. Consider yourself lucky that you didn't wake up with a sore throat."

"The treatment is worse than the affliction?"

"Indeed. For that one, he makes you swallow a slice of bacon with a piece of string attached to it."

"Argh, don't tell me—he then pulls it back up, and makes the victim swallow it again until the sore throat goes away."

"Right. Or until he runs out the door."

Grif was beginning to feel more at ease. "I have a cure for colds you might want to try." He did, too, a "prairie cure" that

Jean had passed on to him. "I hope you have a hat, Miss Polly. You'll need one for this."

"Certainly, doctor." She mimed twirling one on her finger, a phantom hat. "Go on, please."

"First thing, you place your hat on a table. Next, you have to take a drink from a very good bottle of whisky. Then another drink. Then another. The thing is, you have to keep at it until you see not only one hat but two. At this stage in the cure, you must go to bed and stay there until completely restored to health."

"Wonderful!" Her laugh was full and deep. "That one does bring to mind Mrs. Motely, from the village. She's president of the Ladies' Temperance Union, and tenacious on the subject, absolutely terrifying. But she's pickled most of the time herself, as she's a great believer in Dr. Pinkham's Elixir for Female Complaints, which is constituted mainly of gin, Mother says."

"Ha."

"A dreadful woman. With a moustache. Did you know, by the way, that if you take a dried and powdered frog and mix it with water to form a paste, that it makes an excellent depilatory?"

"Perhaps I should try it."

"Father once lured several flies out of Edgar's head by holding a lit candle up to his ear."

She smiled, but his faltered.

"He is a doctor, you know. Some of his treatments are considered . . . unorthodox. At least where we came from. Where we used to live."

And left in a hurry, Grif didn't doubt.

"Every night before bed we strip completely and Father curries us with a brush. A flesh brush it's called; it stimulates circulation and purifies the blood. It's most invigorating, Mr. Smolders."

Grif did not need his blood stimulated, as it had all rushed up into his face. In his experience a young woman, well brought up, veered with expert precision away from indelicate subjects. That a woman had a body at all, and attendant bodily functions, was not widely acknowledged, let alone considered to be subject matter for civilized discourse. Avice's sisters, he recalled, would not eat apples in company, supposedly for the unseemly noise made chewing them, but he suspected it had more to do with the spectacle of full lips on ripe fruit. Avice herself had no such compunction. Nor did Polly Cormany appear to have any qualms about tackling the forbidden head-on. Unless of course she *was* just a child, an innocent.

"Do you know what a man must do," she said, unperturbed, "if he has a bone caught in his throat?"

"Eat a slice of bread?"

"No. He must repeat thrice nine times the words, *I buss the Gorgon's mouth.*" She herself then proceeded to repeat this, several times, her intonation incantatory and sibilant.

Such play-acting. He tried not to grin. He also tried to look appropriately intrigued, and why not, for here was an antique remedy, a physic that might have come straight out of his own journal, a prescription penned in the spidery hand of his fellow author. Then—*damn*, he remembered, the journal. He had left it in that wretched dining room.

Polly made a move toward him, out of the lacy shadow cast by the curtain, and she was twiddling that bright needle of hers between thumb and forefinger. For a moment he thought she was going to stab him with it, and he took a quick step backwards.

"Whatever is the matter?" he said.

"You'll never find me," she said, her voice catching, as though she were the one with a bone stuck in her throat. She then moved briskly around him and strode through the door, slamming it behind her as she went, its crystal knob rattling loosely.

Grif was flummoxed. Something had transpired, but he had missed what exactly it was. More Cormany games—a challenge, a taunt, a bit of fun, didn't the mother say? This one a grownup version of hide-and-seek, down corridors, in a back bedroom. With a flesh brush.

What Grif did not guess was that Polly might be telling the truth. Not the simple truth—the design of it twisted too much out of shape for that—but the truth nonetheless. Once she passed through that door, she was as good as gone, and he didn't find her ever again.

# 13

## WICKEDNESS

Wнат was it that eluded him? Certainly the Cormanys were fine people, charming and amusing, and
God knows that was a boon to any family. They were
just peculiar, and immature, all of them together, which was
excusable surely, living in isolation as they did, keeping their
own company. This, Grif decided (not entirely convincing
himself), accounted for that sense he had of missing something, of not perceiving what it was about them that might
be obvious to another visitor less raw and uncouth than himself. Grasping this revealing detail was like trying to pluck a
single transparent current out of a flowing river. It could be
that what defined them and troubled him was nothing more
unusual than the mystery of childhood itself, with its many
concealed fears.

Yes. (Maybe.)

As the youngest (Master Rumwold didn't count) and the
prettiest, Polly was undoubtedly spoiled, bored, a trouble-
maker. Or simply given to yarning. Many times during the
course of the day he had chanced to observe William Cormany, and had seen only a man with an easy manner and
an unclouded temperament, not a lascivious parent overly

appreciative of his children's physical attributes. Nor had the man offered any occult medical advice, except to comment when Grif enquired about the current state of the medical profession, "My boy, the best physicians you will ever encounter are Dr. Diet, Dr. Quiet and Dr. Merryman."

Grif did not take up Polly's challenge, in any event, but went instead in search of his journal, which was no longer in the dining room when he hurried back to retrieve it. He found Albert there eating a rolled pancake, licking a dribble of syrup off the heel of his hand. Seeing Grif's distress, Albert offered to help search for the missing book, and immediately dropped the pancake on the floor at his feet and began opening cupboards, rifling through drawers, frisking the curtains, tossing aside pillows. It was more of a mock search than a real one, and soon he had exhausted whatever sport there was to be had in the activity. He then suggested a game of croquet instead.

"Your book is sure to turn up. I'll bet you Edgar nicked it for a lark."

This was how Grif's day slid away into distraction. He flew down a winding path of pleasures slick as ice. Croquet in the back garden led easily enough to badminton, until a small black dog appeared out of nowhere and ran off with the only shuttlecock; but no matter, for then it was time for luncheon, and an eating contest, which Victoria won by eating her height in cobs of corn. Afterwards there was crambo and whist—"Hunt the Lady," appropriately enough—followed by charades and conundrums.

"Where did Charles I's executioner dine, and what did he take?"

"Why, that's easy. He took a chop at The King's Head."

Afterwards he helped Maud paint a pastoral scene on a chunk of fungus big as a cow flap. He attended a grammar lesson in the stable, amid much hilarity, as Edgar attempted to teach the rudiments of English to his horse, Enrico, who understood only Italian. With Ina Cormany, Grif spent an industrious half-hour picking apart a dress, *to renew its life*, she said. He supposed this activity actually qualified as work, although it seemed too enjoyably destructive to be that.

Polly did not put in an appearance and join in any of this. He didn't even think of her but once or twice, and then only with some wonder that she was being so stubborn, sticking to her game, staying hidden, her face pressed into the corner of some remote web-wreathed room, while the walls of the house reverberated with everyone else's laughter.

Except Hattie's, of course. She passed in and out of his view, a laden tray in hand, or a duster, fiddle-faced and resolutely disapproving. He wanted to ignore her as the others did, but she seemed to carry—on her back, in her eye—whatever it was about this place that he couldn't fathom. She was a thorn, an irritant, a smarting pinch. Contention boiled in her. One word, the wrong word, and it might rip through them all.

By dinner that evening he was worn out. Amazing how they kept up the pace. It had been like attending a marathon birthday party, a hectic high-energy circus for which only children could have the stamina. The muscles in his face had begun to ache from the punishment of holding his smile constantly and widely in place. A tight band of pressure was clamped around his head, a wasps' nest of anxiety, a headache gaudy and constricting as a turban too tightly wound. He didn't think he could tolerate any more of their laughter. Whether open or insinuating, it whipped around the room like a zephyr. It buffeted and ate away at him. He longed for muffling dullness, for the gloomy repose of his own lost home, even for the seriousness and sanctuary of prayer.

The Cormanys did not preface their evening meal with grace, however. Secretly they might be thanking someone, but God did not appear to be a candidate for their gratitude. Before joining in the scrum that evening—arms reaching, elbows flying—William Cormany did voice an aphorism of sorts that was unconnected thematically to the current table chatter (mesmerism, grape catsup, curling irons) and completely ignored.

He said: "There are none so wicked as represented; none so good as they should be." He winked at Grif, and grinned, giving his saying an equivocal teeter, before he made a grab for the peas.

Grif was surprised when Polly also failed to show up for dinner, although his suspicions about her tale-bearing were confirmed. Not only was Hattie present at the table, but the other missing person from the previous night, the "deceased," put in an appearance. At least that's who he thought it must be, the granny he had envisioned stretched out in the larder, trussed like a fowl. This woman did not at all resemble his conjured picture of her, or any of the Cormany family for that matter, and she might as easily have been their cook or washerwoman. She was introduced to him simply as "Rosie." What she did resemble most was her name, as she was a roundish, red-cheeked, cheerful old woman, warm as the steaming bowls on the table.

If she *was* Grandmother Cormany, death held no terrors for her since she scarcely seemed to believe in it. Her conversation bore this out, persistently. Leaning toward Grif, she confided numerous stories of death circumvented or defied. She knew of a woman, she claimed, who had been roused at her own wake. Sheer indignation had reactivated her heart. The shameful racket the gathered mourners were making, the drunkenness, the irreligious songs, the mud tracked on her clean floor, caused the woman to sit straight up in her coffin and tell everyone to clear out and leave her in peace.

"It's not uncommon for people to be buried alive," said Edgar.

"Go on."

"You do hear of it, some corpse or other being disinterred and then the inside of the casket is discovered to be shredded and clawed."

"Lord, you mean...?"

"Yes, the poor sod snaps out of it, a coma or what have you, and finds himself six feet under."

"Imagine that."

"I know of a man," said Rosie, "who came back to life during his own funeral, and all because his sons were clumsy. They were the pallbearers, you see, and bumped the coffin into a pew on the way out of the church, and then one of them tripped going down the stairs and away it flew. It crashed on the ground, the lid sprang open and the poor man rolled out. And then he jumped up and started to stagger around."

"Maudie, pass Rosie a bun, will you please."

"But the family must have been overjoyed," said Grif.

"Shocked, really. The wife died of it right on the spot."

"And then they buried her instead?" said Edgar. "How convenient."

"No, no. Although they *were* more careful the second time around."

From her end of the table Maud shied a bun at the old woman, which glanced off her forehead.

"Maudie!" said her mother.

"Sorry, Rosie, I meant it to land on your plate."

"Never mind, dear. I know of another woman ..."

"Tell me, Mr. Smolders," said Victoria, "did you find your book?"

"No ... I didn't." He thought only Albert knew about his missing journal.

"Your Wicked Bible," said William Cormany.

"My, what was that?"

"It's old enough to be one."

"Have you heard of such a thing, Mr. Smolders?"

"I'm afraid not. A bible of some sort?"

"An edition that was published in the seventeenth century. There was an unfortunate misprint in it. The seventh commandment reads, 'Thou shalt commit adultery.'"

"Thou shalt *not* honour thy mother and thy father," laughed Albert.

"Thou *shalt* kill," said Edgar, rubbing his hands together.

"A collector's item," said Grif.

"Indeed."

"Where *is* Polly, anyway?"

"Couldn't tell you, I haven't seen her all day."

"How odd."

"Maybe she ran away."

"To the city—she's threatened to do it often enough."

"To become a type-writer, wasn't that it?"

"She wants to be a doctor," said Hattie.

"A *female* doctor?" barked William.

"A witch doctor, more like," said Albert.

"I wonder where she is, though."

"So was I," said Grif, "wondering that."

"You were the last person to see her," said Hattie.

"Was I?"

"Yes."

"Check the well."

"Edgar, really."

"You might be surprised."

"Bah!" blurted Master Rumwold, forgotten as usual in his bucket in a corner of the room, and everyone—almost—laughed merrily.

Conversation soon whisked the subject of Polly's absence away out of reach, as it did seem to do here. Talk was a vehicle more of delivery than of discovery, although it didn't take Grif anywhere but around in circles.

When the meal was over, he excused himself once again from participating in the evening's diversions, and went up early to bed. Before going, he snatched a book from their library, which was meant to suggest that he had no intention of spending all the hours of revelry ahead buried in the tedium of sleep. When he got to his room, he saw that he'd chosen something called *The Finchley Manual of Industry*. His hosts would take him for a serious young man; anyway, more serious than they were. What they actually took him for shortly became a more vexed issue. He spotted his lost journal on the bed, sitting square on the pillow like a precious object on display. Someone at the table knew it had been found. This person had obviously put it in his room and should have said as much.

He set Mr. Finchley's manual on the washstand and walked over to the bed, eyeing his journal for signs of violation. With something he valued so much, he felt he should be able to tell right off if it had been opened, and read. Not that it contained any secrets of his own, unless one considered the titchy details of a butterfly's genitalia a personal matter (as it might well be for the butterfly). He picked the book up and began to flip through it. He saw then that it *had* been interfered with. The empty page he had paused over that morning was now complete, filled in, his day recorded. More incredibly, it was written in his own hand, but was not of his mind, or not of his mind as he knew it. It was a forgery obscene and callous. It contained a thief's inventory of goods in the house, and was interspersed with crude remarks about the family, especially the women. One passage, most fantastic, recorded an unspeakable act:

131

> Cornered youngest in d. room. Made sure beforehand door wd lock. Shoved her up agst. the wall and got my fill. Cd. tell she not unwilling. Gagged her anyway, with her own drawers (ha ha). Promisd to slit her throat if she told. She wont talk. Better than a sporting house this place.

Grif slapped the book shut and hurled it from him as if it were on fire, as if it were alive and scheming, plotting wickedness all on its own. The journal bounced off the wall and fell open again, but at an earlier, centuries-old passage, the ravages described therein long forgotten.

It was only a practical joke, of course. He knew that, and knew he shouldn't let his headache think for him, and make more of it than it deserved. But it was fashioned out of a humour that was too queer and soiled for his liking. Which one was responsible? Edgar, probably. Surely the girls themselves weren't involved. Although Hattie was a possibility. Even Polly herself. Or the whole blessed family. To the very bottom of his sorry soul Grif regretted not finding the front door as he had intended that morning, and he vowed as he put out the light and slid under the covers that tomorrow he would be gone from this place with the dawn, that he'd vanish with the mist.

Again in the middle of the night he was awakened. He thought he could hear someone calling him. He had been walking on a lake bottom, walking for years, it seemed, his shoes encrusted with shells, his jacket trailing fronds of blanketweed, his skin furred a dull green with algae. Around his head his hair pulsed black and silken as he pushed up through currents soft as cloth, up into the sharp night air. He heard then, not a voice calling, but a muffled moaning sound coming from somewhere in the house. The sound defied interpretation. It might have been a cry for help, or a plea for mercy, or an exclamation of enjoyment entangled with one of hopelessness and despair.

What he did know for certain, what he finally understood, was that nightmare in this house lay somewhere outside of dreaming. And knowing this, he held his breath and plunged back to the lake bottom.

Not for long. Shortly after, a bolt of pain shot through his jaw as he was struck with something hard—an axe handle, the butt of a rifle—and he had no choice but to surface once more, breathe deeply, and open his wary and reluctant eyes.

# 14

## NO LIES

W<small>HAT SHE DID</small> was nail him with his own shoe. Vermin in the bedding. She clipped him hard, the full sandbag weight of her personality behind the blow, and might have left a burning crescent on his jaw if the heel had not been so worn. As pulped as he felt.

"Get up," she hissed. Then, "You're not safe here."

So delivered, this was hardly news. He raised a hand, lifted it right out of the depths of sleep, and touched his jaw, waggled it tentatively. Didn't she know he was fragile?

"Hattie?" he said to the figure hovering above him, her features obscured, a silhouette only; but with that raven-tumble of rocks in her voice, and her lethal version of the womanly touch, it could only be her.

"Hurry." She began tossing his clothes on the bed—socks, pants, jacket.

He thought, *I won't.*

What he registered of the night and what was going on in it came in fragments, disconnected, as if perception too had been knocked on the head and shattered: a faint burning smell, a gleam of light burnishing the window, the rasping bark of a fox outside, the Japanese harp on the back porch tinkling,

Hattie's agitated breath falling on him, the taste of fear rising in his throat. No laughter anywhere, none whatsoever.

"They've found her," she said. "Get up."

"What?"

"Polly. In the field."

"My God, not . . . ?"

"Yes, and soon they will know what you did to her."

"I did nothing."

No response. In the dark her face might as well have been missing.

"I swear, I never touched her."

"Don't talk, *just come.*"

He thought, *I will.* Flight being his first and only recourse. He leapt out of bed and dressed in haste, fumbling with his clothing, while she stood, still enfolded in the night's shadows, watching and, he assumed, making her unsparing assessment.

She said, "If Edgar finds you, he'll cut off your balls and make you eat them."

She might as well have thumped him again, his ears ringing with this threat, but it was more her vulgarity than anything that injured. A sickness had entered the minds of women and was pouring out of their mouths like black blood.

"Why him?" was all he could think to say.

"Are you blind as well as simple?" she said. She grabbed his arm roughly and pulled him through the door, although not before he had pocketed his incriminating journal, so infested with evidence, so spoiled, he hated to touch it.

As they crept down the hall and then quietly down the stairs, he listened closely for sounds of distress, for weeping or anger or oaths of retribution; but nothing seemed amiss. The house was discreetly containing its horror, allowing only the usual midnight disturbances: a shifting, settling groan, a tocking grandfather clock, a mouse scratching behind a wall, a sleeper concealed in a nearby bedroom snoring lustily.

"Where is everyone?" he whispered into Hattie's back.

"Quiet," she warned. Even lowered, her voice contained a dangerous mettle.

They were all outside, then, he thought, except for the snorer, whom they must not have wanted to waken. Rosie, he guessed. He could picture the others out in that cursed field, silenced by so sudden and profound a grief, shocked into immobility. It wouldn't last, this reprieve their immediate suffering gave him. This very moment a family procession might be closing in on the house, William Cormany carrying his dead daughter in his arms, his face struck dumb, tears rivering down. Edgar's face the livid mask of a devoted brother. The childish Cormanys in their rage would act like children—impetuously, furiously. They would tear him apart, exact some communal vigilante justice, blind to the knowledge that it was one of their own, slyly concealed in the mob, who was the murderer.

He had no idea why Hattie was helping him (if she was) and no desire to follow her lead, but he was desperate to get out, to escape, and he trailed after her as if she were the ever-receding door he had to reach.

On the first-floor landing he got too close and trod on her heel. She elbowed him sharply in the ribs and he backed off, but not so far from her that he didn't still smell the tang of sweat that rose off of her, her unwashed hair, the odour of camphor in her clothes. They were as married in this exploit as two sneaking thieves, and despite his distaste he stuck to her like the quaking soul she perhaps didn't possess.

After navigating through a series of rooms made unfamiliar by the night, Grif found himself in a summer kitchen at the back of the house. The floor was cluttered with crocks, pots, a pigeon roaster, a buffalo robe, skates tossed over a chair, a bucket—all of which he avoided, only to trip over an empty birdcage. Why they had to take this strewn and roundabout route soon became evident as Hattie stooped to retrieve a wrapped bundle out of a dough box: provisions swaddled in a tablecloth. Clearly, she was decamping too, for she didn't hand this over to him but pushed quietly through the screen door and motioned him out.

"Something's burning," he whispered.

"Quick," she said.

The bundle in her arms grunted.

Master Rumwold. Provisions for the heart, then. Not that this particular package would provide much sustenance for anyone, but he was relieved to know that she had enough motherly sentiment to bring the child along, and it made his flight down the lane with them easier. A small hunted family they might have looked from above, harried and fleeing, but knotted together with loyalty. An unholy family was more like it, improvisational and bound by some sin the nature of which he could only guess at.

A wagon stood at the end of the lane, to which Edgar's horse Enrico was harnessed. This struck Grif as a cumbersome and not overly romantic vehicle in which to make their getaway. They would make better time and be less visible if they both rode the horse. But he said nothing, only climbed up. Hattie took the reins and gave them a snap. She said something to Enrico in his own language, all vowels rolling and tumbling over one another, and he took off at a trot.

As they pulled away, Grif glanced back nervously. Still no sign of life, although the house was backlit with an orange glow, a cloud of smoke boiling up from behind. One of the outbuildings was on fire—the stable or the shed.

"Arson," he muttered under his breath. Abduction. Horse theft. Rape. Murder. He saw his innocence in all this as a blank sheet upon which any number of crimes could be inscribed. It seemed clear that Hattie had roused and rescued him for no other reason than his usefulness and gullibility, his scapegoat's horns and his brute obeisance.

The night was cool, and as they rushed along he felt it sliding into him and through him. Hattie and the baby beside her, wedged between them, maintained a complicit silence. He knew it was pointless to ask for an explanation. If he wanted any answers, he was going to have to provide them himself:

*Now tell me Hattie, did you set that fire?*

*What do you think?*

*Is Polly really dead?*

*I didn't say that, did I?*

*Where are you taking me, by the way? To the town jail?*

*You'll find your own way there soon enough. Why should I bother?*

What he actually asked was, "That boy of yours, does he never cry?"

"He has no need."

By which she meant, he supposed, that he was already so full of sorrow that he was replete. He was like an idol that had received so many supplications and hard luck stories over the years that he was dense with accumulated woe. It was a wonder that the wagon could move at all with him on board; although the axles did creak, and the carriage groaned, and the horse's hooves crunched on the road. And beneath those rhythmic sounds there was another sound, more intermittent and disturbing that Grif was positive he heard.

"Where are we going?" he tried.

"We?"

"You."

No answer.

"Me, then. What about me?"

"To town. I'll drop you off up ahead. It's a short walk from there. You can take a steamer in the morning, take a room, find a job. You are free to do as you wish."

Free? Before long he would be swinging free, no doubt. If he did have a wish, just one wish, he would ask for a more desperate and truly criminal hand so that he might strangle her with it. If he was going to hang, then he wanted there to be a genuine and gratifying reason for it, and not just because he was fool enough to be caught in some woman's malevolent design.

Grif heard it again, that noise, coming from the wagon's box behind. Attending closely, he could hear a rustling and shuffling, then something knocking against the side of the box, the sound someone might make if tied and muzzled and struggling to break free. It was the very sound he was making himself, if only in his head. He had been slow to arrive at it but knew now that Hattie had taken the wagon because she had human cargo, other than himself, to transport. Nor was it necessarily someone who was hog-tied and restrained—only wanting him to think so. This unknown other might just as easily be hovering at his back, ready to spring if he made the wrong move, his favourite move. He glanced quickly aside, considering it. A leap and a slide, a rolling tumble into the ditch, and he'd be out of the wagon and across the field, gone like a hare.

Hattie murmured to the horse, words that sounded so soft and sweet.

He sat listening, waiting, watching an arc of moonlight curving like a blade on Enrico's flank. He knew that there was enough light to peel away at least one layer of the mystery. If he turned quickly and looked back, he would see who the third—no, fourth—member of their party was. Even if that person were completely bound, he would have a good idea. But he didn't want to know. Knowledge was an implicating business, and he didn't want to be dragged even further than he already was into this strange game of Hattie's. Instead, he stared straight ahead and concentrated on absence, on closing down his senses—hearing nothing, seeing nothing—like a man riding in a tumbrel and about to be parted from his head, getting used to it.

Not long after, Hattie pulled at the reins and drew Enrico to a halt. "*Caro sposo*," she said. The foreign tongue, the softened expression, made her seem warmer and more accommodating, more an actual member of the weaker sex. On the other hand, maybe it was the horse she preferred above them all, her son included.

"This is where you get off." The road had come to a fork and she indicated with a curt nod which way he was to go.

Obediently, he climbed down from the wagon, and was about to set off, without speaking, without looking back at her, when she called to him.

"Griffith," she said, his name in her mouth a shock, a sickening intimacy. "Here."

He saw a flash of silver, and thinking *knife*, he spun away, dodging the hit, then turned to glare at her. Astonishingly, for the harm it might do her face, like a wound straining, she smiled at him. Looking down at it, he saw that what she'd thrown was indeed a precision weapon, but one aimed for his open palm and not his back. He stooped to pick it up. It was a pen with the heft of solid silver, but slender and delicate, its embossing so ornate it felt like scar tissue as he ran his fingertips over it. Intended for a hand far daintier than his own, though no less cunning, it was a lady's pen, and in such a hand would have been used to record all the politic detail of a busy social existence.

"No lies," she said, and smiled once again, briefly. Then, with a flick of Enrico's reins, she moved off down the other road.

He stood watching until the wagon diminished into a sliver. Two smiles he had gotten out of that woman, neither of which he knew how to interpret. One for innocence, one for guilt? Or one for life, one for death—both sides of the vise that was closing in on him.

He slid the pen into his pocket and began to walk toward the only light shining in the distance. Venus, he guessed. It was bright enough, yet it seemed too low in the sky, too earthbound, to be either a star or a goddess.

# 15

# CALL US
# NOT WEEDS

F GRIF were music, he'd be a dirge, moving down the road at a balked, funereal pace, a mourning tempo. *Lento, retardando ... fin.* Anything in pursuit could easily have snatched him up and devoured him, and he would hardly have noticed. Or cared. He felt so weary and flightless, it was all he could do to move one dead man's shoe, rotted as a face, in front of the other. He slurred his steps as he walked, and what filled his lungs was more lament than breath, what he exhaled a sorry and pointless tune. His life the theme of it.

He arrived in Little Current about the same time as the dawn, and descended a hill following the smell of water and wood, fresh-cut. A port and a mill town. He wandered by houses hushed and sleep-wrapped, past stores with boomtown fronts and signs in limb-high lettering that identified them as Carruthers' Drugs, Turner's Dry Goods, Vincent's Bargain House. A store for everyone. His footsteps made hollow rattling sounds on the wooden sidewalk, and as he waded through patches of morning mist, his pant legs gathering damp, he might have been taken for a revenant, something flushed out of the night and about as substantial. A skunk ran toward him, and then straight across his foot. Even to the creatures he was nothing more than an unravelling patch of grey, fading like the dawn. If it were possible, he would do it—melt into the atmosphere, or become the day's weather, or even that blasted skunk, if he could figure out how.

He passed by a blacksmith's, a photography studio, a combination confectionery/butcher shop—another odd union. Outside of a barroom he saw a man curled up in a wheelbarrow, his digested dinner—or someone's—from the night before piled *deja spew* in his outstretched hand. He walked quickly by; the man smelled rank.

The place was dead still, although surely not for long, unless it was Sunday. He pictured the bustle and surge of noon traffic in the street: wagons, horses, dust roiling up, people weaving in and out, a medley of voices, a joke tossed across the road and returned with a laugh. Farmers, fishermen, mill hands, Indians, tourists—more men than women. At present he appeared to be the only actor on this stage, and his performance wasn't up to much, his soliloquy stuffed so far down his throat he'd never get it out. Someone likely *was* watching him, someone standing at a window washing his neck with Windsor soap, or sprucing up his hair with Butler and Crisp's Pomade Divine. He could feel the eyes fixed on him like a gun's sight, the crosshairs dividing his face like a pie. A drifter, a stranger, anonymous as dirt.

A wanted man. But only for a legal and concluding formality. He surveyed the facade of a large hotel on the corner. The Mansion House, it was called.

He scanned the windows to see if anyone *was* watching him and imagined a curtain twitching as a shadowy form stepped back out of sight. No one really—he was only seeing himself, already registered in the hotel's black book, a party of one standing up there staring out at nothing, scouting for the courage to do away with himself. Surely it wouldn't be that difficult. He felt so tenuously held together, it could only be a matter of a nick, a slice, a minor undoing.

Taking in the rest of the street, Grif noticed a much smaller building that was stuck like a skewed hyphen between two taller ones. Stealing a few moments from what he regarded as his rapidly dwindling stock of them—insolvent in time as in much else—he wandered over to see what it was.

The building's clapboard was painted Prussian blue and fixed on at a slightly drunken angle, aspiring upward like an optimist's handwriting. The shutters were a goldenrod yellow, the door green as leaves. The place was too colourful entirely. Grif craned his neck to read the sign that swung above the door, its lettering flowing and molten. *The Dancing Sun*. A sun was depicted, too, painted against a black background and bouncing along with its rays sticking out like stiff hair. A barbershop, he thought, or an old-fashioned apothecary, a medical hall. Maybe a public house for foreigners, or pagans, as it was plainly not the Talbot House, the Wellington or the Queen's, where the subjects of the Crown could drink and bellow at one another in a civilized tongue. What lay behind that green door might be another country altogether.

He stepped forward and gave the door's brass knob a tentative twist. It turned easily, invitingly, and so he entered.

Once in, he was disappointed to find that it was only a saloon, and one that was as sparsely stocked as it was decorated. There was one table and one chair, and behind the bar one bottle of whisky, unless you counted as a second the reflection of that bottle in the mirror—the single ornament in the room. Also visible behind the bar was the furry nub of the barman's head. He was obviously seated, as custom in this spare watering hole was not going to be overwhelming at the best of times, let alone first thing in the morning. The barman was singing a song, or rather snatches of several, meandering like a bee along some erratic melodic course. The voice was sweet and high. Grif cleared his throat. This wasn't, after all, some foreign country where you could air your feelings quite so freely, belt out a tune in public as if you didn't have a care in the world.

Heading toward the bar, he found himself taking it on the run like a rolling alley. The floor had a considerable tilt to it, and he arrived suddenly, both hands splayed, as if the thing had been tossed at him. The singer, he now saw, was only a boy, a short round boy of about twelve or thirteen, who was busy entering some figures in a ledger. Practising sums for school, Grif supposed.

"Yes sir?" The boy abruptly stopped singing, snapped the ledger shut and regarded Grif pleasantly. He had dark hair and eyes, but fair skin that looked almost polished, overlaid with a sheen of confidence.

"Is your father in?" Grif asked.

"Dead," said the boy. "As a doornail."

"Your mother?"

"Gone," he said. "Like smoke." He smiled widely, as if at this lark of parents disposed of so easily in a phrase or two, gotten rid of in nothing more cumbersome than language—good place for them.

"Who, then…?"

"Roland Avery, Esquire." He offered his hand and gave Grif's a quick, cursory shake. "The proprietor of this fine establishment. How may I be of service? Would you care for a drink?"

"Have you a glass, Mr. Avery?"

"One."

"A modest investment." Despite everything, Grif felt his spirits begin to lift. "What I need is a room. Do you have any here at The Dancing Sun?'

"Oh, yes." Roland flipped open the ledger to a different page and placed it on the bar. "Sign here, please."

Grif retrieved the pen that Hattie had given him, choosing to use it rather than the boy's proferred one. He might have been tempted to lie otherwise and sign a name not his own. He saw that there was plenty of space to do it in, for he was apparently the only guest registered.

Roland watched with delight, as though Grif's penmanship constituted some fascinating stunt. "You have relatives in town, Mr. Smolders?"

"No." Christ. "That is, none that I'm aware of."

Both he and the boy stared momentarily at the name he had signed in the register, *his* name, and no one else in the world had a right to it.

"Your room is up the stairs, first on the left," Roland said. Grif snatched up the key, gave the young hosteller a grateful nod and made for the stairs.

Roland Avery turned back to his book and found his original place in it, smiling to himself in the way an accountant might if an unexpected and diverting figure had arrived suddenly in the columns of his ledger.

The ceiling of Grif's room was painted a deep green, the floor done in a checkerboard pattern of red and black, and the walls had been papered with blue roses against a pin-work background. The doorway was stencilled with grapevines and sage leaves, and the Zommo—the cabinet for the chamber pot that sat beside the bed—had been mahoganized, almost successfully. A marine picture, an ambitious garden collage made of shells, crayfish claws and driftwood sticks, decorated one of the walls, and beneath it was inscribed a verse that Grif stepped closer to read: "Call us not weeds; we are flowers of the sea, And lovely and bright and gaytinted are we."

All in all, the room was comfortable and welcoming, but a bit cockeyed and out of proportion, as if built with a lax and carefree hand. The paint was slapdash, the baseboards not quite flush, the window frame crooked. He liked it.

In one corner, on a child's rod-back chair, sat a homemade doll with a nut for a head—a walnut painted with tiny black eyes and red, pursed lips. Her facial features were derived from the nut's natural bumps and ridges, which aged her some; she looked like she knew a thing or two. Grif regarded it closely, but from a few feet away. Having a rag body, it slumped in the chair. Lost? Left behind by some child travelling with a parent? The doll wore a perturbed expression, yet he decided that it was not blaming him for its own misfortune.

He seated himself on the bed and took off his shoes, so worn and mulish, the things had no flight left in them. If he tried to run away now, to walk or even crawl, his shoe leather would rebel; it would dig in what was left of the heels and hold firm. The room had a coil of rope on the floor by the window, but Grif knew that rope was not going to save him this time. It might even be the end of him, the last thing he'd feel while swinging out of this world. He required something far less homey and practical to get himself out of the fix he was in. He needed something miraculous.

He emptied his pockets, taking out the pen, the purse, the journal, and placed them beside him. He removed the Reverend Bee's well-travelled ecclesiastical rag, and laid it across the foot of the bed like a tired and dusty old dog.

He waited. This could take a long time, he realized, as long as walking the length of the province. He might wait and wait and wait. He might become the very state he was immersed in, suspended, taut, never released by an arrival.

He did not think this would happen to him. Eventually, someone would come and settle his life for him. The actor, possibly. Fenwick Nashe. He'd glide through the door, dapper in Grif's own name, that still-unspoken plan wavering on his clever, dissimulating lips. But more likely the police, clattering noisily down the hall, pounding savagely on the door, then bursting in. A brutal eviction.

When it did come, it entered silently, without knocking, without warning, recognition a sudden knife sliding into his chest.

Her, of course. His wife. Avice walked into the room as if only this moment she had slipped out of her bridal chamber at the Belvedere Hotel in London to see what was keeping her husband from coming in to her. Time lost, distance travelled, humiliation suffered—it all might have been nothing more to her than some vile mess on the threshold, easily evaded with one deft scene-splicing step.

She was stark naked. Her body white and smooth, perfect as a stripped and whittled branch of cedar. Unblemished, except for that splatter of moles on her cheek, a faint bruise on her left breast, a crescent-shaped welt on her thigh. Her hair was shorn like a boy's. She was beautiful. She smelled like a saint, of roses and sweat. She was beautiful, more so than he would have imagined—had he bothered to do such a thing.

But her expression, frankly, was not one a young husband would want to see approaching. Her look was not tremulous and open, a bride blushing with a newfound boldness and excitement, but one that Grif had not known until this moment a woman could possess. Her face was as rigid and hard as the granite he had often run his hands over on his travels with Ned through the North Channel. He did not think he would be running his hands over her features, warming them into a softness, a renewed sympathy and humanity.

Avice, he thought, her name a wick he was about to light with his tongue. He could not even remember what had driven him with such force away from her, why he had run so far; but now, finally, he knew he was ready for her.

And she was ready for him.

# PART 2

I'm sure if I were free again,
　　I'd live a single life;
And not be such a simpleton,
　　As to become a wife.

*— popular nineteenth-century rhyme*

# 16

## MR. AND MRS.

I T WAS a marriage of convenience. Hers. And necessarily so, for she was the one who had been stuck with it. Stuck with the galling *in*convenience of having a husband so rare, so scarce, that he did not even fill his own shoes.

On the morning after her wedding, Avice Drinkwater, still metamorphosing into Mrs. Thomas G. Smolders, the glinting dust her marriage had stirred up hardly settled around her, found that already in her new life she had to take stock. *This was it*: a morning coat, a pair of men's dress shoes, and a small brown cowhide valise containing a shirt, three collars, two pairs of socks, a woollen union suit with a moth hole in one sleeve, a bar of soap, a razor and an ivory-handled toothbrush. This was it, what she was married to, the modest props and costume of a husband, but no husband—her mate nothing more than a bone-handled, bristle-headed object.

She might have smiled at this, one of her sharp and self-depreciating smiles, sharp enough to pare down the edges of what was a full and substantial self. Except that she was not in the mood on this particular morning for self-deprecation, or for diminishment of any kind. She had absolutely no intention of being whittled down by circumstance into a whining sliver of a woman. What she felt largely was something hot in her blood, lapping her heart, boiling it, burning her inner layers, scorching her from within. If she were to run her tongue along her wrist and into her palm, she knew that she would be able to taste it even, this searing and poisonous fury. This bitterness. Let other women suffer from vapours: what she exuded—noxious fumes, scalding steam—would fell anyone who came too close.

Her sisters. How they would rally and flutter around her when they heard the news of his decampment. How sympathetic they would be, how enraged on her behalf. There would be much talk of a search, perhaps a private investigator, a lawsuit, an annulment. And how secretly thrilled they would be, wallowing in the muck of her shame, sucking through their teeth the fetid waters of her misfortune. Their warnings about her disastrous choice would be vindicated, their unkind and unacknowledged wishes gratified. How they would simper and cluck . . . and chuckle in her ear.

Like hell they would.

Back to stock-taking. All right, she was married, she did have a husband, and she would *not* be done out of one. Unless, of course, she herself were to do the deed. The deed—*yes*—that would strike her marriage through with a theme, would outfit it with a purpose. It would certainly give her a sense of resolution, if not comfort.

Avice had been rash about Grif, she realized, but not wrong. She hardly knew him, true, but she knew herself, knew the kind of appetite he provoked in her. He was unclaimed treasure, standing so handsomely behind a pile of less splendid goods on display at Kingsmill's, and she had immediately wanted to (and did) lay claim. Her desire had been to hoard him, or to spend him freely, as extravagantly as she wished. She was *interested* in him in a way that felt as basic and elemental as a rough wind blasting her on an open shore. She was still interested in him—in how, precisely, he would look throttled, mangled, slit from tip to stem.

She wished she had a wedding photograph so that she could study it, and him, more closely. She had been too cavalier, too certain of herself; she had missed something about him, and now she wanted to find it, that intimate and revealing detail, the tiny pore in his person through which his regard for her had disappeared. She determined to find whatever reason he could possibly have had for leaving her, no matter how deeply, and surgically, she had to delve. First she would ruin him, then she would be his personal archaeologist, picking and sifting through those ruins.

In the morning light that fell through that treacherous window in the Belvedere Hotel, the one through which Grif had made his escape, Avice again surveyed what remained— the trappings of a husband, without the trapped, as it were. Her marriage definitely lacked substance, but as this was something she herself had never lacked, the problem did not seem to be insoluble. Watching the light pour in, creating an empty spotlight on the floor, a notion occurred to her. She did not need an archangel to materialize in this light, to fill her ear with revelatory news. The gist of that news probably hadn't changed much since Biblical times, anyway. What Mary was told, Avice had already figured out: husbands consist mostly of illusion. So occupied were they with their jobs, their clubs, their recreational and civic duties (or their divine ones), that wives scarcely saw them. Occasionally, a husband might wander through the house like an animal and leave behind droppings—cigar ash, mud on the rug, a pittance to manage the household with—and while there, beget a brood of offspring, the delivery of which would eventually kill his mate. Work and grief, that was what a woman really married. When you considered it, as Avice was intently doing—her brow as rippled as a washboard, but her thoughts slippery as silk—an illusory husband might be more useful than a real one, not to mention more agreeable. If the good Lord could create a man with a pinch of dust and a little sleight of hand, then surely she could do the same with a morning coat, a pair of shoes and a toothbrush.

So pleased was she with this inspiration that when the arrival of the newlyweds' breakfast was announced with a tactful and muted knock at the door, Avice lowered her voice a register or two and ordered that it be left outside. For good measure she also murmured an endearment, sleepily, contentedly, and then held her breath, listening, waiting as the footsteps retreated down the hall. She jumped out of bed and ran over to the door, cautiously peeked out, then wheeled in a laden tray—fried eggs, sausages, potatoes, ham, toast—and ate it all, every last crumb, his share, hers, theirs. After all, she was eating for two.

As she drank down the last of the coffee, allowing herself to slurp it, to lick the saucer, to belch—all husbandly habits and prerogatives—she gave some thought to what sort of couple she would make, and just how she might round out the masculine half. She knew that there had always been women who had taken the part of men in life, such as those who had fought, disguised as soldiers, in the American Civil War, or that brilliant and dashing physician in the British army, James Barry. A whole successful life in the male arena and only after death was it discovered that Dr. Barry was female. How very gratifying, and evidently not impossible; but Avice wanted more than that. Half of humanity was simply not enough for her. She wanted to be, and would be, complete.

Pacing the room, as her husband had done only the night before, she circled his shoes, once, twice, then stopped before them. What *had* seized him so suddenly and plucked him out of this room, right out of his shoes, it seemed? Surely there was no idea so strong that it could have blown him through the window. It must have been an agency of some sort, an abduction; but then she had heard no shouts, no scuffle, no protest coming from him. There had been that noise, a gunshot she had thought, but perhaps only a trick a child might play—an air-filled paper bag slapped open. A craven, despicable trick: the deserting wretch had wanted her to think him in trouble. Well, he was *that*.

She slid a questing foot into one of Grif's abandoned shoes and wiggled her toes widely. *My what big feet you have.* Didn't her friends long for fairy-tale weddings of their own? What would they make of hers, she wondered, which had turned her into a Cinderella who was required to fit the boots and role of the prince (with no want of ugly sisters, either)? She slipped her foot into the other shoe, then clomped over to the valise and dug around in it for the socks. Both pairs might help, but when she tried them on, they drooped, garterless, like rags around her ankles. Likewise, when she pulled on the shirt and coat, they hung loosely on her slender frame. She looked like a dressed stick.

Vexed, she kicked at a chair and her foot moulted the socks, which flew off into a corner. It wasn't so much the sight of her ill-fitting male costume reflected in the dresser mirror that annoyed her, for she had funds and resources of her own (her father had not trusted Grif on that score for a moment); to procure a more suitable outfit, and one of better quality, would be an easy enough task. No, what truly and deeply irritated her had more to do with the liberty this masculine clothing afforded. He had not been required to bind and cinch and hobble himself with corsets and straps, with hooks and endless buttons and yards of heavy, imprisoning cloth. Eighteen-inch waists, skirts that dragged in the mud, sleeves that ballooned so hugely they required supporting structures underneath. He had not been stopped, paralyzed, by his very clothing. A woman's blood could scarcely even circulate in her body, so tied was it in place. To think that he had all this freedom ... and it had not been enough.

Tears sprang to her eyes, but with a tide of will she called them back. She promised herself, her better and her worse half in this union, that she would find a more useful and less feminine release for these emotional waters. Let there be no more leaking through the eyes. She was going to learn how to *spit*.

By midafternoon the chambermaid, had she been allowed into the room, might have wondered if a rainstorm had lately passed through, so gob-flecked and damp had it become. By then Avice had mastered the art of expectoration, and felt she could hawk with the best of the boys. Not that she could put out a fire, but she could send a foaming globe of spittle whizzing through the air and pinging on target with a crackerjack accuracy. If Grif just so happened to appear at the window, his miserable, pleading face bobbing into view, she'd christen it all right. She'd daub him smack between the eyes with a wet and shattering kiss of contempt.

This thought warmed her and gave her cramped feelings some range, as had that flask of courage she had discovered in the pocket of his coat. Drink, spit. Drink, spit. Really, a man's life was a wonderful thing. She knew she had the wit to manage it, tacking such a life onto her own as one might add an extension to a house, a porch that stood open to the world. She took another pull at the flask, delighted to have found it when she frisked Grif's abandoned coat, her fingers searching the garment's cheap criminal cloth as if he himself might be hidden somewhere in it. (The *louse*.)

She had also found two train tickets concealed in an inside pocket. How could she have forgotten, having planned most of it herself—their getaway, their honeymoon? It had been intended as an adventurous lark, and a rebuke to her family: a week in a rough American city known more for its industry than its romance. What a shame if they both missed it. Of course, she *was* both now, but did she honestly think she could get away with it? Avice was aware that a woman travelling alone attracted too much of the wrong kind of attention. Such a woman, brazen and depraved (for otherwise she would not be travelling unescorted), was considered fair game—the very game that she herself had been so eager to be, and play, only the night before, at least the sanctioned version of it, which was supposed to make all the difference. So much for that scruple, she thought (drink, spit): new game, new rules.

She took a turn around the room, trying out a few manly walks. She sauntered and strolled. She mastered the strut, the swagger, the hemorrhoidal hobble, the caveman's lope and lunge. The drink had ignited a votive flame in her belly, and she had begun to have a good time. She mimicked with her feet male pride and arrogance, and walked for miles, it seemed, keeping herself entertained while searching for her own ambulatory style, the style of her other. She wanted to make a signature with her own two dissembling feet that was self-assured and forthright. Nothing creative, nothing exceptional—what she wanted was a standard and dominant masculine tread. If a woman's walk, whether helpless or seductive, was designed to attract attention, then a man's was purely territorial, staking claim, measuring out in footfalls what was his. It was this she practised over and over, pacing it to perfection, working it into her whole body, schooling her muscles, until the artificial and adopted walk came naturally. Defense and camouflage. When she was at large in the world, she would invite neither prying nor preying eyes. No more gracious swaying and lilting for her. No more being rooted in place like a bloody useless flower.

As for her hair, that was merely a question of redistribution. Not all men were hirsute, shaggy as apes. Grif had packed a razor and so must needs shave, although Avice had never taken the opportunity to run her hand along his cheek, to discover for herself how far from boyhood his face had advanced.

She stood before the dresser mirror and gazed at her own, then grabbed two fistfuls of her long, dark brown hair and held it up, tangled and in disarray after her troubled and sleepless night. The colour of muck, she thought, of mouldering leaves. Dark was better than fair—but what was to be done with it? If she wanted to play both Adam and Eve, she'd need to step back and forth through the screen of this hair. She could try to keep it tucked under a hat, but knew that the stuff fed too directly on her brain for that: it was wilful hair and was bound to make its own escape no matter how firmly she secured it in place.

She snapped open Grif's razor and began to cut, but carefully, preserving every strand, laying it down on the dresser. She decided to have it fashioned into a hairpiece, perfect for when she was the missus. Who knows, at some point she might even require an infant, a hair baby with knots for eyes, tightly swaddled and held close to her breast.

Avice worked slowly and made a beautiful job of it, even she had to admit. Her hair lay in a curled mound, an animal newly formed. Light-headed, she leaned toward the mirror until the tip of her nose scaled its cool surface. A shrewd-eyed imp stared at her, close enough to kiss.

She couldn't help it. She arched back, hands gripping the dresser, and let out a yelp of laughter.

By late afternoon a bribe or two had been dispensed, a few purchases made, bags (his and hers) packed and sent ahead. She was packed, although not in the usual sense, for she had stationed herself inside *him*, her male equivalent. She felt a bit like a tourist in her own body, peering out, ready to take in the sights with a fresh pair of eyes. Admittedly, she was nervous, fussing with last-minute preparations, straightening a cuff, dusting off her lapel, surveying the room one last time to see if there was any telling clue, anything of herself—or himself— left behind. She was ready, more or less. Smoking, swearing— she'd get the hang of these in time, these and whatever other useful male practices of bluster and release there might be. It was funny, when she thought of it, how women were expected to be so contained (as she was now) despite their reputation for sociability, for nagging and chatter. But no more.

Pausing on the threshold of the honeymoon suite, she was amused to think how she would be carrying herself over it, like any bride entering a new life. Except that she was heading out, not in.

She supposed that she had Grif to thank for this, but she was not planning on thanking him. Naturally, she would honour her marriage vows. How did they go ... *until death do you part*, wasn't that it? Fine. That was one vow she'd keep, the sooner the better. What had been conceived on their wedding night she'd gestate and nurture in the darkest, foulest part of herself.

She stepped out the door, her new, pricey boots fitting like skin, adding a dash of confidence to her debut. She sailed down the hall as one, a happy couple united in boldness, a pair who couldn't have been closer, and more married, if they tried.

# 17

# FREE SPEECH

I F CERTAIN LADIES in the colonies were given to "hearing voices," it was only because they were doing their best to keep up with the current spiritual fashions and predilections of their clever, trend-setting British sisters. With their heightened sensitivities and delicate equipment—ears cunningly designed, auditory canals slender as pinkies, receptivity sharp as that of bats—it's not surprising that such would be the chosen conduits for heavenly news and information. It was a time, after all, when scientific theory caused many to turn a deaf ear to messages from above, and the telephone, fast becoming the newest appendage to the head, had no lines laid to the realm of the supernatural.

Avice's sister Cecile, dutiful and pious, was a woman who had the time and the inclination to heed the word of the Lord, or at least that of His minions, as direct speech from the Almighty might incinerate one's head altogether. On occasion she did hear voices, and in fact, much to her dismay, one particular voice had become attached to her. This would not have been a problem, her faith being capacious enough to entertain the phenomenon, but the voice that dogged her was *not very nice*. It was brash and grating. It was full of boasts and brags.

At times it wheedled and bullied her. It had a dry, sarcastic sense of humour. It lapsed into inferior foreign tongues in which it said, she was certain, the most disgusting things. Nor was there any predicting when it might happen along, when it might come to whisper its vile nothings in her ear, forcing itself and its unsavoury views upon her.

While having tea one day with Mrs. Archibald Brunt and reading aloud from a letter sent by her newly married sister, Cecile shuddered slightly, recognizing the familiar irritating snicker of her unwanted spiritual attendant, its warm breath tickling her earlobe, inflaming her cheek. It was bad enough that she had to censor and "translate" most of Avice's letter, without also having to listen to an undertow of rude commentary, a subversive counter-interpretation of it. Mrs. Brunt, she knew, would be shocked to hear descriptions of factories, of tenements, of streetcars packed with immigrants. Her sister had sent postcards depicting the insane asylum, a giant Garland stove as large as a house, a beer garden, a dance hall, a *bath*house, an establishment in the Merrill block that displayed freaks and oddities—a Wild Man, a Tom Thumb, a woman dressed in snakes and *nothing else*. Why Avice did not choose to write about the distinguished commercial buildings, the university, the churches, or even the art gallery—and surely there must be one even in *that* city—was beyond Cecile. It was not beyond her, however, to describe these more elevated sights herself to her flesh-and-blood guest, while fending off the undermining insinuations of her immaterial one.

*Don't go to Michigan, that land of ills . . . the word means ague, fever and chills.*

With the letter before her, gripped perhaps a bit too firmly in hand, Cecile recounted the finer theological points of a sermon that Mr. and Mrs. T. Griffith Smolders had attended in the beautiful cathedral of St. Paul's (surely every city had one) in that delightful, if unusual, honeymoon destination—

Detroit. But, *au contraire*, Cecile heard a murmured disavowal, and tried her best not to listen as it recounted in sickening detail how the young couple had been enjoying other delights entirely, and had scarcely stepped outside their room in the Hotel Cadillac.

*In nomine fillii . . . et spiritus sancti . . . et furor uterinus.* Noting the red blotches creeping up Cecile's neck, not to mention her fixed gaze as she read the letter (was it memorized?), Mrs. Brunt secretly sympathized. It was not easy being an elder and unmarried daughter, and Cecile Drinkwater was stepping with some dignity into the comedic role of spinster. Soon—figuratively speaking, of course—she would disappear entirely, which in Cecile's case might be an improvement, as she was alarmingly plain. A boiled potato had more evident charms. Mrs. Brunt was pleased to hear that Avice, the most spirited of the Drinkwater girls, certainly the most intractable, had finally come to her senses. Marriage had obviously done her some good, even if the husband was not exactly the sort of person you would want to invite into your own home.

"The Russell House is the leading hotel in Detroit, I believe," she said. "It's where the Prince of Wales stayed in '60."

"Fully booked, I understand."

"How unfortunate. Did you say they attended the opera?"

"Oh, yes."

"And what was being performed?"

*Fellatio.*

"Something . . . Italian."

"Fidelio?"

"Yes, that was it."

*Porca Madonna!*

"Are you feeling quite well, Miss Drinkwater? You do look a bit feverish."

"A slight earache, I'm afraid, Mrs. Brunt. I should perhaps retire."

Indeed it *was* trying for a proper young woman to maintain the required genteel glow while livid, or to retain her demure composure when all she wanted to do was smack herself on the side of the head, or tear off those coiled and tightly wound braids that were clapped onto her skull, serving her ill as mufflers but rather more as antennae sensitive to this most undesirable presence. How was one supposed to be an angel in the house when a devilish informant persistently tattled in one's ear? And yet Cecile realized that there was truth in what she was hearing. She knew her sister was too headstrong and contrary to have become the sudden possessor of retiring wifely virtues. Nor did she believe for a moment that Avice was as blissfully wedded as she claimed to be in her cards and letters home. Lady Pride mounted on her high horse was the author of those.

Equally incredible was her claim that she was having a glorious time in . . . *Detroit.* In an industrial city seething with filth and crime, teeming with socialists, and blacks, and *Americans*—people who spoke much too loudly and told you everything about themselves at the drop of a hat. The land of free speech; and heavens, it was that—too free entirely. Who in their right mind would go to Detroit for their honeymoon? A Fabian? A factory girl? The Drinkwater sisters had all urged them to go to Niagara Falls, and the fiancé had been willing enough, but the inarguable reasoning that everyone goes there had only caused Avice, typically, to declare that in that case *they* would travel in the opposite direction. Her decision—and it could only have been hers—was pure spite and perversity.

What would become of her young sister? Cecile had to wonder as she watched Mrs. Brunt march down the front walk, her stately progress about to be undercut by a little mess that Pepys, the family dog, had deposited there. *Nothing good*, Cecile heard herself thinking, *nothing good at all.* For once she and her disembodied adviser were in complete accord.

Mrs. Brunt slipped and went down with a loud shriek. Cecile clapped a hand to her mouth, trying to contain the wild shout of laughter bursting in her head.

Avice herself would not give the time of day to any form of intercession from a higher power. The very idea! She was temperamentally incapable of receiving advice, whether from an earthly father (or sister) or a heavenly one—*or* from one of His tedious, prating go-betweens. Whatever religious sentiment she might have possessed as a child, she had chucked years ago. The Reverend Elias Bee was largely responsible for this, having sermonized her into an apostatic stupor. Sunday after Sunday, corralled in the family pew of St. Paul's, she had listened to his righteous blather and sanctimonious twaddle with a glowering and growing resentment. Besides causing her a sinful amount of boredom, he did not even present a sample of manliness worth her study. His face was too large for his features, as if someone had given his nose a good yank and pulled his tiny mouth and eyes inward. It was like a platter with an insufficient serving of character upon it. He had child-sized hands that fluttered about like moths as he spoke, and a peculiar vanity about his feet, which, in moments when he thought himself unregarded, he gazed at with undisguised admiration. His voice was a vessel that spilled over with an unguent hypocrisy. Christian virtue? Justice? Prudence? He no more believed what he preached than she did. Except when he got onto the subject of Quebec and the French menace. That was his real religion: inciting hatred. He'd incited hers, anyway. So, while her sisters faintly sighed their affirmations, their *Amens* and *So-be-its*, she was given to muttering more unseemly expressions—"Good *God!*" and "Oh shut *up*, you fat arse"—against which the family who sat in front of the Drinkwaters had to close their ears and stiffen their backs like shields.

The only voice Avice was going to listen to was her own. Not that this exercise hadn't gotten more complicated of late, what with marriage and wanting to get to know her husband better, the onus being on her to generate that knowledge. She knew she could do it—why not? She wasn't so encased in her own person, her own views, that she couldn't entertain the prospect of his. She would be the very bridge (iron) linking the happy couple, the unifying structure (or steel) upon which their shared soul could shuttle back and forth. *Any* woman can dress in the guise of a man, but that was not enough for Avice. She wanted to *be* the mate who had deserted her. She wanted his endearments, his loyalty, his protection. She wanted to be the beneficiary of his masculine intelligence and authority (which she scarcely believed in, but in this case she would give him the benefit of the doubt). And later, when she caught up with *him*, her real husband, she wanted his hide as well. She wanted to hold up his shorn ears and tail and shake them triumphantly in the air. You bet.

Accordingly, when she was he, she tried to see things differently, exactly as he might. Cecile Drinkwater would have been gratified—her attendant voice chuckling away like a spring in her ear—to observe how her brother-in-law recoiled from the sights that met his eye, and the smells that flew up his nose, the moment "he" stepped over the American border. While his fellow honeymooners in Niagara Falls thrilled to the spectacle of tons of water thundering past, misting them to a state of damp, romantic receptivity, he found himself less enthrallingly engulfed. In the spring of 1898, Detroit, Michigan, was home to over nine hundred factories, and to all the social enlightenment that went with the times. The air was yellow with sulphur, thick with dust from streets not yet macadamized, clogged with the traffic of human misery: the halt, the sick, the insane, gaunt beggars, children dressed in rags, girls selling themselves for a meal. He was jostled and shoved, nearly run over by a rattling, clanging streetcar, and swept into a stream of striking workers who were surging down Woodward, bellowing and throwing rocks, a simmering violence barely contained. The women in this country, he noted, were large—and brassy. A herd of them nearly trampled him to death trying to get to a sale of shirtwaists—twenty-five cents each—at a towering store called Mabley's.

Most of the time he stumbled around, his new boots sealed with spats of horseshit from all the droppings on the streets, his skin furred with soot, his lungs bursting with "seegar" smoke, his head rattling with Yankee boosterism. Mrs. Smolders' husband in honesty had to conclude that he had entered some rank, discordant underworld, and screwing his derby tighter onto his head, resolved to get his wife out of this hell-hole as fast as their little heels would take them.

Mrs. Smolders, on the other hand, was having a fantastic time. It's not that she didn't take in the noise and dirt and degradation, the sorry human scenery, but she knew that a person could see much the same in the shantytowns of Toronto or Montreal—if they cared to look. She simply responded more directly and fully to the spirit of the place, to the bustling commerce and confidence and American self-delight. The whole city, wealthy and poor quarters alike, crackled with life; everything seemed to be electrified and in motion. Striding briskly down Jefferson, she marvelled at how the fad of wheeling had overtaken this city. Surely every citizen who could get their hands on one owned a bicycle, for they skimmed by in packs—one a tandem built for ten—and were parked and piled everywhere, leaning up four deep against offices, stores, saloons, even churches. She saw Bloomer Girls by the score—all manner of women, as old as forty, wearing those "bifurcated nether garments" that old Bee had fulminated against so fiercely from his pulpit. Not only bicycles, but there were also numerous wheeled and unidentifiable vehicles, some with gasoline-powered motors attached, that flew by at phenomenal speeds. Fifteen miles per hour, or so she was informed by a waiter when she was in Swann's Chop House on Larned, sampling a stimulating brown beverage called Pemberton's

French Wine Coca and trying the new flaked wheat cereal invented by a Dr. Harvey Kellogg. "Eat what the monkey eats," Dr. Kellogg apparently advised. And, more ominously, "A housebroken colon is a damaged colon."

Invigorated, her appetite for novelty aroused, she climbed the two hundred and ten steps to the top of the city hall's main tower and, along with the four Amazonian stone maidens stationed there in niches, gazed out over the city, taking in the clean streets, the elegant homes flanked by groves of shade trees, the river surging with traffic, Belle Isle, and the Dominion beyond—distant, cold, stodgy. What she saw below her, though, was a cauldron of a country, hot and bubbling, rich with possibility, throbbing at this very moment with war fever and patriotic ferment. Even that strike her husband had briefly gotten enmeshed in was exciting, and appealing. She would not have ducked and run as he had, turning away the moment the police arrived with their truncheons and revolvers. She would have marched in inviolable solidarity with the workers, demanding her rights, demanding a ten-hour working day—never mind that she had never worked a day in her life, or that the laxity of such a shortened day, as her father insisted with an undeniable rationale, would cripple the economy and destroy moral resolve.

Thinking of that strike, and of a few other of her forays into the city as Mr. Smolders, she bit her cheek to stop herself from grinning inanely. Truly, it was a joke, what she had gotten away with, and how she had so readily been taken for a male. Slap on a man's hat, fasten a high collar over your plucked Adam's apple, some loose clothing to dissemble the want, or largesse, of other telltale bumps . . . and you're in, you've joined the boys' club. Given her experience with this, she had to conclude that people didn't notice much, really, outside of themselves. They saw what they expected to see. But she noticed; she was aware. Alertness was absolutely essential as she moved undercover and warily through the city. If it weren't for her, he'd be lying dead on the street. When those officers appeared, revolvers flashing in the sun, she hustled him out of there, slipped him swiftly down an alley, made him desert the strike as precipitously as he had joined it. Surely she wasn't expected to be her brother's keeper as well as her husband's.

She glared at him now, turned inward on himself, folded primly on the lyre-back chair in their room at the Cadillac. How insubstantial he was! She thought of that sculpture she'd seen at the Museum of Art, a stone man in a pose of thought, not wearing a stitch, and her blood quickened. Her husband simply could not compare. She wondered if she could do without him entirely, then supposed not. Without him she'd never be allowed to do half the things she'd done that day, including the trip out to Bennett Park to watch a baseball game. Reluctantly, goaded by his portable wife, he had paid his fifty cents to climb the scaffolding erected around the outside of the fence, a perfect vantage point from which to hurl insults and rotten vegetables at the team from Chicago, and spew wads of Mayflower "eatin'" tobacco on the hats of the fans below. Not that he had joined in any of the fun—oh, it was galling in the extreme.

Was *this* marriage? Slight as he was, he dragged her down. He was a dead weight that she was yoked to, her silent, disapproving Siamese twin. Indignant, frustrated, rebellious—she could have torn out her hair, if it weren't already halfway across the room, a dark, brimming mass stuffed in one of his shirts like a submerged head. If she had had an intellectual acquaintance with Charlotte Perkins Gilman, or Susan B. Anthony, or even Emma Goldman, Avice might have burst out of her cozy cocoon at the Cadillac and stormed the streets as a fully realized New Woman. If she had stooped to pick up that trampled and spattered copy of *Free Society* she saw during the strike, instead of buying the *Detroit Times*, Mr. Hearst's eye-popping, salacious rag, revolutionary and liberating ideas might now have been zinging like bullets through her head. She had often enough mocked the reformist and do-gooder clubs her friends joined—the Dominion Order of the King's Daughters, the Girls' Friendly Society, the Anti-Corset League—and yet she had more spunk and a greater independent nature than any of them; otherwise what was she doing here?

Progressive? Of course she was. That's why she had picked up a *Vogue* magazine along with the paper at the newsstand. Lounging on the bed in her silk robe, smoking, drinking, chewing gum, cramming as many liberating habits as she could into the afternoon, she began to flip through it, and was dazzled once again by American dash and ingenuity and style. Even the name of the magazine, *Vogue*, was chic and alluring. Arriving at the final pages, she sat briefly, absorbed in contemplation, then leaned over and stubbed out her cigarette in one of his shoes, for she had suddenly been taken with a desire to embark on a defining and advanced cultural activity. She decided to get dressed as the missus and go shopping.

A gift, then, a honeymoon souvenir for Mr. Smolders. This is what she resolved to find while trolling the aisles of the Newcomb-Endicott Company, a department store she had discovered after following one of its red-and-gold delivery wagons to its source. What to choose? A moon calendar watch in a silver case? A solid gold vest chain? Or one made of braided hair? Perhaps a fob, an ebony cane, a gent's charm—a tiny anvil, or a bicycle lamp set with a ruby for the light. How about collar studs, a stamp box, a hat mark, a moustache comb, an umbrella plate, an autoharp, a hunter's suit made of marsh grass, an ear cleaner (spoon and sponge combined), an electric ring—or a castrating knife from the veterinary department? A book might be useful. One on the subject of faciology, or *Dr. Hood's Plain Talks and Common Sense Medical Adviser.* Dipping into the latter, Avice was a little shocked at its author's forthright modernity, addressing as he did the effects of sexual isolation on old maids, and the prevention of conception "for those who would enjoy a higher and better love." Dr. Hood also tackled the problem of unhappy marriage and how it destroyed the tone of the nervous system. Certainly her husband *could* use such a book, but she found herself incapable of deciding whether or not to buy it, for the tone of her own nervous system had tightened to an almost painful pitch.

The volume of choice in this compound store was overwhelming. Aisles and aisles of goods—stockings, vests, jewellery, dishes, trinkets—all gleaming and new and desirable. At first, dazzled and a bit greedy, her heart had pounded at the sight of so much; but then, after a short while, roaming up and down, touching, marvelling, only her head pounded. Everything seemed to crowd in upon her, exhorting her to purchase. She turned a jaded eye upon a pair of gorgeous kid gloves, a hatpin set with pearls and a large turquoise, and even stared blankly at a Princess Bust Developer (with Bust Food) that formerly would have made her snicker with delight. She tried to imagine the eventual destination of all these things, who on earth was going to buy them; and once they were gone, she supposed that even more of the same would appear in their place. More and more.

*Oh, don't be such a nit*, she upbraided herself. *This is perfectly wonderful. The more ear cleaners there are in the world, the more there will be for everyone. Humanity will be better served, and better for it. Everyone's hearing will improve. Maybe they'll even begin to listen to one another.*

She couldn't wait to write home and tell Cecile about this place. Poor old Cecile, who won't want to know, who will only plough her head further into her bible so that she doesn't have to hear anything about progress and business and filthy lucre. Yet, *God the Father does not bring Cecile damask piano scarves and berry sets*, Avice thought, as she ran a finger over the smooth, cool belly of a silver teapot. *Father does, courtesy of the Merchant Bank and the stock market.*

That resolved, and her moment of consumer's despair conquered, Avice thought she might as well get herself something instead. Or something that she and her husband could share—like, say, a *gun*. Perhaps that pearl-handled pistol her eye had lit upon and lingered over, entranced. It was displayed in a glass case with several other derringers and revolvers, and was an instrument of such compact beauty that even she, who knew nothing of guns, could appreciate the workmanship involved: a Colt House model with cloverleaf cylinder, four-shot, single action. It had a three-inch barrel, a bronze frame, and ivory grips inlaid with silver bands. *Why*, a tiny voice seemed to twist like a worm in her head, *it might easily be concealed in a pocket, or in one's palm, its fit snug as a child's little hand.*

Death's little hand.

Avice longed to touch it, only fractionally as cold as what it promised to deliver. If she did, she knew she would have to buy it, the perfect souvenir from a nation that settled its problems so promptly and efficiently. Hearing that crack of gunfire earlier, during the strike, had sent an undeniable thrill up her retreating back; how many of her fellow marchers lay bleeding on the street, she had wondered. She recalled Kit Coleman's piece in the *Mail & Empire* about international styles of murder and how stabbing was not a British habit, stilettoes and daggers being the favoured choice of Italians and Spaniards. The weapons of the Britisher were his fists, whereas the American used the revolver ... but surely it could be customized to fit the colonial way of doing things. She imagined taking a more conservative approach to the exercise by shooting first one limb and then another. And this her real husband, not the surrogate she'd been trailing around. Put out an eye, blow off a finger, all the while apologizing to him, like a good Canadian, for the inconvenience. *So sorry, Grif*—BANG—*do forgive me, dear*—BANG—*my fault entirely*—BANG, BANG!

While she was entertaining herself thus, happily and murderously musing, a salesman approached her from behind. It was an appreciative approach, too, for she cut a fine figure. He was accustomed to ladies stopping at this case, attracted by their own reflections in the glass. They adjusted their hats or patted their hair, fixing a stray lock, or simply made quick, satisfied assessments of their appearance. Women, all frills and vanity. Take this one—she was a peach, he thought, and she knew it, too. She was staring at herself with such rapt intensity that he could scarcely keep a chuckle out of his voice when he cleared his throat and asked, "May I be of some service to you, Madam?"

"Yes," she answered, without even turning around. She knew what she wanted, but out of the habit of deferring to masculine expertise, or perhaps only to follow a commercial ritual, she solicited his opinion. "I am going to kill my husband," she said. "Slowly—he must be made to suffer. Please, which of these fine instruments would you recommend?"

# 18

## FLY

ALL RIGHT, she'd keep her own counsel if she had to. She'd keep her secret, hard as a knot of gristle buried in her chest, a sliver driven deep where it could fester and leak a steady stream of poison into her system. Wherever Avice spent the night during her travels, from Windsor to Toronto to Barrie, in whatever hotel room or berth, she slept with her fingers pressed to her lips. Nothing was going to escape from her. Not a single word, not even one spiked and spiny that might tumble out of her mouth while she lay on some dark shoal of sleep. There'd be no gnawing admissions from her to bore like scarcely audible parasites through the walls and into the heads of the other sleepers, to shock them into wakefulness and alarmed action.

It's not that she didn't savour the gobsmacked expression on the face of that clerk at Newcomb-Endicott's. How smug he had been, his face tight as a nut cracked open once he fully comprehended what he had heard. And it's not that she even had to say anything, really. For some reason that she herself didn't quite fathom, she often inspired a frisson of alarm in the men she encountered—a shudder of disturbed certainties, a shadow of doubt passing, the ominous sensation of a grave disrespectfully trampled over.

A man seated a few tables over from her in the Collingwood Inn had been observing her, quite openly, as was his right, he felt. He watched as she plucked an apple off her plate and stabbed it with her fruit knife, as if through its very heart. Such indelicacy he found abhorrent. He knew women—what they were like, what they were for, what they were capable of. Essentially, there were two kinds. This woman had the appearance of one but was obviously the other, and as he refused to dine in the same room as one of those, he tossed a coin onto the table and left.

Avice hardly noticed. He was of no interest, a stout packet of stale opinion hustling through the door, a man dead and buried in his own body. He didn't even have to open his mouth, for she knew the type from her many forays into male precincts—smoking cars, saloons, clubs—revelatory as a quick tour of Bluebeard's forbidden room. She had come to understand that violence was often cleverly accomplished, disseminated as facts that circled and circled a woman like a pack of menacing guard dogs. For instance, it was well known that education damaged a woman's reproductive system; it had been proven in the medical journals. The higher a woman ascended in learning, the more her womb withered in response. Also, only prostitutes were capable of sexual feeling. (Judith, the Drinkwaters' maid, had neither the leisure nor the skill to read these journals and had informed Avice otherwise during their bartering session on the eve of her wedding.) The "truth" of the matter was that a woman's cranium, like an overbred animal's, was simply too cramped a space to entertain thoughts of any depth or proportion. It was a cavity as small and empty as the teacup Avice presently drained, although her own cranial reservoir overflowed with ideas—bloody and seditious. She now knew not to show her hand or they would have it off, cut at the wrist. In her own anthropological studies she had found civilized gentlemen not that much different from the labouring brute who sinks his fist into his wife's face on a Saturday night—only in his methods, and at times not even in that.

Avice stared into her teacup, turning it this way and that, trying to read the leaves, what pattern they formed on the bottom. This hardly qualified as brain work, she realized, but all the same was a prophetic game that she was good at. She used to read the leaves for her credulous sisters, and although she liked to tease them, she had more often than not—and weirdly—made accurate predictions of future events.

"I see a tall dark stranger . . ."

"Go on, do tell, Avice."

"He has a hooked nose."

"Oh!"

"A club foot, a hump on his back."

"No, no, what's he really like? You can see him, can't you?" Yes indeed, and she had been the one to claim him, the handsome stranger, the envisioned man. And look where it had gotten her.

The way the tea leaves were arranged, clumped wetly one upon another, reminded her of the expression on that clerk's face—so gratifyingly dumbfounded when apprised of her unruly plans. She had gotten out of that store fast, hotfooted it before he had time to sound the madwoman alarm, or to call in the police. She had wanted none of their instant Yankee justice. What mischief had possessed her? What inspired garrulity had taken hold in that cathedral of commerce? Perhaps, she thought, it was only the confessional effect of the country itself, the looser, more voluble atmosphere in the land of the run-on sentence.

She felt safer here, back home, where shames were kept secret, where crooks and killers at least had enough manners not to brag, and her countrymen had enough sense not to make heroes of them. Besides, she *knew* that he, Griffith, was here somewhere. The further north she travelled, and the deeper she ventured into this cold province, the warmer she got. So intent on her goal was she, so determined and clear, that she had developed a whole other sense that was trained on him alone. It was no use his dodging, his dissembling, for she would witch him out like a hidden spring that crawled through the earth. She'd gather intelligence of his passing, follow his scent no matter how faint, step on the very stones he had stepped on. She'd step down hard, too, as if upon his very face. She'd grind her heel into his stupid sightless eyes.

It was too bad about that gun, though, which in her hasty retreat she had not been able to purchase. Her name had been practically inscribed on its hilt, and her husband's name on one of its bullets. How perfectly, how flush the two of them fit together. A weapon made for marriage.

No matter, she sighed (while another male customer fled the premises), there were enough materials in the world with which to do harm. Knives, axes, clubs, bombs, garrotting cords, poisons, acids . . . and those were just the obvious ones. Once a person began to take note, began to look about her, it was truly amazing how many lethal instruments there were, even in the most innocent and upstanding locations. In a church, you could brain someone with a crozier, run them through with a pastoral staff, strangle them with a rosary. (Catholics obviously enjoyed much more latitude for harm, with all their ecclesiastical props and clutter.) Or in this establishment itself. Her eye now swept the room like a scythe. A chair swung with enough force would knock a man down, then you could finish him off by smashing his head in with that crystal pitcher. You could slice him up like a roast with a broken bottle or a water glass. Cut a vein or, if you were very ambitious and domestically assertive, saw off his head with a carving knife. Smother him with a tablecloth, drown him in the soup tureen, gouge out his eyes with a spoon. . . Avice laid aside the cup she had been turning dreamily around and around and picked up the silver fork from her place setting. She ran a finger lightly over the tines, then absentmindedly used one to clean a fingernail. Was it possible to kill a man with a fork? She supposed he would look terribly stippled when done, like a baked potato too avidly pricked.

Surveying the dining room once again for dangerous inventory, she was a bit taken aback to see that someone else was seated at the table that the other fat-headed gentleman had vacated. She must have been very deeply engrossed in her thoughts, for she had heard no one enter. This man's face was obscured by a newspaper, a screen of words, that he held up before him. The fingers that held the paper were tapered and long as a pianist's, and not at all like the blunt, bloated digits of the other man.

A heading in large type on the front page of the paper caught her eye: ECHO *LOST. ALL PASSENGERS AND CREW DROWNED.*

Avice shuddered as she conjured up the horrific scene, what those poor people must have experienced. All lost. She hoped that she would be able to avoid boat travel where she was going, wherever that might be. Terrible, a death like that... Of course, it was not to be discounted for someone else. Someone deserving.

Lately, in her lonely rooms at night, tourism beginning to pall, she had taken to killing off the man she had made with her arts and craft. She was starving and fretting him away. And not because she didn't like him; the trouble was she liked him overmuch. (Is it possible to fall romantically in love with oneself?) She was far too comfortable and easy in his skin. It was fun being him, and, as him, she felt herself to be more credible, more bearable, a better human being. Marriage had changed her. As the wife she was sharp-tongued and cruel, a harridan, a nag. As him she lounged and idled, whistled little tunes, snatches of popular song, incomplete as his very self, yet all the more carefree for that. When she was *she*, her eyes hardened and narrowed, letting in less light, and her mind darkened. She was full of anger and resentment, she steamed and whistled like a kettle boiling on a hob. It was just so tempting to be him. He was an intoxicating sweetness, an addiction. He drifted through his days aimless as smoke. He pissed them away—but, alas, not against the wall. Possibly the worst thing was that he had room for forgiveness and she did not. He ate away at her resolve, he was on his side—most treacherous self!

Why *would* anyone want to be married to her, and be ruled by her? (In his kindness, he had not said this.)

So Avice had begun to step far less often into the guise of her husband. This took some effort, mending the breaks in her identity through which she had let herself go. She endeavoured to wean herself from him as a personal form of temperance. As a mere woman, though, she felt unsafe. Not so much because she was travelling alone and searching in the disreputable places where she had to search for scum like him. It was not an outward threat so much as an inward one. At times, in her abandonment, she thought it possible that she might choke with rage—and she feared what that rage might lead her blindly into.

He wasn't perfect, her improvisational man, so maybe it wouldn't be so troublesome to give him up. Self-sufficiency had its limits, especially in the bedroom. Here she was, married for weeks, and the union was still unconsummated. Virginity clung to her like a transparent, skin-tight garment that she could not for the life of her peel off. She would gladly divest herself of it, a woman's most prized possession, and rip it to shreds. She was more than willing to toss it away in a tumble of arms and legs and slapping, pumping flesh—rend it utterly in a storm of effort, if not pleasure.

Nights, with only her hand for company, she had gotten to know herself very well—better than most women of her station, she suspected, whose bodies were usually buried beneath mounds of cloth, and whose minds floated in some other realm when necessary, heads and bodies severed. She had taken a real interest in herself, a lover's charged interest in which no physical feature was too insignificant for a fond inspection. She conducted a census of her moles, freckles and toe hairs, and concluded that she was populated, especially in her rural regions, with a pleasing density of human insignia. She traced veins, contours, dips and mounds. She explored every orifice—aural, nasal, vaginal. She might have been a cartographer, a physician . . . or simply a shockingly indecent woman. She licked her kneecaps. She trailed a pinky over her lips, then ran it up her nose. She smacked herself soundly on the behind, then glanced slyly over her shoulder at her own lovely, blushing bum. (He might not be perfect, but she was damn close.)

With such physical knowledge and bravado it's no wonder that Avice so casually terrified any number of gentlemen as she blazed a trail through the province. The current one, her fellow diner, did not appear to be of this timorous brotherhood. He had lowered his newspaper and was watching her closely, almost as if her private thoughts were flickering visibly through her head, a peep show in a kinetoscope.

Waking from her self-starring reverie, Avice realized that she was being observed, and so she observed right back, sending the man that bold and icy look of hers that usually did the trick. Although not this time. He inclined his head in a slight bow and parted his lips, as if to speak. No words came out, but she watched, more fascinated than appalled, as something else did. A fly emerged from the man's mouth—a large, glistening, blue-black, fully disgusting fly. Once it had crawled out, and over his lips, it progressed through the thicket of his moustache, then walked slowly up his cheek. He didn't flinch, only looked steadily at her.

Avice wanted to scream with laughter, but he did frighten her a little, this man. He was strangely dressed, she now noticed, all in black: his suit, his cape, his top hat on the chair beside him. He had black, slicked-back hair, and his moustache was waxed to bull's horn points. He looked overdone, contrived and artificial, not quite real, as if he had just stepped out of some book or someone's overwrought imagination. Hers, for example.

And there was something else about him besides. A secret. One she would do well to keep to herself. Or rather, she would do better not to keep it at all, for she had no idea what it meant. It was this: she knew from reading the leaves in her teacup that this man, with his mephitic, if stagy, odour, was in her future. He might even be her future. She had read the portent, had seen his face staring up at her from the bottom of the cup, belligerently, even as it now stared at her from across the room.

*No.* She wouldn't have it.

Avice stood abruptly, knocking her chair over and snagging the tablecloth, which made the cutlery and porcelain tremble. She snatched up the teacup, then threw it with force onto the floor, where it exploded into flying splinters and shards. Then she marched out of the room.

If he was real, let him pay the bill.

# 19

## HUGH

H E WAS IN-KNEED, cack-handed and hircine. An unusual migration had occurred on his person, in that he had a mound of orange pubic hair growing on top of his head while a silken straight-as-a-gut sporran bewigged his manhood. His facial features were like parasitical entities that had nuzzled into his skin and clung there with a bat-like tenacity: flame-rimmed eyes, nose-stump, mouth-slash, ears that rode as flat to the head as scabs. Generally speaking, if he was a horse, you'd pass him by, a goat and you'd say no thanks, a dog, you'd head in the opposite direction.

But he was a man, and of all the men Avice could have chosen, she chose him.

He saw himself as a piss artist and a real piss-cutter, but he was really just a pisshead. A dumb cluck born in a garboil, plucked out of a tumult, a chaos of flying boots and fists that in other circles is known as a family. He was too mean for a name.

"C'mere *you*," his mother would say as he tried to skulk out the door.

It was almost impossible to get by that brute of a woman without receiving a ringing clout on the head. It's no wonder he was so physically contracted. His stature was foreshort-ened from ducking, his ears flattened protectively close to his head, his nose retracted telescopically into his face. *You*, that's all he ever got; a pronoun knuckle-dusted into his skull, which at least evolved over time out of the pre-nominal muck into *Hugh*. A proper noun, if not a proper gentleman.

He looked solid enough, was built of enduring material, and was covered in freckles that overlapped like mail. But he tended to slosh when he walked, like a half-empty bottle. He leaked. Water ran out of his eyes, his nose. He drooled. He sweat. He pissed cataracts in the morning. (He woke piss proud.) She thought of him as containing a lake, the pressure of it bursting though his seams, the damp impression he left on the sheets, which was a bit too poetic for her to think, and for him to be. He was well lubricated was all; and she called it out of him, made him weep like a boiler, with pain mostly. Her rising heat, her prickly female dander, made him gasp and sneeze. He was a beached carp on the hard shore of her.

Avice found him behind a blockade of bottles in a dark back corner of the Mansion House barroom. She had to step over a dead man to get to him, and cut her way through a lay-ered curtain of smoke. Not to mention the obstructing stares of the other patrons, tough, bruised, beak-faced locals, mill hands and sailors, who were stunned by her sudden presence among them. A *female*. How easily she strode through the door, how coolly she surveyed them all. The dead man, well, they were *used* to him, but she trailed trouble after her like a widow's black, entangling weeds.

"*You*," she said, sinking her fingers into the russet wool on Hugh's head and jerking it roughly upward, pulling it into what thin annunciatory light there was, to peer into his face. "All right, you'll do. Come with me."

They all marvelled. Pat Sloan, the farrier, crossed himself twice—forwards and backwards—appealing to whatever deity, God or devil, might be attending.

*How did she know his name?*

He should have swaggered back in afterwards, hitching up his trousers with a satisfied manly yank, giving his recently buttoned fly a fond pat of approval. A virgin, after all, and a lady. How many times in one man's low life does he get a piece of that? But Hugh tried his best to be inconspicuous. He shuffled back into the bar like a stick of furniture shifting on the sly. He couldn't quite figure it. He attacked the problem over and over, using his brain like a blunt instrument. What he finally figured out was that *she* took something from *him*, and not the other way around. He didn't know how she did it, or even what it was. (Not *his* virginity. Heck, Uncle Nort got that years ago.) He had the sneaking suspicion, though, that it was something important, something he hadn't even been aware of possessing before she took it. But what?

*Hoity-toity bitch. Fucken hore.* As this was all his quiet moment of reflection had to offer, Hugh walked over to a man drinking at the bar and served up his fist into the guy's empty face like a portion of pig knuckles on a plate. He felt better then.

Her pucelage, she dealt with it.

More to the point was how she had found her way to the Mansion House, to the island and port town, the *x* on the map, the stitch (if not the kiss) that would soon reunite the sundered and drifting couple. Fate had nothing to do with it. Grif could have been caught in its ensnaring strands as he wandered along, thinking himself entirely free, but Avice was more independent and resourceful than that. So. Where does one go in the late nineteenth century when looking for a needle—or needlehead— in a haystack? Where else but to a spiritualist.

Fleeing down the walk after quitting the Collingwood Inn—and Avice did bolt once she was out the door and beyond the avid, mocking eye of that strange man—she ducked quickly down a side street, casting about almost desperately for some place to hide. She suspected, rightly, that he might follow. In a small, tidy clapboard cottage she noticed a sign propped in the front window that read: *Mrs. Betsy Wolf—Theosophist, Clairvoyant, Hydromancer*. Mrs. Wolf evidently had many eerily vibrating strings to her bow, but as long as she had a curtained and concealing room, Avice was content. She dashed through the door of the cottage and locked it behind her.

She had entered a sparsely decorated front room—presumably an interior design preference of the dead and immaterial, as she had once for a hoot visited a similar psychic lair with one of her sisters. The only appointments were a round table, two plain wooden chairs, a pine trunk pushed up against one wall, curtains of a heavy maroon cloth that dressed the room's two windows, soon to be dramatically drawn on the scene within. On the table sat a single unlit candle in a pewter holder and a clear glass bowl filled with water. Lowly props, but sufficient in their modesty. Three doors led into the room from the other parts of the house. All were closed, and Avice tried to guess the one through which Mrs. Wolf was to make her entrance.

She waited… longer than she liked. Surely if the woman was clairvoyant, she would know she had a customer.

She ran her hands up her arms, a chill seeming suddenly to pass through her. This reminded her of her sisters quaking in the darkened parlour at home, while one produced raspy scritching sounds by dragging a bow across violin strings and another whispered ghost stories. It was the best she could do at the time not to ruin the mood of the evening with her sceptical, spell-breaking tongue. Silently she endured their wide-eyed amazement as they breathlessly described the uncanny happenings that occurred at seances they had attended, or what it was like to have their vibrations read, or how they had seen with their own eyes evidence of the supernatural in spirit photographs. Hook, line and sinker, they swallowed it all, including palmistry, levitation, spirit rapping. They had even tried automatic writing, taking dictation from deeply anonymous authors. Fakery and fashionable nonsense. All the same, Avice knew that mystery had to reside somewhere if life was to have any thrill at all, and she was willing enough to seek it here.

Whether Mrs. Betsy Wolf could pull it off was another matter. The plump and matronly woman who finally appeared— and not through the door Avice had guessed—had an air more of domestic dabblings than of otherworldly ones. She had a smudge of flour on her cheek and was wearing an apron, on which she wiped her hands before taking it off and tossing it across the back of one of the chairs. A distinct aura of liver and onions trailed after her, and there wasn't even a speck of foaming ectoplasm left bobbing in her wake. Her dress was a plain brown serge, her white hair gathered up hastily into a knot, her smile kindly and slightly hesitant.

Avice tipped her nose up and held it at a disapproving angle. The theatrical demands of the profession were not being met here. She had been expecting someone sleek and unsettling, with Romany black eyes, pale skin and a hot red mouth full of tangly foreign syllables. She did not want to consult her *mother*, or any of her mother's substitutes at large in the world.

"What *is* theosophy?" she challenged, skipping even the most cursory of pleasantries.

"I haven't the faintest idea, my dear." All business, Mrs. Wolf dug in a pocket and produced a match, which she ignited by striking it on her front tooth. She lit the candle, then walked over to each of the windows and briskly snapped the curtains shut. "Not much call for it in these parts, you see, but one has to make a show of keeping up. To be quite honest, I'm just an old-fashioned fortune teller." She took a seat at the table and motioned for her client to do likewise. "Now, what can I do for you, dear? Wait, don't tell me. You are looking for a man."

"Yes, I am," said Avice, surprised enough to take the offered seat. But then, all the women who came here probably were looking for "a man."

"Your husband."

Not a question, but she nodded anyway.

"Are you certain you want to find him?" Mrs. Wolf herself was thrice widowed. (Mr. Blair, an unfortunate accident, Mr. Dunlop, ditto, Mr. Wolf, "something" he ate.)

"I do."

"In that case I had best have a look at your hand." Mrs. Wolf took Avice's strong, resistant hand in her own warm and pliant one (which felt lovely to Avice, and comforting—maybe she *did* want her mother), and announced after a brief, concentrated study of her fingernails, their high burnish in the candlelight, "You are a virgin."

Avice gave a little gasp, more impressed than taken aback.

"And not a very nice one, either."

She had to smile at this. Perhaps the old bird did know a thing or two.

Mrs. Wolf did not necessarily know that much about onychomancy, a rare form of divination, for she had only been reading the obvious: the *dirt* caked under those nails! She turned Avice's hand over and began to study the lines scored in her palm, which were more deeply etched than was usual for someone of her age; perhaps the girl clenched her fists overmuch. No immediately useful information was available there in any event, for the fortune teller sniffed and said, "I don't see him. Not a trace of him, not even in your heart line. We'll have to look elsewhere."

"All right." Avice withdrew her hand and sat back.

"Do you believe in spirits, my dear?"

"Not really, no."

"Good, then you should have no objections if I try to contact one. Some of them are nothing more than disembodied gossip floating loose in the world. You never can tell, someone may have spotted him. He might even be a spirit himself by now. Save you the trouble, if you know what I mean."

She did indeed know, and had begun to warm to this plainspoken and homey medium. "What must I do?"

"Oh, I do most of the work, you simply ask the questions."

Mrs. Wolf closed her eyes and let all of the expression, and colour, drain from her face and down the thick spout of her neck. Inwardly, she had opened her mind wide enough to accommodate whatever unengaged spirit might happen by—and with the recent disaster of the *Echo*, a mind as expansive as a ballroom might even be needed.

No sooner had she begun this exercise than Avice became aware of a strange noise in the room, a thumping and scratching that was coming from the vicinity of the pine trunk. A light, apprehensive shudder rivered up her back.

Mrs. Wolf cocked open one eye, then both, which she turned—balefully—in the direction of the trunk. Huffing with annoyance, she got up, marched over to it and flung open the lid. "Luther," she said, "scat!"

A white cat, a puritan if not a phantom shade, shot out of the trunk and through the one doorway that Mrs. Wolf had left open when she entered the room.

"My apologies, dear." She resumed her seat. "I never know where that one will turn up next. Let's proceed, shall we."

Avice shrugged, her interest in this whole business seriously diluted. Likely there were other little helpers on hand to knock on walls or rattle chains, and she chided herself for being gullible enough to consider that something might actually be revealed here. This session better be entertaining, she thought, if nothing else.

It was, but only in the way that Hugh, still in her future, was to become: a dire amusement.

While Avice sat and smirked and nothing much happened, Mrs. Wolf once again sank into a trance. And then it happened with bewildering speed. The air began to tighten around her. She felt a pressure instantly building, as an embracing force pushed her eyes back into her head. It tried to ram her jaw up into her skull, to crush her ribs, to flatten her legs like sheets of paper. She was pinned to the chair. She couldn't move or speak—and she was absolutely terrified. Her skin was about to burst open, and her bones explode, and her frozen blood shatter.

Horrified and helpless, she watched as the lit candle flew out of the holder as if hurled by an unseen hand. It struck her on the chest, and landed in her lap. A flaw of fire zipped up the front of her dress. She heard an unearthly scream—had she made it?—then a wave of water hit her and she was standing, shaking, drenched but free of it.

Mrs. Wolf was also standing, the empty glass bowl clasped in her hands. She used water sometimes for scrying. It was like a liquid tarot that could be swirled and swished, a handy lubricant used to unlock a few of the secrets that the future so tightly held. This time it had served the present better, leaving a wet, unreadable splatter on the front of Avice's dress. Mrs. Wolf, a workaday medium, was accustomed to a more civil and prosaic association with the otherworld, as if the Dominion of the dead, the Canadian contingent of the supernatural, was likewise populated with the polite and reserved, spirits who were content to rap on the table or rustle the curtains as required. Never before had she been host to such a vicious presence. Old world, she thought, with an axe to grind.

"My," she said, gamely enough. "I think we've both earned a good stiff drink after that. I wouldn't take what happened too seriously, dear. The mind can do strange things. You're too smart to believe in this hocus-pocus."

Avice nodded, still a bit dazed, and meekly followed Mrs. Wolf through the open door into her kitchen at the back of the cottage. There, as the day wore on, and the greenery outside the window swayed with increasing animation, and a top-hatted stranger knocked on the front door and rattled the knob, trying fruitlessly to gain admittance, the two women communed with another spirited substance altogether (for Mrs. Wolf had another string to her bow: she was the town bootlegger).

One thing leading to another, the fortune teller eventually suggested that Avice travel to the very port town where Grif was headed—but not because she could see him going there. It was more a joke prediction, a glinting piece of warped, but hundred-proof, lucidity that she had inadvertently conjured up. It was a lover she saw, not a husband, and her description of him had them both in hysterics: the hair, the face, the walk, one knee on a crash course with the other. They giggled and snorted like schoolgirls. At one point Avice slipped right out of her chair and accidentally sat on Luther, who howled loudly enough to protest for all mankind. Oh, that stump of a man, that hilding, that affront made flesh.

That Hugh.

# 20

## SEVEN FRIARS
## HUGGING A NUN

F GRIF SMOLDERS were to describe the material out of which his prison was made, he would have to say *women*. Women—their skin and arms and thighs—composed the walls and ceiling and floorboards of his room. How strangely papered it was, in pale cheek-pink matter flocked with warts and moles; how terrible the tooth-white paint, the chair built of limbs, the bed spate-boned and narrow as a back. He woke in the mornings with a woman's spittle congealed on his face, with a woman's icy hand slapped across his mouth, with the words he needed to say wound like a woman's long hair around his tongue. And he felt sick, as if he'd been drinking urine—and blood, hot, thick and bitter. A woman's.

On the shock of seeing her, his wife, she had seemed to scatter in his eyes; she had leapt like a multiplied reflection around the room. With a scraping look, like a key twisting in a lock, she had turned his sanctuary into a cell, but one with a pressing feminine physicality. She was everywhere, his multiple mate, his terrifying harem, and yet he couldn't lay his hands on her. What did she want from him?

He knew it couldn't be anything as straightforward as an explanation or an apology. She did not want to hear a confession of cold feet, an admission of inadequacy, of a failure of nerve, a mistake—a simple, *forgivable* human error. His sin against her was not venal, or even mortal; he had achieved a new level of transgression, a singular sinning apotheosis, the penance for which he did not want to consider. What would satisfy her? A pound of flesh, his right arm, his foreskin nailed on the wall? Plainly, she was going to make him pay for every mile he had put between them, a toll to cover the cost of the treacherous road he had built between his side of the marriage and hers. The road out.

He knew that she was going to keep him trapped in this room at the Sun like an insect in a jar, so that she could peck at him. The woman was going to *feed* on him. Or—not. Possibly she only wanted to keep him off balance, destabilized (that was easy enough), suspended in a solution of uncertainty. Possibly she didn't know herself what she wanted. Although, God, she had an air of knowing. She had been stunning, radiant with offense, glowing as if newly forged in a furnace before entering his room; her body a weapon, keen and dazzling. She had filled his eyes completely. Blinded, he could see nothing else. Not even after she had gone.

Not a word. She said nothing while there, only cruised around, studying the room's contents and the peculiar souvenirs of his long journey. She sauntered casually, comfortably, as if fully dressed, as if encased in one of the usual boned, frilled and wired outfits that women wear. (No bustle was needed, he couldn't help but notice, no strapped-on horsehair pad, to draw the eye to her gluteal charms.) In her survey she took in the Reverend Bee's jacket, over which she briefly paused, frowning; then Grif's mismatched shoes, his gunmetal purse, the silver pen . . . his journal. *This* she fingered with an instinctive knowledge of its value. She wanted it, and took it. She would not have taken him, on the other hand, if he had been offered to her on a golden platter—or, in the cuisine of revenge, skewered on a stick. She had good reason, too, for Grif suddenly drew on an unexpected reserve of stupidity by saying, when she laid a hand on his book, "*Amy*, don't."

Polly, Hattie, Amy . . . too many women. They thronged the room like her ghostly attendants, chill drafts that had followed her in. She might be cloaked with these invisible others, but he recognized his own wife when he saw her, and now that he was seeing so very much of her, he decided that *yes*, he wanted her. A mere slip of the tongue, even a slit in his tongue, had caused him to speak duplicitously, to see one and say the other—Amy glossing her, haunting her skin, so white and inscribable, with only that colophon of a bruise on her breast and that circlet of . . . what was that on her thigh that so resembled teeth marks?

His remark had stopped her as surely as if he had shown her the back of his hand, brought it up viciously against her jaw, slammed her face shut like a drawer. She had been about to speak, perhaps even to lay down the terms of his sentence. At the sight of him—did ever a man look so vulnerable?—a hair-thin crack had appeared in her resolve. Incredibly, she had felt moved to see the pathetic state of the shoes that had taken him so far from her. How they gaped with exhaustion and sadness: mismatched yet presenting two very similar faces. But Grif had healed her weakness and misgiving with a word. *Amy?* It clanged in her ears. She pressed her lips so tightly together, they might have been made of stone.

She gripped the journal. The book seemed frozen to her hand, as if it were the missal of a crazed priest (albeit defrocked), and like someone possessed and driven by hectoring inspiration she immediately strode out of the room, her bare feet slapping across the checkered floor. The door clapped shut behind her.

The silence she left him with was heavy. Suffocating. It seemed to plug every hole and crack in the room, caulking it so thoroughly that Grif couldn't even hear the young proprietor of the Sun whistling as he swept the hall.

He stared helplessly at the nut-headed doll that was still slumped in the chair, but her gaze was aimed askance, her tiny black eyes misfiring.

Roland Avery knew that Grif's room was not constructed of women, nor was it female-infested, unless you counted a few maternal roaches snug in the wainscotting, or the drift of slut's wool under the bed, or Norma, the doll. He knew it was not a prison constructed of female flesh and bone because he had driven every nail into it himself and no one had screamed bloody murder. With his tireless boy's hands he had mixed and poured cement, framed and sided, painted and shingled, decorated the rooms, and installed rain barrels on the roof in case of fire. Out front he had hung a shingle of his own optimistic design, upon which the sun danced with the buoyant and animate spirit of youth.

Roland had scavenged and bartered for materials, rooting through the dump and hanging around outside the mills and on the dock. He worked, moonlighting at the cooper's and the undertaker's, and on long nights, when the moon itself rolled slowly across the sky, he played poker and blackjack in the smoky back room of the Mansion House with men who took him for a boy but somehow were unable to take him for a fool, or a ride. He was a boy, but one of many parts that, when fit together, made him as round and industrious and capable as a beaver. While other boys were running free in the street, or leaping naked into the lake, or plugging stray cats in the alley with rocks, Roland was busy rolling carpet down his stairs, or scrubbing sheets, or feeding those clever, dodging strays saucers of milk at his back door. He *had* a back door—he'd installed it himself with his own trusty and trustworthy hands. Not only that, but it was a door through which he could come and go as he pleased. Unlike the liberties enjoyed by the other boys in town, his were absolutely his own, uncompromised and fully paid for.

If Roland Avery's hotel had a certain lilt and sway to it, that was most likely because he had raised it on the strength of his own voice. He sang as he went about his work, tunes like "Sweet Rosie O'Grady" and "A Hot Time in the Old Town" or, when the mood took him, songs from *The Pirates of Penzance* or *The Mikado*. He hummed and whistled as he hammered and sawed, mopped and polished. Even the day his voice broke, like the day he fell through the roof, he simply picked up where he had left off, a few octaves, and floors, lower. While most visitors to town preferred the other hotels—the Huron, the Royal, the Mansion House—the odd traveller was drawn irresistibly to The Dancing Sun. Its structural alignment might have been skewed, its colour scheme mismatched and overenthusiastic, but the place had a protective, sheltering charm. A warmth seemed to emanate from its walls, so lovingly constructed, and at times an almost audible tunefulness could be detected, as of rogue notes drifting high and free, detached from whatever lullaby they had been born in. Orphaned, as Roland himself was.

His father lay encased in concrete in the Trent Canal—a functional tomb that Roland could at least visit if he were so inclined, or if his father, while living, had given him some reason to. As a baby, his mother had kept misplacing him, and then finally she misplaced herself, ending a relationship that might have been pleasant enough had it endured. Roland could claim only a single day of schooling to his credit, but that one day had provided him with sufficient educational ballast to sail forthrightly into the workaday world. *Carpe diem*, his teacher, a Mr. H.H. Fudger, had thundered from the front of the one-room schoolhouse in Bidwell Township, and Roland took him at his rhetorical word. Before that very day slipped like water through his fingers, the boy stood and walked out of that dank, sour-smelling room (spilled milk, wet woollen socks) and never looked back. He *did* seize the day, every day on its arrival; unpacked it like a box lunch and savoured every last radiant crumb. His hotel was his invention, his family, his investment and the theatre where he hosted each of his days, which never failed to unfold with entertainment and interest. He wore all of the hats in the Sun, not only out of frugality but because he genuinely enjoyed being the chambermaid, the desk clerk, the accountant... He had still been working on his books when Avice appeared, shortly after Grif.

Her reputation preceded her, and after she had gone, it lingered, a cool, disturbing presence. It was as if a black bird had drifted ominously through one of the windows, stolen something indefinable in the Sun's construction, a glittering filament or thread, then swept out again.

The woman had not been in town long, and had given out her name as Smolders. Men went to her room in the Mansion House, he had heard, and didn't necessarily come out satisfied or much inclined to go back in.

"Have you a guest named Griffith Smolders?" she had demanded at the bar.

"Yes, Ma'am. And you are—?" His sister, Roland guessed with a determined innocence. This would explain Grif's arrival, come to rescue his sibling from depravity.

Answers were not a service she provided, and she was gone up the stairs so swiftly she might have flown, her feet hardly touching down. Anyway, he didn't continue to think her so sisterly once he discovered her heap of discarded clothing outside Grif's door, which she must have shed with a breath-takingly immodest efficiency. A fine linen blouse, a black ribbed-silk skirt, silk drawers, lisle stockings, garters, no corset or corset cover, no rustling petticoat, no hat or gloves, but shoes of black kid with decorative steel beads and black bows. Roland folded each garment neatly, studying the make, running his hands over the materials—the beads on the shoes, the pearl buttons on the blouse, the lace that rimmed the high collar, even the yellow celluloid collar stays. He inclined his head toward the door. Not a sound within. He placed the shoes on top of the clothing and slipped back downstairs.

When she charged past, not long after, he noticed that her skirt was on backwards and that she was carrying a book in her hands. He wondered if he should go back upstairs and check on the health of his guest. He dearly hoped that Mr. Smolders still possessed it, and that his visitor hadn't taken more than her proper share of it with her. The song he had been singing quietly to himself, "Please Say You Will" by Mr. Scott Joplin, died in his mouth. He blinked his eyes like an animal peering into the dark. Despite his bold entrance into adult country, Roland still felt himself to be a distant and puzzled observer of much that went on there. Often he was amazed by the huge harm that the older and wiser seemed to inflict so avidly upon one another.

He decided to go upstairs and sweep the hall, which might at least erase her passage through it.

The book was cursed. She read it back to front, and thereby encountered first the anathema that was scrawled on the back inside cover. Latin, as much else, was no barrier to Avice, and she was able to translate it as easily as moving from one room to the next: *Whosoever shall take this book from my household or damage it, let him be* anathema maranatha. *Let him die the death; let him be frizzled in a pan; the falling sickness and fear shall rage in him and he shall be broken on the wheel and hanged. Amen.*

Nicely put, she thought. She wished that she had devised a similar hysterical warning for the books in her own library at home, her copies of Defoe and Thackeray that her sisters were so free with, giving them to their empty-headed friends who used them as props, devices left lying around their sitting rooms to impress prospective mates. A good strong curse this one was, hardy enough to travel undiminished through time and damn all those who dared touch the man's nasty jottings. Even her, doubly damned.

She next read Grif's recorded misadventure at the Cormanys. She examined the hand closely: the aspirant serifs, the unclosed o's, the dots on the i's scattered carelessly on the page, as though even through his writing he were trying to escape. She deduced finally that, although it was very cleverly done, it was not his, not the same hand that had signed his marriage certificate, not the same that had penned the speech she had discovered in the pocket of his morning coat and had read about a hundred times before tearing it to bits, the paper trail, the ellipses, that had led her here. Nor did she believe a word of it, although she conceded it might be strategic to pretend otherwise. Only a gloating idiot would record such an incriminating act; it was ridiculous. But then she had married an idiot, a handsome fool. (Very handsome, annoyingly.) Perhaps *he* believed it. So self-deceived was he that he might not detect in that sly dissimulation of his own hand the mimicry of his character. What an obscene flowering of self it was, too, sprouting suddenly out of pages and pages of evasive, scribbled notes about . . . bugs, mainly. What, did he think he was some sort of natural scientist, someone completely different from the uneducated clerk she had taken notice of in Kingsmill's? All he had done was de-feature an antiquity by trying to see his own face in it.

She wasn't quite sure yet what to do with the thing, how best to use it. She could feed it to Hugh, force him to eat it page by page, then make him shit it out, deposit it in thick quires back between the worn calfskin covers; a new, updated version complete with its own stinking review. In this revised form she'd be pleased to return it to her husband, a little gift.

Avice!

Who said that? It couldn't have been Grif—he didn't even know her name, apparently. Nor her conscience, she believed, for she had taken some pains to beat that into submission. She was determined to think what she liked and do what she liked. Hers was a discipline in disorder. There are fallen women, pushed over the edge by unfortunate circumstance, and there are those who willingly jump, plummeting straight into satisfying ruin. Her diary was written on her body. If Grif had been less stunned by her arrival (and less stunned generally), and more observant, he might have read the story of her days and nights with Hugh. Or did he think that all women came with ink black bruises and indentations as deep as the mysterious signages of the Lord? Ah, the visceral love letters that Hugh delivered. For Hugh did love her. He wanted to marry her. Marry her to the wall, at any rate. He wanted to open her up like a wedding present just to see how much love for him she concealed so deviously and quietly inside.

What should have deeply frightened Avice, and made her wary, only served to make her more incautious. She should have gotten rid of Hugh, and fast, but like the journal she held in her hands—caressing its covers, riffling its pages with her fingertips—she knew he was potentially useful. He was even comparable to the book in a way—an artifact, a survivor from a bawdier and more riotous age—and she could read him as easily. And Hugh did have his tender moments, as when the scavenging nub of his nose snuffled the whole length of her as if she were a field scored with the erratic pathways of the small and hunted.

Love—he got the worst of it, anyway. She had singed him from toe hair to hairline, given him a wayward waxing, by studying him too closely with a burning candle. (*Jeezus woman!*) Her affectionate punishments were usually more artful than his—but then it was not beyond her to give him a good swift kick in the backside, sinking the sharp toe of her shoe like an arrowhead into his buttock. He had been vivid with vermin, almost pixilated, and she had subjected him to the cruel indignity of a bath, shearing a crawling, fly-specked layer off him with a stiff bristle brush while he howled and struggled and eventually rose from the tin tub raw-skinned, reborn, streaming water and potency.

Glistening, slick as a baby, he was not the tempter in the garden, nor even the male bait, but the fruit itself, forbidden and delicious.

Even her eyes were wet by the time he had taken himself off, back down to his job at the mill or to the tavern, where the other men no longer whistled and winked when they saw him, but stared at him in wonder. He might have left her feeling bluff and proud, but by the time he got to where he was going, he would have that same sense of diminishment, of being robbed, of being somehow less than he had been. He was deeply troubled with the discomfiting notion that soon there would be nothing left of him at all.

Always as happy to see the back of him as his jouncy, pelted front, Avice would lay in the bed afterwards, reflective, sore in body and mind, mouthing her knuckles softly as a nuzzling colt. She allowed herself then to look ahead, and within—but not too far in either direction. Too far was more alarming even than Hugh.

She now read some entries from the earlier part of Grif's stolen journal (how else would he have come by it?) and found herself increasingly taken with the writer's irregular occupation:

Haveril In Suffolk, January the 6th: 1643 Wee broke down about one hundred superstitious pictures and seven Fryars huging a Nunn and the picture of God & Christ and Divers others very superstitious and two hundred had been broke down before I came. Wee toke away two popish Inscriptions with Ora: pro: Nobis & wee beat down a great stoneing Cross on the Top of the Church.

At St. Gregory's, January 9th Wee broke down Ten Mighty great Angels in Glass and about seventy small ones.

Feb: 3rd Wee were at the Lady Braces House & in her Chapel there was a picture of God the Father of the Trinity of Christ & the Holy Ghost the cloven Tongues which wee ordered to be taken down & the Lady promised to do it.

The iconoclast's approach was remarkably businesslike for a zealot, and Avice felt she would do well to emulate it. She did not want her own potential sources of comprehension, sympathy, tolerance or pity to undermine her intentions—but rage was such a surprisingly difficult and costly emotion to keep stoked. She had to keep feeding it and feeding it. Loss of conviction was inevitable, fury burned itself out. Her aim had been so pure, so true, and yet somehow she had not been prepared for the fact of him. Theirs had not been the confrontation she had long imagined. She had meant to strike a blow with her guise of wantonness; she had meant to be seen as ruined. *His most grievous fault.* She had wanted him to recognize the shade of his own death in her pallor.

She had only to snap her fingers and Hugh would smash him to pieces like a pile of sticks, and, conveniently, be the one to pay for it. Grif had certainly stood there as secure as a pile of sticks, trembling and uncertain. Her very appearance before him should have been enough tinder to ignite him. He should have been consumed with contrition, widowing her on the spot. But no. Instead he had called her . . . *Amy*. That name had whistled straight through her like a bullet, and might even have grazed her heart. She knew it was a mistake, that he hadn't taken her for someone else; but how do you flash your identity in a man's face and afflict him with the revelation of your wronged self when you are nothing, and told so—only part of some female jumble in his mind? Her nakedness, worn as boldly as armour, had been revealed to her then as only nakedness, pitiful and imperfect, her threadbare suit of humiliation. Even her exit from the room had been disgraceful, ungainly, for the damned floor seemed to tilt and she had to take the door on the run, her bare arse waggling like a clown's cheeks.

So. She resolved to stick to her original vow, cleave to it with the closeness of a religious infatuate. *Let him die the death. Let him be frizzled in a pan. He shall be broken on the wheel and hanged.* The Lady promised to do it. *Amen.*

# 21

## RUE

WHAT Grif had thought was only a word, a compact summary of his state of mind, his woeful, melancholy funk, he now consumed in liquid form. At The Dancing Sun he imbibed a quotidian cup of regret, a daily measure of remorse to wash down his daily bread. This, naturally, was not how Roland Avery saw it, as each morning he carried to Grif a cup of pale greenish tea, an astringent infusion, that sluiced over the edge of the Spode cup and into a Wedgwood saucer. Spilled over as did "Buffalo Gals" from the boy's own plump lips. Rue was indicated for nervous headache, giddiness, spasms, palpitations, earache and jail fever. In the past it was also used in rituals of purification. Priests at one time sprinkled holy water from brushes made of rue before the celebration of High Mass. As an infusion it made a sharp, cleansing drink, as spiritually medicinal at least as confession. And, not incidentally, it was said to be very handy for warding off witches.

Roland gave his guest's door a brisk one-knuckle salute, then entered the room without waiting for an invitation, proving that a door is just a door after all, and nothing to get hysterical about and hide behind for the rest of your life.

"Morning, Mr. Smolders. Beautiful day." Roland walked over to the bed and offered Grif the cup. "'There's rue for you' …" The herb of repentance and grace.

"Mr. Avery," said Grif, "I cannot."

"It's very good for you. The name comes from the Greek *reuo*, to set free."

"I don't trust Greeks."

"They say it gives you second sight."

Grif would have been grateful for first sight, a cure for opacity and dim-wittedness. He shook his head. "Too bitter. The stuff tastes terrible."

"It will protect you from serpents, scorpions, spiders, bees and wasps."

"I haven't encountered too many serpents in your hotel. Or scorpions."

"And fleas."

"Those I have encountered." Grif sat up, baring a shoulder, and revealed five flea bites, red as buds, dotted across it. He regarded his hovering landlord, dapper in his double-breasted suit, his glossy black hair parted in the middle and slicked down. "Which goes to show that your medicine doesn't work at all."

He was well aware that Roland's doctoring was working, though, for what this capable youngster brought him every day was really a cup of common sense, every sip a curative for a fevered imagination, a brain that sizzled in his head, cooking up a seven-course meal of doom and disaster, none of which he had so far been served. After all, the law had not come to clamp him in irons or string him up. Nor had his wife returned to bait or torment him, or simply to finish him off. On the contrary, she seemed to have forgotten him.

"Don't scratch them."

"I can't help it."

That was the problem. *She* had bitten him. Her poison was in him, and how could he not worry it and make it worse.

"They say it will drive away nightmares."

Grif held his hand out for the cup. "Sold," he said.

He couldn't understand why Roland had taken a liking to him, why he bothered. A few other guests had signed in, which had to be keeping the boy busy enough, but he still brought Grif this godawful tea every morning. He made him meals besides, and let him do odd jobs around the hotel in return for his room and board. Some of those jobs were more odd than others. Carrying down the slop pails and chamber pots in the morning, Grif had the opportunity to ponder the correlation between a man and his excrement, his signature in the pot. It was a subject that invariably brought to mind his wife's satellite, her pet manling, the hairy vassal who trundled by her side. Standing in the bar, hard by the frame of the front window, motionless as a curtain and peering out, he had watched them parading up and down the street. *Where* had she found him? In what backhouse, workhouse, asylum? You had only to look at the creature to tell he was not in his right mind. Only the day before, having been handed a broom and gently shoved out the door, Grif had been toiling away on the stoop when they walked past. Avice had appeared suddenly, out of nowhere (a style of arrival she seemed particularly skilled at), and with her, a few steps behind, came her hulking companion. Her Caliban, her leering Rumpelstiltskin. Grif had been forced to step back abruptly or she would have marched right overtop of him, her face perfectly composed, head averted, his existence not an issue worth considering—or so her manner implied. Her stumpy friend caught Grif's eye, grinned, and flicked a cigar butt at him. It hit his shirt front and bounced off, soiling it with an ashy smudge, a demon's thumbprint.

This incident Grif recognized as being colder than a snub, and more troubling than an insult or a challenge. He was sure it didn't signal his dismissal or indicate that she was finally done with him. Basically, it told him that he was still in trouble, submerged in it about as far as he had imagined, and that there was no escape. He knew, insofar as he knew anything, that if he were to flee to another town, or another country, or even halfway around the world, she would be there at his back, or hanging menacingly over him, but never at his side.

He drank his rue.

Roland was running his hand over the wallpaper, humming to himself, completely liking the way one pattern barked up against another.

"She's not my sister," Grif said.

"No," Roland replied, "she's everyone's sister."

At this, Grif was surprised to experience an unexpected stab of loyalty. He felt he should defend her, as he felt he should protect her from that orange-haired gnome she'd picked up. That fellow's eyebrows met in the middle—a sure sign of simpletonism.

"Speaking of sisters," Roland said, "there have been some unusual happenings on one of the farms outside of town."

Very carefully, Grif replaced the cup in the saucer.

"What do you make of it? One night the eldest son in the family was discovered tied up in the barn—not a moment too soon either, for it had been set on fire. And two other family members, daughters, were missing, along with a wagon and the brother's horse."

"Two daughters, you say?"

"I wonder what his crime was."

"His crime? It was a game."

"Attempted murder? Some game. But that's not all. There was a guest staying with the family when this happened, a young man who also went missing."

"They think he did it."

"And abducted the daughters. Obviously. Although, who knows, maybe they abducted him—there were two of them."

"The police are looking for him."

"I don't think they even believe in his existence. Old Wilkin, our town copper, was here asking questions. Not the most reliable crew out there, I've heard."

"What does he say, the one who was tied up, the brother?"

"Nothing. Refuses to speak. Anyway"—Roland smiled—"you don't fit the description Wilkin gave. I don't think so, that's what I told him."

Grif stared into his empty teacup, so relieved he could have refilled it with tears. But then, "No one missed the baby. Did they say?"

"What's that?"

"Wait a minute." He sat up straighter, looked around the room. "That doll is gone, the one that was on the chair. What happened to it?"

"Norma? I'm afraid she moved into Room 4 with that travelling salesman from Sprack's Flypaper Company."

"The guy with diarrhea? This is hard to bear, Mr. Avery. Why do I have this effect on women?"

"Not on some of the ladies in town, I bet, if you'd only give them a chance. Why don't you go out for a while and look around. No one will bother you. We only have old Wilkin to keep an eye on things, and he's also the truant officer, the dog catcher, the street commissioner and the fire warden. The law is stretched so thin, you can step right through it without even noticing, or being noticed."

It was possible, Grif reasoned, that he was wrong about Avice. (Wasn't he usually?) She could be done with him for good. This might be the single, artless point she'd been trying to make with her new friend and her withdrawal from their marital contest. If only he could do the same. Roland's exorcising libation might yet sweep her out of his own head, purify it like a chapel.

"All right," he said, handing the cup and saucer back to his young friend. "I will."


During the time that Grif had spent holed up in his room, he had formed an aural acquaintance with the town that he presently stepped into with all his senses open. During the night he had often enough listened to rowdies cursing beneath his window, to fights and scuffles, drunks bellowing or retching, occasionally a woman's rough and bawdy cackle. He heard snags of conversation, more intriguing for floating up to him incomplete, out of context, and more revealing as such. *His rod . . . a straw in a cow's nosril . . . d'ye hear, Mrs. Coat poisoned her husband . . . touched with the slime of animalism . . . Julius Caesar with a Scots accent? . . . it's alive, I say . . . so when her eyebrows vanished, she pasted on black felt strips . . . the divine spark . . . it's a question of affinity.* In the early morning he wakened to the sounds of the town cows lowing, ready to be milked, a rooster crowing, a horse pounding down the street, the leather of its harness creaking. Once he'd heard the clamour of an escaped team, people shouting and running, then a tremendous crash, the noise of glass exploding as the team went through a storefront window.

Outside now at midday, he wasn't sure if even this had prepared him for the vigour of the place, its full sensuous immediacy, the medley fleshed out. It was no longer the silent and empty street he had at first walked down, or the same underpopulated one he had dipped his toe into the other morning when Avice had swept by with her nose in the air and her animal at her heels. This day the street was thronging with people, shopping, milling around, lounging, gossiping, going about their business. Up near the Merchant's Bank a crowd had gathered, some spectators hooting, others shouting encouragements or disparagements, while a bald man wrestled with a bull.

Grif struck out in the opposite direction, leaping aside as a shower of water shot out of the open doorway of the Bargain House, followed shortly by the tin bucket itself which bounced clanging into the street. He saw a man with a jerk to his head, and another one wearing a Turkish fez. Breathing more confidently, he trailed after a tendril of lavender fragrance coiling through the air, and found himself walking directly behind a woman who had a mayfly riding on her back, perched on the narrow isthmus of her shoulder blade that stretched against the cotton cloth of her dress. Here was an insect that Ned had described as being "uncommonly delicate and graceful." In the height of their season, abundant in their brief lives, mayflies papered whole walls, or lay thick as carpet on streets and walks; you could slip on them and break your neck. As Grif reached out to pluck this one off, to hold it by its fragile, transparent wings, to watch its tail twist and its legs writhe before letting it go, he sensed the woman's back stiffen. She quickened her pace, and soon both she and her passenger had moved far ahead of him. He then stopped to look at a petrified foot that was on display in the window of Carruthers' Drugs. A wicker pram was parked beside the store, and he glanced into its blue velvet interior to tip a wink to its occupant and saw that it was a crow, dressed in a bonnet and christening gown.

"His name is Handsome," said a voice at his side.

Grif turned to a girl of about eleven, who was wearing a white dress, a straw hat, black stockings and shoes. With her composed expression and perfect pale skin, she reminded him of a statue, a particular one in fact, that had been in the church of his boyhood, the church he had polished with his hide.

"His parents were shot." She shuddered.

"That's dreadful," Grif said. "He is very well named."

"Are you?"

"I'm not sure."

"I have two pet muskrats at home, Muriel and Fern, a beaver named Mr. Woods, an albino deer—that's Ambrose—and a freak calf that looks like an owl. It was born with its nostrils beneath its jaws. I haven't decided what to call it."

"You could exhibit your animals and make some money."

"I could. Do you know that Sarah Bernhardt sleeps in a coffin and has a python for a footstool?"

"I've heard that, yes. An unusual woman."

"Women are."

"I couldn't agree with you more."

"Can you say this as fast as me? Try it, it's not easy. 'A canner exceedingly canny one morning remarked to his granny a canner can can anything that he can but a canner can't can a can can he?'"

"No," Grif laughed, "I *can't*."

"You shouldn't drink, then. It's pure wickedness."

"But I don't. Not like that fellow over there, anyway." Grif indicated a man near them, propped up against a post, sleeping it off.

"Goodbye, then." She gripped the handle of the pram and began moving off.

"Are you well named?" he asked after her.

"Yes. My name is Rae." She kept going. "That's short for Raewyn."

"Good day, Miss Rae. Goodbye, Handsome."

At about ten feet away she called back over her shoulder, "I'd watch out for that person who is following you."

Grif didn't turn to look. Nor did he try to feign indifference by sliding his hands casually into his pockets and continuing his nonchalant progress down the walk. What he did was bolt. He sprinted straight across the street through a moil of dust raised by a passing buggy. He skimmed by the undertaker's (crossed himself—habit), ran by Boyter's Shoe Repair—two men inside playing checkers paused to watch him fly past— then scurried down a narrow alley between the post office and the Royal Hotel that led to the dock. Given this, it might have seemed that his goal was to hurl himself into the lake, to bury himself in its depths, to drown himself once and for all; or, if he could only stretch the tale of his life taller, to swim all the way to the States. He didn't know what he was doing, outside of reacting instinctively. Balanced on the very edge of the dock, he searched around anxiously for some clue, some salvation that might rise out of the water itself. All he saw were thick, clotted patches of sawdust floating on its surface and, further out, log booms that stretched far into the channel. Some boys were streaking across them, chased by a man who was shaking his fist at them and wielding a grappling hook.

Not a sound behind him. No footsteps approaching, however stealthily. The girl had been mistaken or teasing: no one was following him. As Roland had declared, it was a beautiful morning, and Grif could see that it was free of menace. The lake was calm, the air pure, every stone and blade of grass articulated with a clear wash of sunlight. It was all of a piece, every sight and sound and smell woven together in a way that, for once, Grif, by the scrawl of his presence, did not feel he was ruining.

He had to stop running, he thought. He had to make some sort of peace with Avice, if only in his own mind. He wanted her, yes; he didn't want her, also yes. But his budding affection for this town was unequivocal. He wondered, can you marry a place? What he should do was adopt Roland and settle here. Or more realistically, Roland should adopt him, and then Grif would have the singular advantage of a thirteen-year-old father.

He stared at the floating islands of sawdust—what the fish ate for breakfast, or what they choked on. It was a sight that shouldn't make a man hungry, but he immediately saw himself with knife and fork in hand, tucking into a big greasy platter of bacon and eggs and fried bread. He glanced up, realizing that he was being observed. A man with a bushy black beard was standing on the deck of a sidewheeler moored nearby, studying him. The boat Grif recognized. It was the *Northern Belle*, the same he had seen while idling on the dock in Owen Sound, shortly before Amy shanghaied him. The man, apparently the captain, had an air of recognizing him as well, giving him a shrewd look that gradually turned into one of alarm as his eyes focused on something just beyond Grif, some darkness condensing in the background. A black form taking shape.

The captain didn't have to shout a warning—although he did—for Grif had already dropped onto the dock and flattened himself out. A bullet whistled overhead and hit the water with a hissing *thuck* as the lake swallowed it. With his face pressed into the wood of the dock, his lips kissing the grain, the smell of tar coiling up his nostrils, Grif had to wonder about the gift of second sight Roland had promised him. He couldn't see much from this vantage point. He couldn't even see the breakfast he had envisioned only moments before. Instead of that knife and fork, all he could picture grasping firmly in his hands was Avice's pulsing throat. As he rose from the dock, legs rubbery, fingers twitching, he decided that he was going to have to forswear his telling cups of rue, and his breakfast, and *do* something about that woman. His hands were working already as he walked briskly away from the water's edge.

# 22

# BLUE RUIN

HUGH LAY on her bed. The peanut balanced on his throat-boll kept the room from rocking. His face was stretched tight as a drum and each dust speck that drifted down from the ceiling hit it with a loud *ping* that hurt like a pinprick. Hugh was thoroughly gin-rinsed, addled, pickled, half eaten by a spirituous solvent. There was nothing left of his brain but lace, and his body was a jumble of spare parts stuck so loosely together that, if he moved it even an inch in an effort to puke in the bucket Avice had put by the side of the bed, he would collapse into a pile of screws, rat turds and loose change.

Her pacing. Back and forth, back and forth. Every time she walked by the bed, he could feel her passing right through him. Her intensity was painful. Even at the best of times, to touch her was to get a shock of spirit conducted through metal—direct contact with hell's heat. She was enough to make a man's hair howl. And his toenails. *By God*, he was sure they were going to shoot off the end of his toes and stick into the wall.

He should have listened to that little angel in the barroom. White dress, straw hat, ten, eleven years old, bible clasped to her breast, and singing so sweetly ... *Jesus the water of life will give.* The water of life—whisky. Hugh *knew* that; why else was it called corpse reviver? But the Lord as distiller? This was a whole new angle on religion he hadn't considered before. Then she sang "Rock of Ages" and some prohibition song . . . *The drunkard shall not perish, in misery and pain* . . . her voice so pure that men were falling on their knees, praying and singing along and shouting out the abstinence pledge. After she left, everybody felt so virtuous and worthy that they jumped up, slapped the sawdust off their pant legs and hollered for another round.

But whose slack-witted notion was it, anyway, to send such a pretty young thing into that filthy place? The temperance hags, that's who. Too chickenshit to enter the tavern themselves, their long, pointy noses turned up in disgust. Temperance! Got nothing better to do than ruin a man's pleasure. Somebody ought to cork their yaps with a good thick fist. Man works his arse off all week, nothing wrong with a few drinks. Only . . . it was the thirty or so following the first few that Hugh wasn't feeling too confident about at the moment.

Take Avice. She's different, she *don't care.* Kill yourself with the stuff, it's all the same to her. *There she goes.* He shuddered. He could swear that woman had walked ten miles in this room already. You'd think it was the road to happiness.

If Hugh had had the physical means, he might have craned his neck, lifted his head just enough to watch her whip her hairpiece out of the wash bowl where she kept it and attach it onto her boy cut with a few deft, artful motions that often looked to Hugh like she was sticking pins right into her skull. He loved to dig into that bowl of hair himself. He loved the silky feel of it in his fingers, loved to rub his face with it and drink down its smoky fragrance, her hair that smelled like no other, like a field on fire. Never mind that the stuff made him sneeze. *Shit*, if he sneezed now, he'd blow himself apart.

Her tireless pacing disturbed the air, roiled it like a pool. It had been washing over him ceaselessly, the rhythmic torture of it so relentless that it took him a while to realize she was gone. What *relief*. Sleep—he dropped into it like a grave. Once there, not even his dream of being a log fed through the sawmill—his own snores ripping through his head—could wake him.

If Grif and Avice had taken to stalking one another down the same alleys and passageways, they might have actually met and resolved their marriage one way or another—inventively or disastrously. Although they were currently living within the same half-block, on the same street, in the same small town, Avice could not find him because she was lost in a labyrinth of revenge, and Grif had even less luck locating her, for she had become strangely elusive. Finding her was like trying to isolate a lick of wind for observation. And once the desire to throttle her, to take her neck in his hands and halt the pulsing life in it, had dissipated, he did want to observe her, in taxonomic detail, from claw to wing tip. He needed to sift through her to find what it was that held him. He understood that she had changed. She was fierce, wanton, remorseless, and possibly, unaccountably, more vulnerable than ever—but the change that interested him involved something far less obvious. It was almost as if they had consummated their marriage and thereby become inextricably mixed, trapped in each other's bodies. They were married just enough to be snagged, caught on one another by something broken and ragged—a nail or piece of bone, a vow pointed and sharp as a fish hook.

The allure of what she withheld, like an unacknowledged impregnation, disturbed him, and drew him.

If he was searching for something scarcely perceptible in her, and willing to construct her cell by cell around this mystery, she had her sights set, less fancifully, on the whole man, whom she would gladly break down into the smallest of pieces and scatter far and wide.

Grif had learned to be careful when entering his room after his chores at the hotel were finished for the day. He had learned not to propel himself with too much eagerness toward his longed-for bed. A man too avid for comfort might leave his head behind, suspended on the threshold where some- one had strung a thin wire; his head served up like a block of cheese, the only smile left the one topping his neck. He had learned not to use the water from the pitcher on his wash- stand without first dropping a roach in it to see if the creature dissolved like a tablet. He had discovered that in standing too close to the window, one not only got air, but aerated: his walls had acquired several bullet holes during his residence. And his bed was always more welcoming without the broken glass concealed in the covers; likewise the leghold trap. At times deliberation was required, and at other times its very opposite. When entering Turner's Dry Goods on an errand for Roland, he had the disconcerting experience of seeing the better part of his earlobe precede him, skewered on the tip of a stiletto, his own skin racing him to the counter.

His skin in fact was getting a real education—that being the only way it could save itself. It had developed a keen sen- sitivity to murderous intent in the immediate environment, and ever seemed to be yanking him, its contents, this way and that to safety, pulling him behind posts, making him sprawl on the floor. Grif found himself ducking and diving, jerking around like a puppet, but for the life of him he couldn't nail down her intent. Did she want to control him, make a fool of him, unnerve him, or simply drive him into the hands of the law? She had his journal and yet had not used it against him; she had his life in her hands and had not yet taken it. If she really wanted to do him in, surely she would have done it already, without the provocative foreplay. Or her thuggish friend would have.

Roland, like Jean and Ned before him, wanted to tell Grif stories (was there something about him, he wondered, that stimulated the anecdotal impulse?), and he was generous with his one bottle of whisky, although the boy was not a drinker himself. While they sat together that morning in the front room of the Sun, its lobby and bar, he told Grif about a woman who used to live in town, who for her entire life believed she was being followed by someone. The unsettling thing was that she could never catch sight of this person. If she turned quickly, she might almost see him. This invisible other always remained on the very edge of her vision, the merest fraction away from being seen.

"He?"

"She was certain it was a man. She could feel his breath on her neck. Could smell it even, and it was like water, she said. The smell of the lake."

"She was crazy, of course."

"She got there eventually. He drove her to it."

"And when she arrived, did he finally reveal himself to her?" Grif wasn't taking this too seriously.

"No. That's not what madness is like."

The story was a parable, Grif concluded, a coded warning. Although he wasn't sure if he was supposed to be the one on the periphery playing the part of the shadowy predator, the illusory stalker stepping out of bad dreams, or if he was the one being driven mad. Avice *was* following him, but every time he turned to catch her at it, all he saw of her was a glimpse of her black dress disappearing around a corner, or a faint heel print in the dust. She left very little evidence behind of her presence, his newly shy and retiring wife. She had withdrawn into unreality, and was luring him there, over the precarious edge of his sanity. Hugh, on the other hand, was all too visible. Grif had watched him reeling pie-eyed down the street. Hit by white lightning, drenched in panther piss. He saw him propped up against the Post Office, chewing his tongue, slack-jawed and stupefied, or leaning over the balcony of the Mansion House, staring down at him, puzzled. And pizzled. It disgusted Grif to think she could bear to let him touch her. Adultery with an ogre. He was nightmare material, fungus-faced, something that might surface in a bog. He was the dark slub in the gut of the alley, the town's malignant growth, its tumour completely cut and floating dangerously free.

Grif understood that Hugh was her rebuke to him in sub-human form, the agent of her dirty work and his would-be assassin. But assuming that she wanted him more unbalanced than dead, which seemed to be the case, he was not consoled. As far as he could tell, the guy was plastered about one hundred percent of the time, his aim not true. If she wanted to maintain the margin, however slim, between his living and his dead self, he did not see how Hugh, with the finesse of an enraged bull, was going to manage it. Grif had guessed (correctly) that she had not told Hugh anything much about him—or *them*; and that alone was what probably kept those bullets on a wider trajectory, or the knife from finding a slot in the very centre of his head. Whatever shreds of information she fed him, it must have been enough to keep him in the background, menacing but more or less satisfied, not hungry enough to come forward and make a meal of Grif. Not yet.

Poor maligned Hugh. Sure, he had performed a few services for Avice. She was a lady, and ladies expected that. She was not like his ma (fat sow) or those prune-faced old maids who were fighting to make this a dry town—dry as their shrivelled twats. He wasn't blind (blind drunk was a different matter). He saw how Avice had taken a disliking to that mollycoddle who was staying at the Sun. Hugh didn't much like the looks of him either. He wasn't respectable. His clothes didn't even fit. *He weren't no reverend, neither.* For Avice, Hugh would gladly rearrange those looks any way she liked. If she wanted the clown to dance, Hugh would make him dance, right into the ground if need be.

For the time being he had his own business to attend to. He was still trying to fight his way out of that sawmill dream. *Christ*, now he was a stack of planks! If he didn't wake up soon, that faceless figure in his dream, that man running the mill, in top hat and cape no less, was going to cart him away and build something out of him—a shithouse, his gaping mouth for the hole. Mind, he figured he could always drive a sliver up the guy's arse. Hugh wasn't without tactics, even in the most trying of circumstances. He was not as stupid as he looked, which in itself would have been an accomplishment.

Avice too might lately have dreamt herself into some architectural form (although nothing so humble as an outhouse), for she had been spending her days in the company of buildings, at times clinging to them like paint, while spying on Grif, tailing him or avoiding him. She had gotten to know this town intimately from its material substance, the quality and texture of its wood (how chinked and dovetailed), its brick and stone (the workmanship in its assembly, or lack of it), her hands sliding across cool surfaces like pond striders. In her strategy of concealment and pursuit, she had adhered so closely to the sides of stores, houses, hotels, that she often felt the life that pulsed through them—sounds and vibrations and heat routed through her. She drank in the fragrance of pitch and turpentine, whitewash and dust, while her face was pressed into cracks, her nose a blunt root, probing. Once, she almost inhaled a moth, its powdery wing clamped like a dun shade across her nostril. She had nicked her tongue, cut it on a shard of tin, and no wonder, for she had driven more than a few choice words deep as nails into these walls when from her hiding place she watched Grif neatly sidestep some carefully constructed trap. How she hated to see his unscathed back moving away from her. How she hoped it was only the fact that he was unharmed that pained her.

Anyone inside these buildings listening to her angry murmur might think the walls were infested with wasps.

This day, having left Hugh to sleep it off, she stationed herself across the street from The Dancing Sun, behind a stack of fish boxes that had been left out in front of the Customs House. The boxes, stacked six and seven high, formed a narrow wall with chinks to peer through. From this vantage she was able to see the hotel clearly without herself being seen, even though she felt more than a bit ridiculous, as if spying on a husband suspected of infidelity . . . but of a commonplace variety, not Grif's particular brand of faithlessness. Her surveillance, she found, had become necessary; she couldn't let it go. He was having a little dalliance with death and it was fascinating to watch. Five minutes and he'd step out of that door. He'd become so predictable. She couldn't understand why he came out at all, and so punctually, when he knew that his life was hers, and that she was not to be trusted with it. Unless he didn't take her seriously. Unless he knew something about her that she didn't know. If this was his thinking, she would have to differ, would have to apprise him of her true character; but she wanted him fully alive to appreciate it.

Alive, yes—and this is where Hugh presented a few problems. Though not at the moment. She had left him behind, so sodden that he was flammable; toss a match on him and he'd light up the room. Hugh was her obedient oaf, her big doggie, loyal but not entirely reliable, and not patient enough to fuss with the intricate machinery of her design. He did have a mind of his own, however meagrely provisioned. She liked him, to be quite honest, but she did not think that her faint feeling for him, genuine as it was, was going to do any of them any good.

Waiting, she caught her breath. The small street sounds around her stopped. Grif was going to appear. When he did, her heart would beat faster and harder. She was thrilling only to the chase, the game, and not to the man. Not that. Although he was . . . beautiful. Was she the only one who had ever seen that in him? Odd, that he never wore a hat anymore. A slovenly habit and one that left his head pathetically exposed, an obvious target. She pictured a bullet, shaped like the end of a woman's finger, skimming along his scalp, tracing a part right down the middle. In their former life together, their ex and non-existent one, she might have done that, raked her fingers through his black tangle of hair, not painlessly. Did he think she would have been a modest and reticent bride, their lives circumscribed by convention? At-homes, clinking cutlery, lustres and knick-knacks, the smell of lemon polish, the constant nickering of her sisters: the stale interior of marriage would not have defined what they made together. Theirs would have been something wholly uncontained and shockingly pleasurable—no words for it.

She grew very still. *There he was.* He had stepped outside the hotel and was glancing around, cautiously. Good. Then he looked over at the fish boxes. He was glaring, darkly. Surely he couldn't see her? She crouched further down, willed herself into a tight, unrecognizable form. He began to cross the street, walking straight towards her, as if she were plainly visible. She was appalled by his expression, determined and purposeful, as if he had something of consequence to say. As if he were carrying words in his mouth that could only be passed on directly, physically, pushed down her throat, like a bird feeding its young.

Avice made a dash for the alley between the Customs building and a warehouse, slipping away like water, and Grif followed. And followed.

# 23

## THE LADY PROTESTS

GRIF THOUGHT it was the moon, knuckled and white, bunched like a fist, that had flown down out of the sky and popped him one. He raised his hand slowly to touch his face, to explore with his fingertips this new terrain, swollen and cut, and so unfamiliar that it might easily have been stamped by the moon, or excavated by it. *Her* face had been washed in it, the moon's light. She had been bleached to a spectral shade, her features ghostly pale, when he had finally cornered her, caught her up against the wall of May's Livery Stable, after hours of hide-and-seek. Confound the woman. Escaping through windows, down stairs, through trap doors, she had managed to evade him like the immaterial and ungraspable moonlight itself. Like quicksilver. What was she made of? Gall for one thing, and bloody raw nerve. So many times it had been only the trailing sound of her voice he managed to catch—laughing at him.

He almost nabbed her up on Robinson, past the newspaper office, but then she eluded him by walking straight into a private home, right through the front door, without a hitch in her step or a second's hesitation. Grif expected her to be chucked out on her ear, but she stayed for hours. When he crept up to one of the windows to see if he could find out what in the devil she was up to, he saw her seated at a large table, dining with the residents of the house, an unexpected but not unwelcome guest. She was sipping a glass of wine and chatting spiritedly, spinning them quite the tale, he didn't doubt; earning her supper, the hearty meal spread out before her, while her husband starved in the forsythia bushes. Her audience certainly looked captivated, and likely hadn't enjoyed such entertainment since those roving minstrel boys performed in blackface at the dance hall. He settled in for a long wait. She had to emerge sometime. And did, but he never saw her. Snuck out the back way, he guessed, but for all he knew, she might have gone up the chimney and dispersed like smoke.

It was only by luck, and not necessarily good luck, that he caught up to her when he did. She had grown careless, or weary of the game, or she'd had too much to drink, for she had stopped to take a piss in front of the stables. She didn't even crouch but stood with legs astride like a soldier, skirts hoisted high, her strong, warm stream splashing into the dust. That's not how women usually went about it, surely?

"You sound like a horse," he said, stepping out of the shadows to confront her. "Or Niagara Falls."

"*No*," she said.

Just that? But *no* to what? To his sally, his unasked questions, or to him in general, to his whole existence? (Was she always going to deny her young husband?) Then again, she might not even have been speaking to him. The negative might have been meant for her moonling, her lumpish, hair-hearted pal, who had crept up behind. *No*, she said as he knocked Grif to the ground, and kicked him in the back, and then brought his huge fist, all rock and crater, down again and again, pounding Grif into the dark side of the night.

*No*, she had said. Defending him? He was touched. But much too hard.

As he shifted carefully, testing to find out which part of him screamed the loudest when he moved, the stale but comforting smell of the bedclothes rose around him. He could smell linseed too. He was swathed in bandages, around his chest and head, and on one hand. Roland had been trying to stick him back together with his salves and poultices, his healing compounds of raccoon lard, resin and beeswax. Bless him, but the boy had his work cut out for him. Grif was a pile of rubble. He tried to think back but couldn't even recall peeling himself off the ground. The last thing he remembered was sucking a mud pie through his teeth, a dessert (just?) that tasted mostly of his own blood and his wife's urine. He'd taken several servings, his face slammed into the stable's muck. She must have intervened finally, called off her hound and saved his skin for another day. Or Roland, concerned about his long absence from the hotel, might have gone searching for him and scared them off.

That Grif was not alone in the room was information that seeped into him slowly, like the arrival of the morning light through the windows. Gradually, he became aware of a faint scratching noise and the sound of paper being shuffled. The odd sniff. A muted humming. Roland, he thought, fondling the wallpaper again, the skin of his beloved building. He'd be waiting patiently for Grif to come round. They would have tea and their morning chat. *So, what happened to you last night?* Grif wasn't so sure he could chat. It would hurt his mouth too much, like picking shards of glass out of his lips.

He raised himself slightly to greet his friend and saviour, uncertain as to how many supportive, non-aching inches he had to rely on. He caught sight of a walking stick propped against the door frame. It had an ebony shaft and was topped with a large round silver knob.

"Lead-filled," a voice piped up. "A handy article, especially for fending off brutes in the night. I do hope your attacker wasn't representative of the local citizenry."

Grif squinted at this person, who was seated at the far end of the room in Norma's tiny chair (he still harboured hopes of her return), occupying it like a giant spider. He had a sheaf of papers in one hand and Grif's pen, the one Hattie had given him, in the other. The man was clean-shaven and wearing a white linen suit, but it was him all right, fresh from the land of scoundrels and smiling benignly at Grif.

"You," Grif croaked. Then all he could think to add was, "You mustn't write lies with that."

"Oh, never. Nothing but the truth." The man smiled even more broadly, while holding up the sheaf of papers in his hand. "Now, where were we? Ah yes, we were about to discuss some business, before you so gallantly escorted that pert young thing out onto the lake and drowned her. I did try to warn you, you know."

"Look—"

"Hmmn?"

"I don't want to hear your damned plan, Mr. Nashe. I don't want to talk business. I have enough troubles of my own. As you can see."

"Do you not want to get your wife back?"

"Get even, you mean?"

"No, you know that's not what I mean. Remember . . . the truth."

"Wait, let's get this straight. I *hate* that woman. She won't leave me alone; she's possessed. Worse, she's insane. Why would she follow me all the way here? She cuckolded me with that truncated halfwit, and God knows how many others. I tried to talk to her yesterday, reasonably, just to find out what she wants from me, to see if we could settle this once and for all, and she almost had me killed."

"A fascinating creature. No wonder you love her."

"I *do not*. And she despises me. She thinks I'm a worm."

"You are a worm. And she's the hook. And I have plans for both of you. Now, look, see what's happened: you've told so many lies already that your mouth is bleeding. So shut up, will you, and I'll tell you what we're going to do."

Moonstruck? *Nah*. Hugh himself was not thinking he had been cracked on the pate by a heavenly body, by some puckish, low-flying celestial object. He was acquainted with all the more earthy vehicles available to your amateur bludgeoner—rocks, hammers, wooden legs, pokers, two-by-fours—and he sensed that it was possibly one of these more humble and ready-to-hand objects that had laid him out cold by the livery stable and neatly rearranged the physiognomy of his skull. The topography of his noggin already a phrenologist's dream, Hugh now sported a goose egg on the anterior of his head that matched a dark, incubating lump of brooding matter on the interior.

He awoke, dew-jacketed and shivering, and lay for some time blinking himself into consciousness and staring up at the crimson-tinged sky. A crow drifted by, wings creaking, and wearing a bonnet. *Christ almighty*, he thought, *that's not good*. He endeavoured to gather his shattered recollections of the day before. Yeah, he had been worried about Avice. At least, he figured the sentiment was worry and not some further stomach-twisting torment compliments of his hangover. That's why he went out, to look for her. She'd been gone all day, as far as he was able to tell, and most of the night. But then what does she do when he finds her cornered by that cringing milksop? She says, *No*. Was she trying to protect the baby, the lily-livered funker, or was she trying to protect him, Hugh, trying to warn him about the guy's partner sneaking up from behind with a brick? Or a bottle, yeah.

That crack on the old coconut had done wonders for his hangover, anyway. Although it might have dislodged something else, for Hugh was feeling more than a little peaky. His various mongrel notions and philosophies did not seem to have the same toothsome grip on his brain as before. As he heaved himself up, he could hear a *tinkling crashing* sound, like broken glass, a whole chandelier sliding to the floor, that seemed to be coming from within his head. He staggered around and gave himself a few smacks for good measure.

He got to wondering what had happened to Avice. It didn't occur to him that she might have stayed to help him out, that she owed him at least that much. She could have fetched the doctor, or some drinking buddy to drag him back to the Mansion House. But that would have been spoiling him. He didn't expect that. Although he did expect something for his gallantry. Stumbling back onto the street, he decided to skip work and go see if he could find it, what he'd earned and deserved. He might even shake it right out of her, like a coin out of a bank, if she had it in her.

*No*, Avice had said. Then *no* to herself and for herself. It was her prayer of negatives, her worry beads, each bead a tough knob of denial sent against him, to ward him off. That face, lit by a slash of moonlight, had chilled her and woken her out of a long dream. When he raised his walking stick and felled poor Hugh, she slipped away with a practised alacrity. She edged around to the back of the stables and fled. The sound it made—enough to split a skull in half, even one as hard as Hugh's. Was it possible he had survived it? She had no idea, and absolutely no intention of going back to find out. She retreated to her room, packed hastily and checked out of the hotel.

Grif, well, he had gotten what he deserved. *No*, she didn't really think that. She should have stopped Hugh. In her confusion and alarm she began to chastise herself for taking part in this whole madcap adventure. Her vendetta, absurd. Her audacity, gone. For the first time she felt genuinely unnerved, stricken, fright boring a hole right into her, a vortex into which all the perils of the world could swirl. The *sight* of him. Twice now—that was no coincidence. He is what sickness calls up. She was responsible, and knew it.

Early morning, not a soul in sight, she ran towards the docks as if pursued. Her jaw was rigid and her voice hoarse from straining through her teeth those small, hard—and useless—words: *no, no.*

Hugh's head was teetering. He was tipping it back and forth, up and down, like a dog puzzling over some canine conundrum that lay before him. It might look as if he were attending to his inner marbles on the roll, but what he was actually doing was reading—Hugh's version of reading, whereby he pinned a word to the page with his eye and then tried to gut it for meaning.

When he had burst into Avice's room at the Mansion House, expecting to see her served up on the bed like a hot meal, all white-skinned and steamy, he was taken aback to find her not there. The bed was cold, not slept in since he'd vacated it. Not only that, but all signs of her presence had been wiped out. No clothing, no bowl of hair, no goddamn slice of pie—his share. He felt like hurting someone, he was so disappointed.

He knew some rumination was required, the better to understand her absence. She might have been abducted by the same devil who had thumped him, although that wouldn't account for everything that was missing here. She was a bit finicky, so maybe she didn't want to sleep in the same bed he'd puked in. Hey, he could understand that, although he *had* wiped it up with his shirt, which he'd afterwards tossed in the corner. Or, *hah*, she might even be hiding under the bed. She liked games, that one. Hugh immediately got down on all fours and had a look. Nope, no sign of his slippery, devious gal under the bed. But he did see something else. That book. That journal of hers that he'd kicked under there the other day and forgotten about.

Imagine being jealous of a book, of paper and cowhide and squiggles of ink. You had to watch her reading it, though, as Hugh had done, his brow pleated in distress. She had been so absorbed in it, her lovely face lit with a delight that excluded him entirely. He had no access. He couldn't see how anyone could get what she seemed to get out of it; you'd think she was sucking the juice out of an orange. That sparkle in her eyes, the smile on her slightly parted lips—what she did with that thing was not wholesome, not right. A very strange and suspect activity.

He sat down on the bed with the book in his hands and began to flip through it. To his thick-fingered, though not insensitive, touch the paper felt like an old man's skin. When it came to the act of literary congress, Hugh was still a virgin, and so he didn't recognize anything unusual about the journal. He did notice that some of the ink wore a fresher face, and that not all of the inscrutable notations were consistent in form. If he had been able to read it, he more than anyone might have appreciated the author's line of work, and even lamented that such opportunities were no longer available for a coming lad such as himself.

His eyes lit upon such words as *superstitious* and *popish* and *apostles*, and wandered overtop of them, and underneath, and all around, with puzzlement and mounting frustration. If only he could split one open, he reasoned, and get at the meat of it, then the rest might come easier; he'd have a method. He decided to start with a short, simple word, and chose—*God*. He studied this word for some time, eyeballing it like a dissenting theologian. And then, because of his intense meditative focus, or the unaccustomed strain of intellectual effort, or simply on account of the recent crack on his head, which must have let in some light, Hugh experienced something very unusual. Something illuminating. He took it for reading, but it was more like a revelation. The word *God* suddenly opened up for him, and displayed itself to him in all its profundity and mystery. All the other words in the journal then followed— quite literally, for they seemed to rise right off the page and clamber over him. They filled his eyes and ears, buzzing, whispering, speaking all of their individual meanings to him. Admittedly, their message was scrambled and chaotic, but all he had to do was sort it out and put it together.

Ah, Hugh. This certainly wasn't the first time a book was misinterpreted and subsequently caused a great deal of trouble. If only Avice had been there, she could have prised the journal out of his hands, gently, as if he were only a child, with a child's hunger for secrets withheld. She could have said, more kindly than usual, *No, this is not for you. Let it go, you don't understand. Not at all. No.*

## 24

---

# 16 FPS

Fenwick Nashe ran his fingers appreciatively over the body of the machine. He was quite taken with the thing. Under sixteen pounds it weighed. Light as a feather compared with that two-hundred-pound brute, the kinetograph. It was of French origin and design—elegant, portable and all the rage overseas. Fenwick had acquired it from a fellow in Quebec. How acquired was of no account, although, recalling it, a flicker of amusement eddied across his lips. Camera. Projector. Film printer. You could even eat your breakfast on it if you wished, or store a box of Mr. Kellogg's healthful horse feed in it. A brilliant invention, a piece of furniture that had the power to seize and transform the world. It was nothing but a curiosity to most, a clever device, but Fenwick saw it as a machine capable of manufacturing dreams and money in about equal proportion, a lucrative counterfeiting indeed. He personally had witnessed the success of Andrew Holland's kinetoscope parlour in New York—and Holland a good Canadian boy, at that. Twenty-five cents he charged to enter one of his peep-show booths, where you turned a crank and watched a single film loop of some trained bears disporting themselves, or a dentist at work (horrors!), or Gentleman Jim

Corbett laying some sucker out flat in the boxing ring. People were entranced, couldn't get enough. And *this* (he patted his machine) was miles ahead in ingenuity, as Mr. Edison, dispenser of light *and* light-fingered—in the realm of ideas, anyway—was quick to realize.

Fenwick began to scrutinize the audience of townsfolk gathering in the hall for his show. He had no hand in the machine's invention, but he could see its potential clearly. As clearly as that mole—no, it was a *tick*, stuck like the head of a hatpin in that fat fellow's neck. The mayor, didn't Roland say? Well, even if these hayseeds didn't see it, an aperture to the future had opened and his sharp eye was positioned in exactly the right place to take it in.

Optical toys intrigued him. Magic lanterns, zoetropes, even those simple paper disks with strings attached that you twirled in your fingers until the pictures on the opposite sides merged—all entertainments that relied on illusion. What a deceiving organ the eye can be. What a trap for the desired. He was partial to early theories on the nature of vision, how light was said to shoot out of the eye and then return to it with captured images, and how, as a consequence, it was given to contamination by fantasy. The communal collusion involved in this day's experiment should prove to be very interesting. When he turned the handle of his *cinematographe*, exposing the reel of film to its light source at sixteen frames per second (well, no fewer than twelve; *he* wasn't a machine), his audience would see, projected on the screen, not what was really there—individual photographs printed on celluloid—but one single picture *come to life* before their wondering eyes. In this hall, which did resemble a church, now that he thought of it, with rows of seats like pews, he, priest of the new technology, was going to perform a miracle. What did visionaries experience, anyway, except their own private screenings, those diverting illusions to which we are all susceptible with the right equipment? St. John spoke of the mind's darkness confronted with the bright light of the Divine, and could not he, Fenwick Nashe, provide a similar—if secular—illumination? For a little fee?

He scanned the room. All appeared to be in order, everyone was in their assigned position and the seats were filling up nicely. There was bound to be a crowd. No one in this rustic thorp, this one-eyed town, was going to miss such an opportunity. Demonstrations had already occurred in Montreal, Toronto, Ottawa, and some here would have read about them in the *Globe* or the local papers, the *Gossip*, the *Expositor*. Fenwick had no great desire to be a cultural missionary, bringing his enchantments to the periphery of civilization, but he had a particular reason for stopping here, and at present she was seated in the front row, about as far away from him as it was possible to get. Her aversion not an obstacle in the least. He didn't need proximity for the kind of intimacy he was after.

Avice fidgeted in her chair and reached up to touch the back of her neck, as if to swish away an irritant, as if she were the one with a tick stuck in it. This was an uncharacteristically self-conscious motion, and a sign of her much larger discomfort. She knew he was staring at her. (Actually, she was garnering more than a few searing looks from a number of respectable ladies, who, fretting about the advisability of these democratic entertainments, were keeping her under close observation.) *Go hang*, she thought, still amazed that he had stopped her from leaving. How overwrought she'd been! It was hard to credit, for he was nothing but a stage ham, a two-bit huckster, which she realized the moment they sat down together in the lobby of the Sun to discuss his moving picture plans. Her initial fear of him had been ludicrous. She'd gotten a bit carried away, but before she could actually sail away on the *Northern Belle* (she hadn't liked the way the captain had regarded her, with such fascinated attention, as if she were a specimen of some sort), she came to her senses. He'd been all deference and courtesy. (No mention of that incident with the fly!) Some of his ideas weren't bad, either, and to these she had privately added a few of her own. Not that she trusted Fenwick one jot—the crook!—but she knew now that she could better him at his own game.

She glanced at the screen they had set up, a pair of sheets from The Dancing Sun sewn together and strung across a line. These would already have hosted more than a few performances in the line of duty, she smiled, although there weren't any telltale stains. How strange that what they were to see today would leave nothing behind, not a trace; that the images which were to appear, supposedly, would then evaporate off the sheets like apparitions. Her eye strayed over to Roland Avery, their sound effects man. A man, anyway, seemed to be concealed in his child's skin, he looked so replete.

Roland was standing on one side of the room, near the front, with a table before him that was piled with a range of objects: a sheet of tin, a bicycle horn, two coconut halves, a whistle, drumsticks, bottles filled with varying levels of water. Most of the aural accompaniment Fenwick had instructed him to provide was to issue out of Roland's own throat, but he'd gotten creatively involved in the project. For the moment he was silent and still, letting the *buzz* and *hum* of the gathering audience fill him with a helium of delight. Levitation was not out of the question. With his keen anticipation of this novel entertainment, and the part he was to play in it, along with the steady sound of coins raining into the cash box that Raewyn (the comely Miss Hays) was commandeering at the door, Roland's spirits had expanded to a gravity-defying degree. He fired a wink in Grif's direction, but his friend's attention had been diverted by a late arrival.

It had taken Hugh some time to scare up the price of admission, but finally he had managed to extract it from a tight-fisted, and currently broken-fingered, kid on the street. One last seat remained unoccupied at the back of the hall, and Hugh threw himself into it like a sack of dead cats, and smelling about as pleasant. There were a range of fragrances already in the air, most domestic and identifiable: cedar from the shavings in a wardrobe, vanilla daubed behind the ears, onions on someone's breath, woodsmoke clinging to fabric, horse liniment on the hands. Pleached together, this formed a kind of aromatic blanket that rested lightly over them all. Until Hugh arrived, that is, and brought with him an essence more troubling that infested the weave, a sweaty, sour, pukey, gaseous, rotting-under-the-porch smell. It was the smell of treachery, if that can be said to have an odour. A bad smell, in any event.

Grif, also seated at the back but on the opposite side, watched with irritation as Hugh settled, like a pile of dung, then redirected his attention back to Avice. If he leaned forward slightly, the woman in front of him, the one in the fancy-dress hat that resembled a camera, no longer obstructed his view, and he was able to observe the white slice of his wife's neck, which was visible above her collar, as well as the back of her own daringly unhatted head. Her hair had been carelessly dressed, scooped up into a tattered knot that was slightly askew, as if someone had given it a smart tug. He knew that the someone responsible was no longer Hugh, although he wasn't so sure about Fenwick, because Avice was now staying at the Sun, and receiving no callers, according to Roland. She had not spoken to Grif. That was fine, he didn't care—as long as he could be near her. That he needed to be near her, he had, to his dismay, recently discovered. An exasperating and cumbersome need it was, too, and not one that was going to improve his health—and he had the bruises to prove it. Indeed, she made him sick. The closer he got to her, the worse he felt. Was *that* love?

Grif wished that Fenwick would get on with it, start the show. He hadn't thought much of the actor's plans, once he'd finally gotten the true gist of them. Fenwick claimed that he could heal the wound in their marriage, the rift, with an application of celluloid. Art as a corrective, a retriever of what was lost. Not that what was lost had existed in the first place. Grif's job this evening was to observe the impact of Fenwick's demonstration on this gathering. He was to take a reading of the audience's response. Easy enough to predict: some would be tickled, some dazzled by the gimmickry, some dismissive. Like the fellow sitting beside him, sucking on the end of his moustache—*suck, suck, suck*. He had a critical and sceptical air. It was going to take more than a fancy new machine from France to impress him, whereas the man on Grif's other side was clutching a missal to his chest like a protective amulet, a prophylactic device to ward off the evils that Fenwick, the sorcerer in the red satin waistcoat, was about to unleash. Grif took a deep breath, and almost choked. Somebody had already unleashed an evil, and *by God*, did it stink.

Coiling, side-winding, it made its way to Avice, a particular pungency that could only be Hugh. Her back stiffened. Who would have guessed that he'd attend an event such as this, with most of the town's upper crust, thin as it was, present: Mayor Reilly (scratching his neck), the Turners, the Vincents, Ted Runnalls, the mill owners and their wives. Who would have thought that Hugh could *attend* to anything. The blow that Fenwick had so smartly delivered had driven him into an incommunicable distance. Not that communication was ever the point. Although she and Hugh had understood one another on a certain low level. But no more. When she spotted him for the first time after her hasty desertion, he showed no signs even of recognizing her. Drunk, she had thought, too far gone to speak. He was leaning up against a post in front of Howe's Ice Cream Parlour, staring into space and mumbling to himself.

"Hugh," she had said, then louder, repeating his name several times but getting no response.

He looked right through her, venting her with his new-found visionary power. He *was* drunk—but with inspiration.

She didn't know it, but he could read now *and* get the message, and the message came directly from the Lord. Almost, anyway, for it was refracted through that journal of hers.

Avice was pained by his absent expression and tried to extend to him a verbal lifeline, mouthing some womanly nonsense that he could not hear. Not a word of it. The Lord's words were sizable and took up most of the room in his head. Besides that, they were scrambled, in code, as one would expect in a communication so private and of such extreme importance. Why, this was intelligence from the highest source there was. Hugh had been chosen to be the Lord's translator, and he understood that it was his duty to spread the word. Once he figured out what it was, he had every intention of doing just that. He'd spread it like paste.

He'd finally cocked an eye at Avice and grinned. One thing the Lord had confided: He didn't much care for women (excepting His ma, of course, Mary, Holy Ma of God). Women had been disobedient right from the start. Troublemakers. Harlots.

Avice had turned and walked quickly away.

Not watching her step, she slipped on a greasy coil of fish guts that a fumbling and chagrined gull had dropped on the planks of the sidewalk. She slid, skated across the walk, arms windmilling, but caught her balance before breaking her own head open. She retreated hurriedly into the shelter of the Sun, mortified. Once in, she couldn't shake the sense of things gone awry generally, as if some unidentifiable force had given the whole town an unbalancing knock. Emotions that she had held in check since her wedding night were surging in her, uncontrolled. Good thing Grif wasn't around. Avice couldn't bear to look at him, his face still a mess from the beating Hugh had given him. She didn't completely trust herself anymore. Hugh might well have stolen a snippet of her own sanity when he had slipped irretrievably through that crack in his head. She didn't even trust her eyes anymore, for when she entered the dim bar of the hotel that day, she caught sight of a ghost in the mirror standing behind her, a young woman drained of life but not of its residual longing.

That was nothing. Fenwick Nashe had a whole cast of spirits preserved in flat tins who were about to dance and cavort at his bidding. The time had come to release them.

He kept his introductory remarks brief . . . *Ladies and gentlemen, what you are about to witness today . . . quack, quack . . .* Just long enough to ratchet up the excitement, but not so wearyingly long that in their excitement they started hurling rotten tomatoes at him. He was a seasoned showman, after all.

At a nod from him, Roland drew the window shades against the waning afternoon light, and Ritchie's Music Hall, venue for travelling vaudeville shows, local theatricals, dramatic monologues and musical evenings, was erased in darkness, the memories of these former diversions instantly forgotten. Everyone sat hushed, curiosity primed, listening to Fenwick in the back as he fiddled with his contraption, clicking something, cranking something, until suddenly a strange flicker of light passed through the screen up ahead, and then a living being appeared there before them. An apparition. Someone in the audience gasped loudly. There were exclamations of surprise as the figure continued to move. It hopped around. It was a demon *God preserve us* with a pointed goatee stuck on his chin, a receding hairline, a dashing cape, tight breeches. Disturbed murmurs snaked through the crowd, then a soft, helpless cry. The prancing figure had pulled off its own head and tossed it into the air. The body continued to caper around without it, while the detached head, hanging like a planet above, leered and chattered wordlessly. Finally, the hideous thing sailed down and the demon reattached it to his neck with the ease of one securing a hat, then vanished in a sudden puff of smoke. (How Fenwick envied the beauty of that trick. Such a clean getaway was virtually impossible, unless you really were a devil.)

Darkness reclaimed the room, as did a total, stunned silence. Even Roland was speechless, his own excited breathing the only sound effect he had produced. It had been a bizarre, thrilling and completely mesmerizing spectacle. Most present had seen amazing things before; the world was full of them, ever since Mr. Edison had flicked on his electric lights and chased all the spooks and shadows out of the corners. But such things, though incredible—Constable Wilkin's talking watch (press a spring and it told you the time of day), the giant Edward Beaupré, who was over eight feet tall and wore size twenty-four shoes, the woman in town whose own hands were given to attacking or fondling her—amazed less, and were less disquieting, than this.

Fenwick had wanted to begin his program with a real stunner, a knockout, and was most pleased with the result. He *had* them, he could tell. There was a definite change in the atmosphere of the hall, a heightened readiness and desire. They wanted more. In the darkened room, tremulous as a herd of cornered deer, their eyes were opened wide, ready for these images to drift in and settle to the bottom of their souls like a layer of fine silver silt.

Fenwick was only too happy to comply. He did not like to disappoint. He set up the next reel, and the next, some of the living pictures lasting under a minute, others as long as five or six. His audience was voracious, and as the show proceeded, they began to enjoy themselves even more. They clapped until their hands were as red as their flushed faces. They began adding commentary to augment the sounds that Roland had begun inventively supplying.

"Very refreshing," quipped the moustache-sucking man beside Grif as they watched a small ship sailing on a rough sea. Roland whistled like the wind.

The next film was of horses galloping (coconuts), followed by workers leaving a factory (footsteps) and then a man feeding a baby (coos, gurgles). This last subject, a marvel in itself to many of the mothers in the audience, caused more than a few thoughtful and appraising glances at mates seated open-mouthed beside them.

A window had been conjured through which the towns-folk could see far beyond their own limited horizons, into distant lands, or into the intimate moments of other people's lives—even if they *were* foreigners and had more of them. Fenwick only wished that he had on hand the first picture to be publicly shown, the one that had caused an excitable Paris audience to flee into the streets. It showed a train arriving at a station, and to such realistic effect, barrelling head-on, seemingly right through the wall, that some believed they were going to be crushed by it and fled. He suspected that his Anglo audience would only grip their seats tighter while waiting stoically for the locomotive to thunder over them, not yet accustomed to the whimsy of iron melting into the air but too proud to clear out of the way.

Instead, to relax their grip, he showed them one called *The Sprinkler Sprinkled*, a simple piece of nonsense in which a gardener is seen watering a lawn with a hose that stops working when a young boy happens by and steps on it. The gardener can't figure out the problem and, staring into the nozzle just as the boy steps off the hose, gets a blast of water in the face. He jumps up and down shaking his fist, and the boy runs away. *Fin.* And how they laughed at this, holding their sides, wiping tears from their eyes. Very agreeable it was to draw this out of them, to be the master of all this lighthearted merriment; master and manipulator, for he was the one who controlled the tempo of the pictures by cranking the projector faster or slower. He had a true feel for the action, he thought, his long, fine fingers on the pulse of these animations, thereby also controlling the tension and emotion in the hall. In a way he was as much a creator of these innovations as the original artists.

Admittedly, Fenwick couldn't control everything, for he was not the one who caused Mrs. Fertuck to screech in alarm during the screening of *The Laboratory of M.*, the evening's finale. Nor was the star and director, Georges Méliès, the guilty one, with his brilliant deviltry, his dazzling editorial hijinks and sleight of hand. No, what made Mrs. Fertuck scream was the man sitting behind her, who, under the cover of darkness, performed his own act of prestidigitation by running his hands lightly, but feelingly, over her rear, cupping the abundance of what her chair could not quite contain. He had always admired a woman who had no need of a bustle, and in Mrs. Fertuck's case he was just checking. *Pure magic*, he thought, while on screen M. Méliès performed it.

"Very clever," confided one of the audience members to his wife when the show was over and they were all drifting out of the overheated hall into the fresh evening air. "I'm afraid it will never catch on, though, my dear. After people see this sort of gimmick once or twice, they will tire of it. Mark my words."

Fenwick marked them, and congratulated himself. One look into the eyes of those who passed him on the way out, eyes slightly blurred and dreamy, blinking awake, bringing everyone back to the real world—of drudgery, hardship, boredom, cruel husbands, neglectful wives—and he knew they would return for more. And more. Why would they not? He had what they desired above all else: access to the impossible.

"Can you imagine!" he overheard another, more astute gentleman say. "You photograph your loved ones with this device and you will always have them, alive, before you. Don't you see? Death will be cheated, no longer absolute."

Fenwick turned to his helpers, to Roland, Raewyn, Avice, Grif, his fledgling company—for every person has their price and is eventually persuadable—and was delighted to observe the same healthy and greedy burnish on their faces. Even the young girl was too het up to make her usual prohibitive noises about inebriating pleasures. One audience member had left early, he noted, a familiar form, hulking and shadowy, that had slipped by him, but not before casting an ogreish silhouette on the screen. That was to be expected, naturally. Not everyone was going to be quite so smitten. Dissent, after all, was never without its uses.

True, Hugh had been completely unimpressed with the show. He couldn't figure out what the big deal was, when an incredible book had already come to life in his hands, and through it he had witnessed wonders far greater than those seen this night. Daily life was already like a silent film for Hugh, composed of jerky, juddering scenes, disconnected and meaningless, sunk into a backdrop of darkness. He knew mystery, was submerged in it up to his hair ends, and what he had seen here in this airless room *wasn't* it.

Fenwick inhaled deeply in preparation for a little victory speech he was about to make, to prepare his friends for the next stage of their venture. But then his nostrils began to quiver and pinch, his features registered an offence, and he said, "Good Lord, what is that *smell?*"

# 25

## TAKE ONE ...
## AND TAKE THAT

THE PEN was dead. In the beginning was the word, but in the end was only the image. Or so Fenwick Nashe mused as he added a few more details to his loosely conceived script, then tossed Grif's silver pen onto the bar. He had no doubt that books would soon be obsolete, at least for the majority of people. Not unlike the Middle Ages, when the illiterate derived their spiritual news and views from the stained glass windows in their churches. Quite possibly some of those pictures had moved too, in those credulous and olden eyes.

"Mr. Nashe?"

"Yes, Miss Hays."

"How's this?" Rae held up her arms and spun around, the better to display her costume to its full effect. She wore a short, glittery shift over orange tights, golden ballet slippers and a tiara onto which Roland had grafted several spiky rays of copper wire.

"Splendid, my dear. Absolutely marvellous."

No lie, that. He did marvel as the young thing performed a backflip, and then another, until she had arrived at the window where Avice was standing, looking virginal and even credibly innocent in the lace curtain wedding gown that Roland had also made. The little girl had brains and would prosper, Fenwick predicted, but she did not have what Avice had. Few people did. He had recognized it the moment he discovered her in Collingwood, and that by sheer luck, by the accidental attraction she had created in flashing her husband's name so liberally around. Very surprised he'd been to see that Mr. T. Griffith Smolders was signed into his hotel. Her drowned husband, Fenwick had thought then, and did still, although Grif was beginning to revive. *Blinking causes us to lose twenty-three minutes of every waking day,* Fenwick had informed him, implying that Grif might have missed a fair bit during those swift, dark intervals in his troubled day.

She was exquisite, standing by the window, light falling around her, moulding her form, playing up her arms, exposing her neck, haloing her hair (of all things). She belonged to the light, and had spread into it, staking out territory of her own that extended far beyond this interior, or any. Captured on celluloid, then released nightly, he knew she'd radiate this provoking quality, this flame she kept alive in her that shone from her face, this achieved liberty. Luminescent, he thought, she'll make moths of us all.

The glory of it was that he had not forced her to stay. She had done so because she thought she could outwit him, silly woman. She had something up her little lace sleeve, oh yes. He could read her thoughts easily, for they were written in the same language as his own. She thought that she could protect herself from him and keep what was hers, when what was hers belonged to all men. Today and in the nights to follow, she would wed every one of them. Providing, of course, that her many intended had the price of admission.

As he had explained to Raewyn, one of the WCTU's star White Ribboners, this too was a mission; they were providing a service, moral and remunerative. Surely no man would return home after a night at the moving pictures and beat his wife senseless. Or would he, Fenwick wondered, once that man saw Avice up there on the screen in all her haunting and inaccessible beauty?

"Rae," said Avice, "you look more like a Christmas decoration than a bridesmaid."

"I'm not a bridesmaid," answered Rae, hopping in and out of the light.

"No?"

"I'm ball lightning."

"Really? What kind of wedding is this supposed to be?"

"A comic one, I think. With all kinds of funny things happening."

"I see. And here I thought it was going to be a tragedy." She touched her chest lightly, where a weapon was concealed, although it might only be venomous, retributive language coiled tightly there. "Where is the groom, have you seen him?"

"Nope. *I'm* never getting married."

"Good for you."

Fenwick slipped his fingers into his waistcoat pocket and retrieved his watch. He enjoyed the sensation of holding it, for it was like a smooth stone that he could skip over the calm temporal surface of the day, but he did not care for what it had to tell him. *Late.* A flicker of annoyance creased his brow. Surely, he thought, our young man hasn't himself skipped. How many times can you run out on the same woman, *this* woman in particular? Grif had no respect for his own skin. Five minutes and he'd have to send the hounds out after him.

Fenwick sighed, slid the watch back into his pocket, and walked over to where Roland had set up the machine and readied it for its alternate role as a camera. A bit of an experiment still. While Fenwick had been pondering the aesthetics of light, Roland had been grappling with the technicalities of it.

"All set, Master Avery?"

"I guess so. I've arranged these lamps here, which should help. We really should be doing this in a brighter place."

"A glass hive?"

"Yes, actually. Some place like a greenhouse. Or outside."

"Too many bugs." Also too many props borrowed from the churches in town. "Do you think it will work?"

"It's worth a try. I've figured out that optical trick, by the way. You know, how to introduce the ball lightning."

"Yes?"

"It's just a question of stopping the camera. You have Grif freeze in position, bring Rae in, get her to do a cartwheel or a jump, and start the camera again when she is in the middle of it. The previous picture will flow right into it, but suddenly there she'll be, as if she'd appeared out of thin air."

"I see, yes. That's certainly quick on the trigger. How on earth did you figure it out?"

"Don't know, it just hit me. I've been studying those French pictures, the zany ones, slowing them down, speeding them up. The one where the bald man sprouts hair on his head after drinking the tonic."

"And on his hands! Hilarious. What about the one where the man pulls a whole room of furnishings out of a trunk and tosses them into place?"

"Including his wife and his dinner." Roland laughed.

"You know, some of those stunts come right off the stage—like those boots that hop all on their own—but the thing is that the wires aren't at all visible in the pictures made by this Méliès fellow. What I don't understand, Master Avery, is why anyone would bother photographing workers leaving a factory, and all the usual humdrum human activities, when like him they could be creating these magnificent illusions instead."

"Like real magic."

"As if the supernatural was actually being documented. I wonder what the Church will make of it."

"They won't like it."

"I expect you're right. Ah, look, the groom has arrived. Another miracle manifests itself."

While nurturing his reservations about this hare-brained venture, Grif *had* been more than a little tempted to take to his heels once again. What made him late, though, was not flight but the need to cool those agitated heels of his while waiting at the undertakers for his monkey suit, the morning coat and trousers that he was renting from them. The original owner of the garments had been buried without them, chattels left behind to defray the cost of his wooden suit. The cursed things smelled of death, and there was even a bullet hole in the chest of the coat. Grif fingered it nervously as he entered the Sun's barroom, where once again, if only fictionally, he was to enter the matrimonial state. His real wife was to become his fantasy wife, which would make him married to her both inside and outside of reality. Was that tying the knot tighter or loosening it so they both might escape? Fenwick had told him that this business, this animated photography, represented a whole new kind of freedom: freedom within the pictures themselves, where the laws of nature did not necessarily have to be obeyed, and without, for those who made the pictures. Grif didn't believe it, but their play-acting did give him one more chance with Avice. He'd be in the neighbourhood of her flaring attention, if nothing else. His heart, he felt, was worn so heavily on his sleeve it was a wonder he could lift his arm ... while in his chest he carried delicately a cluster of flammable materials, straw and husks and twigs. Tinder.

How Fenwick had talked her into it was another question entirely. Grif could only think that the man, although supremely confident, was much mistaken—he did not know Avice at all.

Grif scanned the room, which had been turned more or less convincingly into a chapel. The props were an ecclesiastical hodgepodge, but that was no surprise as he had swiped most of them himself: an altar cloth, a bible, a lectern, a chalice (couldn't resist), a vase of tiger lilies (Protestant), a statue of the Sacred Heart—and look, He too was exposing that most vulnerable and tender organ. The only wedding guest present in this hybrid church was Norma, the nut-faced doll, slumped in a pew that he and Roland had lifted from Holy Trinity. If Norma was playing the part of Avice's sisters, he felt she was a perfect choice for the role, being only slightly less sour in aspect than the originals. As he understood it, the story they were to enact would mend the flaws of the first wedding, the gash he had made in it and through which he had fled. In Fenwick's rewritten and improved version, Grif was to have second thoughts soon after his precipitous flight, which would return him on a wave of remorse to his abandoned and bereft (and fully clothed) bride, that saintly and forgiving woman, radiant with forbearance and self-denial.

*And there she was*, standing by the window, a model of Christian and maidenly virtues, who might just wring his neck at any moment without the slightest compunction.

"Ball lightning?" he heard her mutter to herself.

Fenwick took a breath deep as a drink, clapped his hands once, sharply, and exhaled a command. "Cast, take your places, please. Master Avery, the camera. We are about to begin. We are about"—significant pause—"to make history."

As the officiating cleric Fenwick himself stepped up to the altar, and from the pocket of Reverend Bee's freshly spruced-up jacket (he had given it a good dunking in the lake) he drew the holy book from which he intended to pluck the matrimonial vows like tiny wire snares out of a box. It didn't matter what he actually *said*, unless the audience for his picture were all going to be lip-readers—the last rites would do, or the service for the dead—but he knew that a degree of authenticity would solicit a better performance. Even the right missal was important, and he had searched high and low for this one. Fortunately, he had searched low enough, directly in the gutter, and had discovered it in the filthy paws of that drunk he'd tapped on the skull not so long ago. A religious fanatic the creature was, too, blubbering away about the wages of sin, a currency that Fenwick did not trade in, if he could help it. He felt truly sorry for the lout, and by rights should have whacked him on the bean again—a mercy that might have knocked some sense into him.

He gestured for the reluctant couple to come and stand before him, which they did—reluctantly—and then he gave the go-ahead, a quick nod, to Roland.

Grif stole a glance at the bride. She seemed so strangely calm, settled in herself, her anger in abeyance, that he was confused. She returned his look, not indignantly or fiercely, but with an openness that was entirely new, her expression gentle, her usually tenebrous and unreadable eyes fond. Fond? Adoring, even. Blood rushed to his face.

"I'm only *acting*, stupid," she growled.

"Oh," he said, "right."

"What *is* this?" said Fenwick, who had opened the journal at the Cormany forgery. "My *my*." He flipped to an earlier section of the book, to its very entrails, and dug in. "But . . . how *interesting*," he murmured, unexpectedly caught like a fly in the web of the text.

Grif and Avice stared at one another. They had not been this close physically since the day of their marriage.

Roland was humming Mendelssohn's "Wedding March" as he cranked the camera.

Raewyn was idling, fidgeting, waiting for her cue to enter the scene.

Avice reached out a hand to Grif, an offering, it seemed, a peaceable enough gesture, a bridge to span the hurting distance between them. Cautiously, he extended his own hand to her . . . he could hardly credit this. She ignored his hand, however, brushing it aside, and placed hers flat on his chest. He felt the warmth of it sliding into him. She might brand him with her very touch. She started to move her hand over his chest, assuringly, feelingly, as if she had found a way to return him to himself, to fill him up with all he had lost during his long, fruitless journey. Then, deftly, with practised fingers, she unbuttoned his shirt, his collar. She reached up with both hands and, more roughly, yanked his coat off his shoulders. She unsnapped his suspenders and his pants slid to his ankles. She dug into the bodice of her dress and pulled out a small scaling knife. She studied his body, coolly, for a few seconds, then a bit more energetically began to saw the buttons off his long johns. Buttons zinged this way and that like loose teeth flying out of a smashed mouth. This done, she reached down into the opened gap in his underwear, slid her hand right in, and with it cradled his clenching privates. None too gently, either.

Grif thought she was going to gut him like a fish, and he wore the expression of one, freshly caught and pulled from the lake, shocked and gasping.

To her the act was certainly more surgical than erotic. There was a blackened and tumorous bond still joining them that had to be severed. She'd cut him loose, free him for good. Not that she was enjoying the prospect, or any of this. His mortification had not trumped and cancelled hers, as she had expected, only oddly compounded it. And odder still, he was hardening in her grip, the astonishing sight of which had at least cured Raewyn of her fidgets. The young girl stood transfixed in her fiery costume, chewing her lip, eyes wide, watching them. Roland kept cranking the camera, although he had stopped humming.

Fenwick glanced up from the journal, gave a little snort of surprise and barked, "Cut."

"*No*," said Grif, but he was speaking to the wavering air above Avice's head, the turbid space just beyond her shoulder, where he thought he saw something—or someone—move.

Raewyn screamed. A grinning goblin's face was pressed up against the window, peering in at them.

Grif lurched out of Avice's grasp and shouted, "Roland, stop. The hotel, it's on fire!"

"Why," Fenwick sniffed, "so it is." He snapped the journal shut.

*Huh*, thought Hugh, he'd washed his face that morning, and combed his hair (with his fingers)—he didn't look that bad. Here he figured Raewyn for a sweet kid, too, a kind-hearted girl, but they were all alike, females, all whores. If she was going to scream about something, she should scream about that sap with his mug hanging out as far as his cullions. *Shit*, Hugh had seen more impressive balls on a poodle. Avice preferred him, did she? A very bad woman, he understood that now. She couldn't even wait to get this guy alone in the hotel room.

So he gave the kid a fright, eh? What about that gal standing right behind Avice? Now she was scary, if a tad indistinct, wringing her hands like that, rubbing them together like sticks until they caught on fire. She might be a circus act, or a witch, the way she was waving her burning hands around like torches. And even though she was soaked to the skin, hair plastered to her head, it didn't do her a speck of good. When she buried her face in those hands, it caught on fire too. Her face, her hair, her clothes. Body in flames, yep, she was a hot one, headed straight for hell like the rest of them. That's why he had locked all the doors behind him after he'd decorated the hotel with the kerosene-soaked rags, which had been easy enough, them all so busy. That's why he had a shotgun, in case any of them tried to break through the window. There was a lesson here he was trying to convey: a sinner cannot escape hell. Hugh wasn't so addle-brained, or so struck with the Lord's dazzling regard, that he couldn't himself see clearly what was going on in there. It was diabolical. Mock-church, mock-priest, mock-sacrament. And to top it off, that vaudeville clown had stolen his book, wrenched it right out of his hand when Hugh was feeling indisposed, having a little snooze alongside the horse trough. *Thou shalt not steal, eh?* A straightforward enough commandment, to which Hugh felt bold enough to tack on an additional clause: *and thou shalt not spit (arseface) on the poor drunken wretch thou're stealing from, neither.*

*YOU, C'MERE,* he heard the Lord say, and expecting to receive confirmation of his editorial amendment, or congratulations on his current initiative, he stepped out into the street at the very same and unfortunate moment that one of the water barrels, which Roland had installed in case of fire, came loose, rapidly gained momentum, and began its rumbling, bouncing trajectory down the slope of the roof.

# 26

## VULCANIC LOVE

FIRE, a delinquent guest, more consuming than consummate, loved the little hotel. It toured all the rooms, ran up the walls, blistered the paper, jumped on the beds, cracked the mirrors with one scorching look. It was as wild and torrid as a visiting stage celebrity. It had the melting gaze of a Barrymore, the sultry mien of a Bernhardt. And the temper. It was a sizzling hothead, a hotshot, too hot to hold. Fierce, rampageous, incandescent, it tossed its flaming orange hair and snapped its white-hot fingers. It smoked everywhere. It belched, its manner explosive. It autographed the register, then devoured it, along with rugs, chairs, shoes, a doll (alas!), and a peculiar machine festooned with cranks and reels. Inflamed, it shattered the one bottle of whisky, collapsed the bar, folded the stairs like an accordion, went through the roof, blew out the windows, tossed blazing timbers like swirling cabers down into the street. It drank gallons of lake water supplied by the sweating, scurrying locals. The rest of the town it found simply too banal to kindle even a spark of interest, and it finally checked out with a long, satiated *hissss*, leaving behind quite the mess, a charred and gutted ruin, proof that a real ball was had.

The antic spirit that enlivens the films of Georges Méliès, the pandemonium let loose in his Montreuil Studios in Paris, was an artful anarchy, precisely choreographed and controlled. Even the imp of unpredictability, the afflatus that breathes life into so much art, danced to his tune. Fenwick Nashe had not anticipated the arrival of that imp on his own set, or the disruption that ensued, but he made the best of it, as he always did. The visitation was, in fact, serendipitous.

When Grif, *déshabillé* in mind as much as in dress, spotted the smoking, sputtering approach of trouble, the uninvited extra and show-stealer, Fenwick was himself suddenly possessed of an inspired notion. His unerring instinct for talent had been doubly confirmed in his choice of Avice as leading lady, for not only could the woman act, but she had with her own ungloved and cold, unsentimental hand found the perfect instrument of revenge. When the saucy thing seized her man (what divesting work, what rude improvisational rooting!), she had also opened Fenwick's eyes, sealed and innocent as a newborn's, to the further potential of this marvellous invention. Surely it was not an idle mistake that *photography* and *pornography* were such close etymological cousins, promiscuously entwined if not exactly married in meaning. Give a man a new technology, Fenwick thought cheerfully, conceived with whatever noble, uplifting intention, and that man will instantly use it to plumb the depths of human depravity. It was only human nature. Imagine making moving pictures in which the portrayal of sin was limited only by the imagination itself. Despite the growing heat in the room, the clamour, the cries of dismay, the director of the fracas shivered with delight.

The only matter that gave him pause and caused him to hesitate very briefly was the book still held in his hand. He was tempted to stoke the fire with it, to use this record of Puritan commerce and zeal to fuel the coming conflagration. How fitting it would be . . . but then he recalled an archbishop he knew down in London, an old crony of his, who went in for antiquarian collectibles such as this one. A potential investor in his newest venture, as well. Fenwick slid the journal into his pocket and strode over to the *cinematographe*. Raewyn, confused and frightened, bolted in front of him, and he grabbed her roughly by the arm and hurled her aside. *Self-righteous chit.* As Roland surged forwards to help her, Fenwick cracked him in the face with his elbow and the boy whirled into the side of the machine, driving one of the cranks hard into his eye. Grif and Avice were involved in some sort of tussle. *Good.* Smoke was pouring through the entranceway and Fenwick saw his chance to stage a clean exit by way of it. He grabbed the footage from the day's shoot and snapped it in a tin, trapping his stars forever: Grif and Avice, wedded in miniature, caught on strips of celluloid like two wriggling insects stuck on a coil of flypaper.

"I'll save you," Grif gallantly shouted to Avice.

Unfortunately, his intended heroics were compromised by the trousers wrapped around his ankles. He stumbled, reaching out to her as she turned away from him, and just managed, with all the finesse of a caveman, to grab her by the hair. He sank his yearning fingers into the untidy, upswept knot of it, and then, to his horror, pulled a great hank of it right off. His embrace was too inept, his touch so clumsily destructive, it seemed he couldn't help but pull her apart. He clutched the soft dark mound in his hand as she tossed him a quick withering look over her shoulder.

"*Christ,*" she said, lifting the skirt of her dress to cover her face, a protective veil, as she made a dash for the front door. Then, "Shit," she said, rattling the hot handle, pounding on the door with her fist. "Damn, damn, *fuck.*" Her language sorely reduced in the mounting heat of the room, everything but profanity boiled away. She reeled around the bar, desperate as a trapped bird. She could feel her life spinning out of the ends of her fingers, uncontrollably. Her bobbed hair stuck out like nerves. She spotted another doorway.

"No," Grif called after her, stuffing his pockets with his claim of her slithery, drifting self. "Not that way." He might have forfeited intimacy with his wife, but he knew this hotel, and she was heading not out of danger but for the coffin-sized closet where Roland kept his cash box and his accounts. She didn't heed him, or refused to out of habit. Flinging the door open, she ran in. He hitched up his pants and followed on her heels, luckless as a trailing shadow.

"Get away," she spat at him, "don't touch me."

He had to. There wasn't much choice. They had stumbled into the secluded and suffocating interior of a fire trap, a private prison within a prison. There was no escape, for the door had slammed shut behind them, and they heard a rat-like scratching and scraping noise as someone outside turned the key in the lock. Before pocketing the key, Fenwick allowed himself one last brief, but pregnant, dramatic pause in which he reflected upon the tidiness of this little scene. Death would marry them finally. It would resolve all their problems, and reunite the impossible warring—and wearying—couple. This consummation was to be their ultimate freedom, and they would even enjoy an afterlife of sorts in his picture. (And, conveniently, not be around to lodge a complaint or demand their share of the profits.) Truly, this was a fairy-tale ending for Punch and Judy. Fenwick liked fairy tales—they were so disturbing, and gory. Not that he wanted one for himself. What he wanted, and would get, was *life*, a deep, inebriating draft of it, deep as the lake he was shortly going to cruise over on his way to, where, New York . . . or California? *Yee-haw!* That was the wonderful thing about life: it was not a rigged fantasy, not a dreary melodrama, and in it a villain with talent had a sporting chance. Who said life wasn't fair? He'd get away with this. Already he could hear the rising tide of voices outside, the honest townsfolk come to the rescue, his anyway, as he was soon to slip like a breath of fresh air through the window they were so helpfully smashing open, the very threshold to his new, lavish existence. Once he was through, no one would ever see him again.

Except, perhaps, at the movies.

No one heard them banging on the walls, the door, shouting themselves out of breath and hope. The hotel had been abandoned to its unruly guest, and outside the whole town was gathered and working furiously to evict it, with water drawn from the lake and from horse troughs, with pails of beer from the Mansion House, and even with a few tears. It's not that they thought so highly of Roland's oddball establishment, but they were fighting to contain the disaster, to keep it out of their own homes and businesses.

An elderly man took a moment to crouch over Hugh's prone body, reaching to take his pulse, then raising himself back up with a hurried sign of the cross.

"First one here to help," another man said. "Never figured him for a good Samaritan. Poor sap."

"That barrel sure made a hash of his face."

"Nah, doesn't look much different, you shoulda seen 'im before. You want his gun?"

"Might as well take it, eh? Won't need it where he's gone." Wherever Hugh had gone, and whatever the nature of the reward he was about to collect from his heavenly benefactor, Avice, stubbornly digging her heels into this earthly plane, had no intention of following her makeshift partner, or of lining up behind him.

"Can't you break the door down?" she growled at Grif out of the close, dark and increasingly airless space their marriage had become.

"Too heavy. Roland fixed a good solid one here." Grif bruised his shoulder trying to budge it but had to concede defeat—yet another manly act the groom had failed to perform. He stooped down and with shaking hands caulked the cracks in the door with her hair. He could at least try to keep out the smoke, try to prolong their lives for a few breaths more, now that for the first time what precious air trickled into his lungs came directly from hers. He was willing to think of it as congress, even if she regarded it as one more indignity.

Crouching, penitent, he had to resist the urge to wrap his arms around her legs, to bury his face in her skirt. He knew he should beg her forgiveness, and that this was his last chance to do so. He didn't deserve it, nor did he think she would give it. She would withhold her forgiveness from him because it was all she had left of her own. Avice had opened herself up and thrown everything away—family, future, honour, respectability, ease of mind, lightness of heart. If he had his silver pen with him, some source of light and paper, or even a pale, visible stretch of his own arm, he would write the truth on it as Hattie had instructed him to do. The truth was that he was about to die at her feet like a dog and he was not sorry for it. Singed nails and hair, boiled eyes, skin curled back like parchment, cooked organs, charred bone—he was prepared to bequeath himself utterly, if only as ashes, to his lawful wedded wife. He would never leave her now.

Avice wasn't ready to accept her inheritance—as useless dead as alive, might have been her sentiment—nor was she anxious to etch her own will on her arm. If she had his silver pen, she'd be jiggling it in the keyhole trying to spring the lock. She was intent, listening.

"Did you hear that?" she gasped. "A noise, right outside the door?"

"What?" He rose quickly, facing her, close enough now to catch her tongue, sharp as it was, in his teeth.

"You deserted me," she said. She had come such a long way to say it.

"I did." He wanted to crawl through her pores, each a portal to the unknowable depths of her. He could strain himself through her, and leave the dregs of his miserable being behind.

"And you're sorry."

"I am."

"You are that," she said. "You're a shit." He'd heard worse. He *was* worse.

"But then, so am I." A surprising enough admission, to which she added, "You could hold me, you know, if you don't have anything better to do."

Her words were measured, and ironic, but her body submerged in the darkness seemed to drag beneath them. A dense, compacted grief emanated out of her, out of the blackness of her mouth and eyes, and off her skin. A mortal bitterness. It was unbearable, even repellent. Surely he would not fail her again?

He raised his hands to run them up the length of her arms, to enfold her, but then, by some liberating agency—spiteful or merciful—or simply because of inadequate carpentry, the door blew open and part of the floor gave way. She disappeared out of his tentative embrace as if she were no more substantial than a wraith.

# 27

## BEST MAN

"LOST IN THE FIRE" was a phrase that would stay with Roland Avery for the rest of his life, a familiar saying in his personal vernacular that became a storeroom of sorts, a handy verbal place to locate any number of missing objects. The collection of kidney stones that came to him from Dr. Carruthers, *lost in the fire*, the Spode soup tureen with the cracked lid and the bird-of-paradise pattern, *lost in the fire*, the hand-me-down Lord Aberdeen sack suit, *lost in the fire*. His inventory of perished goods included both the material and the immaterial, as he also lost the sight in his left eye and the particular view of the world it commanded. He didn't, luckily, lose his ambitions, his goodwill, his voice or his spiritual capital. Foolish or not, his faith in humankind came through the blaze scorched but intact; that faith, fed by optimism, he saw simply as a discipline worth maintaining. Nor were all his losses irretrievable, for his stock-taking led in the aftermath of the fire to record-keeping of a different order. He himself began to keep a daily journal, and in doing so discovered the pleasures of living doubly: once in the air and then again on paper, where experience can be rejigged, patched up, or shaken like a child's bank for its concealed treasures.

Grif Smolders appeared in his friend's book often, head bobbing up between the lines or stepping unexpectedly out of the anonymity of the margins . . . as he did presently, in the flesh, turning a corner onto Water Street, arriving like a restless, wind-driven scrap. He spotted Roland, who was standing in front of what was now a blackened gap in the wall of buildings on the street. For days after the fire an acrid smell hung over the town. It clung to clothing and hair, a nesting and unsettling fragrance, an *eau de feu*. The Dancing Sun, capable of housing only the odd breeze now, continued for some time to distribute burned flecks of papery matter that swirled up and floated away like black moths. Grif paused a moment to peel one of these off his cheek, then raised a hand in greeting and headed toward Roland, his restrained smile teased into a looser one, as it always was by the boy hosteller. Landlord of ashes, but Roland wasn't about to dwell on that, or in it. Buildings can be resurrected, but bodies only clandestinely as lumber for doctors' studies. Apostate but still courteous to whatever higher powers might be listening in, Roland murmured a quiet *Deo gratias*, grateful that he didn't have to add Grif to his inventory of losses.

"Roland, that eye patch is very becoming."

"Yo ho ho."

"I'm not sure it's suitable, mind."

"And why is that?"

"Because you're the hero. Seems I'm the one who's always being rescued. I'm helpless as a girl."

"I've never met a helpless one of those yet. Besides, I told you already, I didn't mean to rescue you. How was I supposed to know you two were having it out in the closet? I was after my cash box. Couldn't very well let that go up in flames, could I? Just glad I had a spare." He held up his bracelet-sized ring of keys and jangled them. His hotel might be utterly unlocked, as open and free as the sky, but he could still make music. And not only that—"Can't start a family without funds, you know."

"There's plenty of time for that," Grif snorted. "You'll be a millionaire, I bet, before you don the yoke."

"I doubt it. Unless I have an exceptional week. Been playing a few hands at the Mansion House."

"What do you mean?"

"I'm getting married."

"Ha ha."

"I am. This Saturday. You're invited, of course. Would you consider being my best man? What's wrong?"

"You're serious?"

"Oh yes. Raewyn's idea, actually. And, well ... it's good timing. Her first communion dress still fits."

"I'm ... how *old* is she? Eleven?"

"Twelve in November."

"*She's* too young ... *you're* too young."

"Perfect match, then."

"I thought she was against marriage."

"Not anymore. She's become extremely interested in it." Roland blushed a little at this. "Claims she has it figured out."

"I don't know what to say."

"How about congratulations."

Grif hesitated, but only for the time it took to clear his head of stark surprise, of misgiving, of unexpected envy. He thought of the young nurse, crisp and pretty in her puffy-sleeved uniform, who had ministered to him during his short stay in the hospital. She had healed his burns, the surface ones at least, with the salve of her gentle touch, her kindness, her ready laugh, her undemanding presence. He wasn't mistaken that her attentions to him had been more than dutiful. She had even given him a stylish new jacket that she said her brother had outgrown, but that he suspected had come less indirectly from Turner's Dry Goods. He brushed an ash from the sleeve of this very jacket (it *was* natty), then reached out to grasp Roland's small, plump hand in his own. "I'd be honoured to be your best man," he said. "Congratulations. Even if she is a mick."

"She could be a Hindoo for all I care," laughed Roland. "Or worse, a Presbyterian."

"Will the crow be there?"

"Ring bearer. Even found the ring himself. Somewhere."

"I'll be."

Turning to gaze into the ruin of the Sun, into what charred structural remains were left standing, Grif understood that Roland would have no problem at all in building a marriage and a family, and would do so with the same care and eccentric detail that he had lavished upon his hotel.

"God, I'm sorry about—"

Roland shook his head, decisively, absolution for the crime.

"What will you do with it, this property? Sell it?"

"Never."

"Rebuild?"

"That's the plan. Not another hotel, though. I'm thinking about getting into the moving picture business. A theatre of some sort."

"Ah, you figure there's a future in it, then?"

"Definitely."

"Whatever happened to the intrepid Mr. Nashe, do you know?"

"Not really. Wasn't seeing too straight at the time."

"Some in town are saying that he perished in the fire. No one seems to remember seeing him leave the building."

"I doubt that. I would have found some trace of him in the ashes."

"His wolf's teeth."

"Grinning at me. I'll have the last laugh, though. I'm positive I can build one of those machines, an improved one, with an even better design." And then, Roland might have added, he would have replaced his lost vision with a new projecting eye. He'd have one eye to look inward with and one to look out.

"You know your biggest mistake, Roland? Besides letting me stay at your hotel, that is."

"Tell me. I can take it."

"The name. You should have christened it something else. The Empire, the Queen's, the Victoria—they would never have caught fire."

"I'll bear that in mind when I'm naming the new building. How about The Lucky Dog?"

"The Dream Palace."

"The Croesus Theatre?"

"The Paradise."

"The Pretty Penny? Well, I'll work on it. You know your biggest mistake, eh, Grif?"

"Yes. Letting Avice slip through my hands once again. Failing her—once again."

"Not your fault."

"She could have been killed."

"Ditto. Blame it on the ants. Or me—I should have done something about them. Meant to."

"Ants?"

"Carpenter ants. I thought you took an interest in the creepy-crawlies. The floorboards were infested. Look on the bright side: she took a tumble, got burned some, busted her arm, but she did survive. At least she can't beat the snot out of you now, not for a while, anyway. So . . . I was thinking, since you're winning this round, why don't we have a double wedding on Saturday? You two can get remarried. Why not? Forget what you've been through—she's as much at fault as you, remember—and try it again from the beginning. Clean slate. What do you say?"

Grif exhaled what felt like the whole poisonous cloud of smoke he had sucked into his lungs during the time it took to drag a bellowing Avice (he had her by the broken arm) out of the subterranean pit she had tumbled into when the floorboards gave way beneath her. Remarried? What an idea. A picture came into his head of the two of them inflicting fatal damage on any church that dared to join them in the sacrament of matrimony. Two contrary antipathetic elements. He saw pews crashing, statuary tumbling, heads rolling, guests fleeing for their lives.

"Wouldn't work, Roland. We're not meant for each other." He shrugged. "We don't get along."

"Have you spoken to her since the fire?"

"No. You think she would even look at me?"

"I can say goodbye without having to look at your sorry mug, can't I?" Avice said, staring point-blank at his sorry mug.

She had approached them silently, unnoticed, and stood a little apart. Her right arm was in a sling, the side of her face scored with a strange burn that looked as if a three-fingered hand had raked her cheek. She was wearing a wide-brimmed straw hat and a smart walking dress, the hemline fashionably raised several inches above her ankles.

"I heard your good news," she said to Roland. "I'm sure you'll be very happy together."

"Yes, kind of you to say, I know we will. Are you coming to the wedding?"

"I don't like weddings." She managed to crack a little smile at this. "Or funerals," she said, the smile vanishing. She had been the lone attendant at Hugh's, but had mourned him sincerely, and had left a bottle by his graveside in case the parching winds of temperance had dried even the swampy watering holes of the afterworld.

Grif didn't know whether he was entitled to take this statement about not liking funerals as encouragement, but ventured, "Your arm, Avice?"

"Mending," she said curtly. "No thanks to you." She gave him a warning look, and was clearly not about to budge an inch in his direction. Forgiveness lay that way, and tolerance. It was as if he could hear doors slamming and deadbolts being slapped into place.

"What will you do?" Roland asked. "Return down below?"

She narrowed her eyes.

"To London?" he hastily added.

"No, I can't see myself attending at-homes, and riding to hounds, and shopping for the rest of my life. I may go west, or I might settle here. It's so open, you don't feel hemmed in, I like that. Later this morning I'm going to look at some property outside of town, on the lake. I've been thinking about building a tourist lodge."

A woman operating such a business on her own? Laundry, meals, boats, endless pleasantries and banter with the guests. Grif was sceptical, but figured she had the gumption to manage it. And who was to say how long she would be on her own?

"Goodbye, then," she said, and that was it. "Be careful," she advised Roland, "or you'll end up doing all the cooking."

For Grif, no further word was on offer. She said nothing, left him nothing—no matter how faint or trivial—to hang on to and remember her more favourably by. He watched miserably as she marched away from him as if it were the easiest and most natural thing in the world to do. He had ashes on his sleeve and in his mouth.

"*Grif,*" urged Roland.

"Yeah."

"Go."

"Where?"

"After her, before she's gone."

"What?—she doesn't want me."

"Who's the card player here? She was bluffing. Don't you know anything about women?"

"What do *you* know, Roland?"

"A lot, actually. I've had a busy week. Look, look what she's doing."

Avice, almost at the corner, had stopped and was bending over. Her body was clenched, her free hand grasping her stomach. Grif thought she was going to be sick on the road. That sound she was making, a terrible retching noise. Or was she sobbing? Wait, no, she was *laughing*. She was laughing so hard that she was staggering, unbalanced. She was killing herself, stung by some mysterious hilarity. Was she suddenly recalling Grif in the burning hotel, shouting *I'll save you*, with his pants slung around his ankles and his manly parts hanging out of his long johns? Or was she laughing at herself? Or at the two of them together, at their whole misshapen marriage so far? Perhaps, unburdened, having transcended her fixation, a gust of happiness had simply seized her. A surging uplift, an expansiveness, a guffawing and heavenly breath.

He didn't know, he just didn't know. But when she glanced back once, quickly, anointing him with her keen eye before hiking up her skirts and pelting off, he didn't wait any longer. He saw, flashing on her heels like fiery spurs of light, and snaking up her back, silvering it, that which was most desirable. For the first time in months, and for the first time in his married life, he knew what to do.

# AUTHOR'S NOTE

Although the iconoclast's journal as described has been fictionalized somewhat, the excerpts themselves have been taken from an actual journal kept by William Dowsing in 1643–44, during the Civil War period in England. Dowsing was a "professional" iconoclast, whose official title was "Parliamentary visitor appointed under a warrant from the Earl of Manchester for demolishing the superstitious pictures and ornaments of churches within the county of Suffolk." He was paid six shillings, eight pence for each destructive act.